AND SO BY FIRE

A NOVEL

BRANDON ANDRESS

This is a work of fiction. The characters, places, and incidents portrayed, and the names used herein are fictitious or used in a fictitious manner. Any resemblance to the name, character, or history of any person, living or dead, is coincidental and unintentional. Product names used herein are not an endorsement of this work by the produce name owners.

Cover Design: Rafael Polendo (polendo.net)
Interior Design: Matthew J. Distefano

ISBN Paperback: 978-1-957007-72-4
ISBN eBook: 978-1-957007-73-1
ISBN Hardback: 978-1-957007-74-8

This volume is printed on acid free paper and meets ANSI Z39.48 standards.
Printed in the United States of America

Published by Quoir
Chico, California
www.quoir.com

ACKNOWLEDGMENTS

Special thanks to my tribe of Helpers who offered their skills and insights in the development of this book—Nevie Dewhirst, Clyde Myers, Seja Brumley, Seth Price, Angella Dykstra, and Adam and Jackie Garn

The dove descending breaks the air
With flame of incandescent terror
Of which the tongues declare
The one discharge from sin and error.
The only hope, or else despair
Lies in the choice of pyre or pyre-
To be redeemed from fire by fire.
Who then devised the torment? Love.
Love is the unfamiliar Name
Behind the hands that wove
The intolerable shirt of flame
Which human power cannot remove.
We only live, only suspire
Consumed by either fire or fire.

Little Gidding, T.S. Eliot

The best way to keep a prisoner from escaping
is to make sure he never knows he's in prison.

Fyodor Dostoevsky

PROLOGUE

Night had the appearance of day as harsh, artificial light emanated from the windows of Pangea. But to those who lived on the island, the distinction between night and day was inconsequential. Time was a relative construct based on the reality in which one existed at any given moment. And those realities were as fluid as their laws and truths. Their curated virtual lives lacked any meaningful moral center.

Implicit in its name, the Pangea Corporation imagined a community where everyone was brought together virtually. Their vision was to help users create positive and meaningful lives by making the human experience more integrated yet individualized. As a result, people generated infinite shared realities through the company's technology and superimposed them on real life.

For all of the technology's promised good, people were too naive to see that it also had the potential to control information and shape how they interpreted reality. And they were too trusting to conceive that this technology could ever be used against them. There was a time when people believed information was power. That was no longer true. Instead, power was using information to craft a narrative so compelling people would believe whatever they were told.

An opaque glass door opened as a frantic executive ran into the sterile white, unadorned hallway. Unsure whether to keep running or collect his thoughts, the young man put his hands on his knees, closed his eyes, and attempted to slow his breathing. His bodily motions and gestures were so dramatic and over-the-top one could have mistaken them for being manufactured. He wondered if he had hours or minutes. Either way, he was confident there would be a response.

Standing upright, still breathing heavily, the young man glanced up at a security camera and down the corridor toward the entrance. The lighting inside the building was so bright that the outward-facing windows appeared black. Anyone could be waiting on the other side, he half-whispered to himself before realizing the opposite was true. If there *were* people outside, they could see him alone in the hallway.

Fear.

Fear could silence dissenting opinions and regulate behavior more effectively than any law. And those behind their screens seemed to have perfected this tactic. Most notably, the quasi-hacking group called The Coalescence. With only a few keystrokes, The Coalescence invoked fear by organizing protests and moving antagonizers as pawns in a larger game of heavy-handed influence and control. While the faction initially mobilized against the injustices of the powerful, the movement became a monster devouring anyone who did not abide by its monolithic value system. This delicate tightrope walk kept people in perpetual distress and quieted all opposition.

Only months before, The Coalescence had organized mobs to neutralize politicians and dissolve the established government. It was an easy and popular move amongst a largely disengaged populace that had grown tired of bureaucrats lining their pockets with the money of special interests while ignoring the needs of the people. The keyboard warriors reportedly hacked their personal information and threatened to expose their every indecency and impropriety for public consumption. This was their first big power play, gaining instant notoriety and support.

The Coalescence tore down or, at minimum, rendered the old patriarchal system impotent. They erased everything from that antiquated ideological perspective. By cutting out the cancer of outdated beliefs, they tried to rescue the population from the old way of thinking. The former ways were a plague to their high-minded progressive ideals. Therefore, they purged every document and file, both physical and digital, which had anything to do with the former regime's history, traditions, or values. The Coalescence threatened reeducation or severe punishment for anyone who retained illegal material. That was how the faceless, decentralized entity appeared to shift power from top to bottom.

Despite shadowy movements on the other side of the windows, the executive decided to make a run for it. He was sure the mobs would be coming for him, whether he tried to hide in his office or not. As he went down the corridor, the security sensors detected his identity and opened the doors. He waited. No one came in. He peered around the corner, but no one was waiting for him. Relieved, he ran through the town center. The young man knew they would be watching, though. Cameras surrounding the plaza would detect him. The radiating lights of the Pangea Corporation flooded the downtown area and afforded no shadows. Even the massive video wall that fully encircled the center and played non-stop news flickered and danced, illuminating colors on everything below.

Opposite the entrance of the Pangea Corporation, at the far end of the town center, stood a towering cathedral. The looming granite edifice appeared dark on the inside, but its facade glowed in the artificial light. Broken stained-glass windows, a crumbling exterior, and graffiti were visible to anyone who cared to look. The dilapidated building was out of place compared to Pangea's architectural and high-tech wonder. Although still standing, the church was set to be demolished so the company could build in the vacant spot and fully encompass the town center. But for now, the structure stood and housed one last artifact.

Rushing into the dimly lit church auditorium, the executive picked up a soft mallet at the entrance and banged a deep, resounding bell. The crested arches above reverberated solemn tones as the young man ran down the aisle and into the confessional. He knew this was the only way the priest would speak to him. His heart pounded out of his chest. He waited impatiently, bouncing his knee up and down. It had been years since he had last darkened the building, even more since he sat in the confessional. As he looked around the dark, hardwood booth, anger accompanied the fear he had carried into the room.

Footsteps echoed in the quiet building. The holy man lit a single candle prior to entering the other side of the confessional. His breathing and the sound of his rustling as he got settled made the executive anxious. Quieting, he cleared his throat and uttered a short, nearly inaudible prayer. He paused once more before speaking.

"Please, make the sign of the cross and tell me how long it has been since your last confession."

"How long has it been since your last confession?" the executive whispered in hostility.

"Ah. The wayward son has returned," the priest grumbled as he glanced through the divider that separated them.

"You did this intentionally."

The priest sighed before responding. "I have no idea what you are talking about, Tyran."

The young man turned toward the lattice and stared directly at Father Prodido. "You know exactly what I'm talking about. You were told weeks ago to delete and destroy every file in your possession. It wasn't a joke."

The old man sat back, no longer facing Tyran, and twisted his gray eyebrow as if contemplating the accusation. "I did," he responded. "I destroyed every one of them just like you asked. And I deleted every file, as well."

"Liar!" Tyran raised his voice. "You're the only one who had access to that file! You were in the simulation! Admit it!"

"I will admit no such thing!" Prodido said with indignance.

"When they come to me and ask why an illegal file was activated," Tyran yelled. "I'm telling them exactly what happened. This isn't on me! It's on you! Do you understand?"

Prodido remained silent.

"Years of brainwashing and hurting me wasn't enough, though," Tyran continued. "No, you've proven that you'll do anything to keep people under your thumb. With enough guilt and shame, you can keep anyone in line. Isn't that right? You'll never change. That's why people hate you and why this place sits empty. You're irrelevant. We've progressed beyond your bullshit. You're nothing but a sad, old relic. The days of you controlling me are over. Do you understand me?

Prodido closed his eyes. "At least I didn't sell my soul to that godforsaken fear mob," he said under his breath before turning back to Tyran.

"You son of a bi..." Tyran said, standing up.

"Sit down!" Prodido shouted. The young man stood defiantly as the priest continued. "Even your sister had enough sense to see what was happening and get away from here! Oh, but not you! Oh, no! You're nothing but a lap dog. Do you hear me? A lap dog. Doing everything you're told on command. Oh sure, you're successful, but they're using you and you don't see it. Down deep, you're terrified you'll end up just like the politicians. Exposed and inconsequential."

The hatred in Tyran's eyes burned.

"And the audacity!" Prodido scoffed, adding the last bit of fuel to the fire. "Coming into this holy place with foul language and accusing me of controlling people. Laughable. Who's controlling who, exactly?"

"What's that supposed to mean?" Tyran snapped back.

"You know precisely what it means," Prodido said, standing up. "Now, if you don't mind..."

"Delete it!" Tyran said, punching through the lattice and grabbing the priest by his collar.

"I don't have it," Prodido said as he wrestled away and attempted to straighten his shirt. "Even if I did, I wouldn't delete it. I'm not your lap dog."

"You old fool," Tyran whispered. "You deserve every bit of what's coming."

"Be that as it may," Prodido said, walking out of the booth, "you're a fool if you believe any of this ends with me. As they say, 'A full belly only satiates for a while, but then it is hungry again.'"

Tyran remained quiet on his side of the confessional.

"First, it's Patrida," Prodido said, facing the young man. "Then the next Patrida, and the ne..."

A low roar that became a shrill scream interrupted the priest. A siren wailed from outside, penetrating the walls of the church building. "This is an emergency broadcast," a female voice echoed over loudspeakers. "Due to a breach in security protocol, you must return to your residence immediately." Tyran's eyes grew wide. Paralyzed, he looked at Father Prodido in angry desperation. The priest calmly turned away and retreated to his room for the night.

CHAPTER 1

Thura stared through the soft haze of the mirror. She grabbed her sleeve and rubbed her forearm against the chalky surface, only making it worse. Leaning in closer, she studied the intricacies of her irises and then the infinite black of her pupils. She closed her eyes and replayed falling backward into the dark expanse. She felt the wind blowing violently around her body as the darkness swallowed her. Each time Thura imagined falling, she saw Sophia's kind eyes looking deeply into her own. A dull ache filled her chest and moved upward as a tightness in her throat. A tear slowly rolled down her cheek. Thura placed her forehead against the mirror and stared at the white module on the sink's back corner. A gentle knock came to the bathroom door.

"Hey T," Odigo whispered. "We can't stay here tonight. We have to go." Thura remained silent, gently tapping her head on the mirror. "You okay, Thura? Do you want to talk about it?"

The two stood silently on opposite sides of the door, but the distance felt further than a couple of feet. Odigo knew from Thura's reaction in the bathtub earlier that he would not be able to fully understand what she had experienced in the simulation. He had never seen her as frantic and inconsolable as she had been over the previous hour. While she had only shared a few initial details about the experience, he regretted letting her go into it. He heard a click as the door unlocked. When he opened it, Thura threw her arms around him and pulled him in without saying a word. He could only hold her as she buried her face in his chest.

"How did it feel so real?" Thura whispered. "I feel like I knew Sophia all those years." Odigo knew she was still processing what happened and did not need him to say anything. "She was so patient and wise. I loved her, Odigo."

The young man put his hand through Thura's long, auburn hair and held her quietly while she cried for several minutes.

"You were in it, too," Thura finally laughed as she pulled away to look at Odigo.

"Oh yeah. Was I patient and wise, as well?" he smiled.

"No, you were my cousin!" Thura said, hitting Odigo's chest gently with her fists. "But seriously. You were the one who caused the whole thing to blow up in the first place. You were a stranger from this beautiful community called Salome. These two brothers nam..."

The lights flickered in the house and then went black. Odigo ran to the front window and noticed the streetlights had also gone out. Inconsistent lighting was not an unusual occurrence on the outskirts of the island, away from the town center. The Pangea Corporation and other downtown businesses in the surrounding high-rise superstructures were rarely off-line. But Thura and Odigo had grown accustomed to the irregularities of life outside Pangea proper, where they used to live.

"I guess you can keep talking to your cousin in the dark," Odigo quipped, causing Thura to laugh. "Grab your stuff. We need to get movi..."

A low roar that became a shrill scream silenced Odigo. An alert on his handheld device jolted them into movement as they made their way out the back door. The street was eerily silent once the siren subsided. While most people were already in their homes, lost in their simulated experiences, those who lingered outside knew the routine. During an emergency, you go inside and wait for further instructions. In only a few short months, The Coalescence had trained people from the four districts of the island into mindless subservience or consequence.

"This is an emergency broadcast," a female voice echoed over the houses. "Due to a breach in security protocol, return to your residence immediately." The message repeated once more before the sirens were again activated.

"Stay on the edges and in the shadows," Odigo said to Thura as he pulled her beside him.

"I have been," Thura whispered, "for months."

The two moved quickly, knowing fewer cameras were operational on the city's outskirts. Peering around a darkened house close to an intersection, Thura saw the faint movement of people down the street. The young woman traced their outlines. Despite scattered clouds above, the dim moonlight revealed ten to twelve individuals extending across both lanes.

"We have to move now before they get any closer," Odigo said. The couple crossed the road but failed to see the man riding his bike ahead of the others. Thura turned in slow motion and caught a glimpse of him from the corner of her eye. The man wore a black bandana over his nose and mouth with a black hoodie covering his head. His dark pants were almost entirely camouflaged by night. His legs moved up and down as he circled them and yipped like a dog to those in his crew.

Thura and Odigo darted into an alley nearby, cutting into another side street. They were careful to stay hidden in the shadows between the houses. It was unclear whether The Coalescence explicitly sent this group or if they were some random street militia. Small bands had joined forces to protect themselves and their property without organized law enforcement over the last few months. As they continued to evade the man on the bike, the two reached a chain-linked fence that separated the outer neighborhoods from the cargo loading docks on the waterway. Odigo surveyed the barrier until he found an opening near the bottom. The couple crawled through the hole and jumped down a cement embankment that ran along the water's edge. As they quieted their breathing, Thura and Odigo waited.

"Who do you think sent the file to you?" Thura asked after several minutes of silence.

"I'm not sure. It could have been anyone," Odigo said, peeking over the concrete barrier and placing his finger in front of his lips. "They're about a block away and moving this direction. We can't stay here. Follow me."

Odigo kept his back against the wall and followed it to the loading dock.

"Please make sure your device is on silent," Thura whispered from behind with a half-laugh.

The two stopped again as they heard someone shuffle on the street above them. Thura nudged Odigo and pointed at the water. The moonlight projected the contours of a man on its surface. They patiently watched as a woman joined him. The couple chatted while they each smoked a cigarette, neither appearing to be in any hurry. Thura and Odigo held their breath until they walked away.

"It's not safe to be on the island right now, Thura," Odigo whispered. "I don't know who this group is but there will be others walking the streets all night. And we can't go back to the house."

"Do you think they're looking for us?" Thura asked.

"Who? The mobs?" Odigo asked.

"No, The Coalescence."

"I doubt it," Odigo continued to whisper. "But they probably know who sent the file to us by now. And that it was activated here in the East District."

"So you think they know it was activated here?" Thura asked.

"Yeah, probably. Maybe even down to our neighborhood. That's why we need to get off the island for the time being," Odigo said, walking down to an empty, automated cargo ship. "This thing should be heading out at some point tonight."

The two jumped aboard and huddled in a dark corner. They could still hear several people chirping from the streets above, but they were not as loud as before. Thura pulled her hood over her head and put her head down, staring at the chipped paint on the vessel's floor. It reminded her of the chipped paint on the storage door in the alleyway of Patrida that she hid behind when she first met Sophia. She remembered hearing the footsteps that sent her rushing to hide. Even in the simulation, her first impulse was to always run away in fear.

"Do you want to talk about it?" Odigo asked, interrupting their silence.

Thura turned her head away and stared into the empty space. She wiped her eyes and then her nose with her sleeve. The emotional distance between the dark, dank cargo ship and her experience in the simulation felt like the distance between Patrida and Salome. Memories of her journey flashed through her mind. Thura picked at the gray paint with her fingernails. She shut her eyes. Thura's thoughts went back to the smooth, gray rocks that lined the shoreline near Salome.

"There was this time when you and I sat on a cliff and watched the waves," Thura whispered, wiping the corners of her eyes again. "And then the sunrise. I had never seen one before. In Patrida, I only saw sunsets."

Odigo closed his eyes with Thura. It was the first time since she came out of the simulation that he ached for her. Not only did he not have words to console her, but he also did not have the shared experience. Even though his mind tried to convince him there was no widening gulf between them, his heart told him otherwise. It was difficult to imagine someone having such a profound and meaningful experience without it impacting their relationships, particularly for those who were not involved but trying to comprehend. The young man put his head in his hand and ran his fingers through his long, dark hair. He was happy that he was a character in the simulation for Thura, but he longed for that same deep connection with her in real life.

"I know this will sound weird but everything in the simulation felt like a metaphor," she continued. "That's why I experienced it so deeply. The sunrise was a moment of enlightenment... of clarity. The waves that washed over the rocks symbolized a patient and consistent love washing over people, despite their rough edges."

The gentle, meditative hum of the boat accompanied Thura's words as it released from the dock and began to move. Odigo remained silent and listening. The way Thura described the simulation made him realize he had never had anything as meaningful or resonant occur in his adult life. Folding his arms across his knees, the young man rested his forehead on his right wrist. He could only vaguely remember having those feelings as a little boy.

Growing up as an only child to a single mother in the working-class East District meant they shared a unique bond. He cherished the times when he got to sit on her lap at night and listen to her voice as she read books to him. The memories still lingered, but they felt so far away. His mother had passed away more than a decade ago. And it seemed that heaviness and emptiness, along with the years, always threatened to eclipse those early moments.

"That's when you said something in the simulation I'll never forget, Odigo," Thura said, interrupting his thoughts. "It was about freedom, and it was so profound." Odigo raised his head, curious to hear what she would say. "You said that freedom is a way of seeing the world without needing to judge it. Seeing its brokenness and embracing anyway. Discovering its naked beauty and loving it despite itself."

The two closed their eyes for different reasons. Thura for what she had experienced but lost. Odigo for never having had the experience himself. Their ache and longing were the same, but neither knew it. Pangea's distant, unnatural lighting washed over them as the boat moved farther from the island.

"But here we are," Thura said, standing up. Her grief was not only in her tone. It radiated throughout her entire body. The young woman grabbed the cool railing and placed her head on her hands. Odigo stood but was careful to give her the space she needed. Despite his feelings, he knew Thura was struggling to process everything.

"I think Tyran may have been in the simulation with me," Thura said, not raising her head.

"Why do you think that, Thura?"

"The whole thing felt like it was created from my life and Tyran's life together," Thura said as she raised her head. "Like they were merged. Isn't that how you said it worked?"

"It is, but there's no way he was in it. Why would he, of all people, defy The Coalescence?" Odigo asked. "It's more likely that the artificial intelligence curated a story based upon your own life experiences. And since Tyran is already in your memories, it would make sense for him to be a person in it."

"I understand that," Thura attempted to clarify as she turned toward Odigo. "But didn't you say it was possible for the program to create new characters by merging people who are connected to it?"

"I did," Odigo said. "But again, there's zero chance he was in it with you, Thura. Not after the purge." Thura turned away and stared at the island. "Why would he risk everything by going into an illegal simulation? It just wouldn't make any sense, right?"

"I don't know, Odigo. I don't know," Thura said, frustrated. "I know it doesn't make sense. All I'm saying is that it felt like there was a character created specifically for me and Tyran, together. Like the artificial intelligence merged us and made a character. That's all I'm saying."

"Hey, I'm sorry," Odigo said, putting his arm around her. "It was your experience. You were in it, not me."

The two stood watching the wake from the back of the boat. Odigo, the left side. Thura, the right.

"There's a reason why I think Tyran was in the simulation, Odigo," Thura said, interrupting the quiet. "And I need you to hear me."

"Okay," he said in a patient but curious tone.

"I believe the program created a character to show both of us a different path," Thura said. "In my opinion, Tyran watched this character transform from his perspective..."

"And you watched this character transform from your perspective," Odigo said, finishing Thura's sentence.

"Exactly," Thura said. "Like it was teaching us both at the same time through one character."

"What was the character's name, Thura?" Odigo asked.

"Which one?"

"The character you said was created by merging you and Tyran."

Thura paused but then finally answered. "It was my father."

"Your father?" Odigo asked in a shocked voice.

"I know," Thura said. "The artificial intelligence must have known how powerful it would be for us to be with him again, after so many years apart."

Tyran felt exposed and vulnerable as he left the church and walked along the sidewalk closest to the buildings. He was exhausted but too wired to sleep. Stepping over the legs of a homeless man, the young man looked up to see someone standing at Pangea's main entrance. The figure was dressed in black and carried a dark backpack. His heart skipped and then began to race. Tyran took another ten to twelve steps forward, training his eyes on their face. A young woman held a tiny device up to her mouth and blew a hit. As the cloud of smoke dissipated, Tyran knew who it was.

"Are you here to see how I'm doing," Tyran shouted as he approached the steps. "Or, are you here for some other reason?"

"Not even going to greet me? Damn!" KT said, taking another hit. "I mean it's been... what..." She blew an even more giant cloud. "Almost a year?"

Scanning his retinas, the doors opened.

"Let's not stand out here," he said with quiet urgency.

"You okay?" KT asked.

Tyran turned and faced the young woman, attempting to discern why she had been waiting for him outside. KT had previously worked for the

Pangea Corporation as a senior programmer, writing code for their latest technology. But a few months prior, in an anonymous online chat group, she was contacted and recruited away from Pangea by someone within The Coalescence.

"Look. I'm just going to get to it," KT said. "They know there was an unauthorized file activated. You know, one of those files that shoulda been purged. And there's only two people with access to that particular file—you and the priest. So yeah."

Tyran swallowed, even though his mouth was dry.

"Here's the deal," she continued. "They wanted everyone down here. All the signs and screaming and stuff. The media. The whole crew, man. They wanted some windows smashed and the like. I told 'em I would come down this time. You know, since I used to work with you and all."

"You told them you would come down and do what?" Tyran asked. "Give me a message?"

Tyran was more irritated that they sent KT than the mobs and protestors. When she left the Pangea Corporation, she said The Coalescence better aligned with her values. But Tyran saw right through it at the time and could still see through it as she stood in front of him. He knew that behind her radical idealism was someone desperately seeking something more. He knew all about her family life or lack of it. And in his opinion, KT always seemed to be searching for some sort of connection or purpose for her life. That was why he believed she left the Pangea Corporation and joined The Coalescence. They promised her a community of off-beat radicalism he could never offer her. That was why sending KT was nothing but a slap in the face.

"You're a smart one," KT said, wagging her finger. "Yeah. To give you a message." Tyran shifted uneasily. "But look. They still need you. They need all your polish and shine at the big event. You gotta make us all proud. Especially me. I put a lot of sweat into that tech. But man, you gotta listen to me. You're on a short leash. Like, really short. You feel me?"

"It wasn't me," Tyran said, appearing flustered. "I thought he deleted it! And even if I knew he didn't delete it, why would I activate it? It wouldn't make sense. Why would I do something so stupid? Haven't I done enough to show them that I'm on their side?"

"Yeah, man. I don't know," KT said. "Just get focused on your thing. We'll deal with all the file stuff after that. Short leash. Got it?"

"They know it was the priest who accessed it, right?" Tyran asked, continuing to shift blame and absolve himself.

"Look. I'm just the messenger, man," KT snapped back. "Has it been delivered?"

"Yes," said Tyran.

Thura and Odigo walked to the other end of the empty cargo vessel. The light pollution of Pangea no longer entirely obscured the night sky's brilliance. From Pangea proper, locating a star was a rare occurrence. The intense luminosity bleached the upper expanse. But from the sea and away from the veil of artificial life, one could finally see clearly. The island's beauty from the ocean's vantage enamored the couple, but it was nothing compared to the resplendence above them.

Odigo had been careful not to push Thura much more. She seemed content watching the stars, but she was emotionally spent. When he had first received the encrypted file and instructions for Thura to be connected, he did not anticipate it affecting her this deeply. Odigo had been hesitant telling her that someone had sent him the file because of her absolute antipathy toward the technology. However, he felt obligated to share it because of the message that accompanied it.

Thura abandoned the system because she knew how easily a person or group could misuse Pangea's technology. She saw what The Coalescence was doing and did not want any part. For that reason, she had never been connected or even in a simulated experience. However, Thura's disdain softened when Odigo shared the anonymous message with the encrypted file. The note stated that someone had recovered the file through an audit. The contents were supposedly a historic cache of her late father, Ochi Kala. They thought the file might have allowed Thura to reconnect with her father, even if the experience was simulated. In retrospect, Odigo felt guilty that they had believed the message and that he had subjected Thura to the entire thing. Nevertheless, he was curious as to who sent the file and why they sent it.

"I grew up in Patrida," Thura said, breaking her silence. "But Patrida wasn't just the name of a church like it is here on this island. It was the name of the *whole island*."

Odigo listened intently, trying to understand. "So you're saying that the artificial intelligence took the First Church of Patrida, the church here on *this* island, the church located downtown in the West District, and made it the name of the *entire island* in the simulation?"

"Yes," Thura said.

"Whew," Odigo said. "Okay, yeah. Hopefully it wasn't much like the church."

"It was exactly like that, Odigo, maybe worse," Thura said. "And that's where I grew up. My father was the leader of this tiny community and Father Prodido was there trying to control everything and everyone."

"Sounds horrific," Odigo said. "No wonder you tried to run away."

The two stood silently, thinking about that last comment and their current situation.

"The town was super old, though. No big buildings. No technology. Just houses and structures made of wood and stone. I even wore a dress," Thura said, attempting to lighten the mood.

"Okay, yeah. That's old school," Odigo laughed. "I would've absolutely loved to see you in a dress."

"Yes, it was quite becoming," Thura smiled as she punched Odigo in the arm. "But seriously, I think the program purposefully stripped away everything."

"What does that mean exactly?" asked Odigo.

"I'm not sure," Thura said. "I just saw everything so clearly. Nothing was hidden. I saw how people abuse power to control others and how it turns people against one another. But I also saw how people can ultimately live in peace. And I saw how a person can be transformed from one to the other."

"And that's where the O..." Odigo began.

"The Ochi character came in, yeah," Thura finished. "But I didn't get it immediately. Not until the very end. We were in a cave with carved rock stairs leading down to the water. My father got on his hands and knees and stared at his reflection. It was like he saw himself clearly for the first time. Then he asked me, 'What keeps my *no* from becoming a *yes*?'"

"That was his question?" Odigo half-laughed.

"Yeah, but it wasn't *his* question," Thura said, her eyes opening wide. "It was *our* question. Tyran and me."

"You and Tyran," Odigo clarified.

"Yes!" Thura said. "Ochi was being pulled between two worlds just like me and Tyran. He was showing Tyran how to get out of the system and stop being controlled in order to find peace and freedom. He showed him how to stand up to fear and how to break the cycle of violence, even though Tyran didn't do it in the end."

Odigo did not immediately respond as he contemplated Thura's explanation. "And what did Ochi show you about yourself?" he asked.

Thura paused momentarily and then changed the conversation. "It looks like we're almost there," she said as the cargo ship shifted gears and slowed.

"We can pick this up again when you're ready." Odigo said.

"Okay," Thura responded, moving back into the dark corner where they had started.

"Have you ever been here?" Odigo asked as he sat down beside her.

"To Villatic?" Thura asked. "Only when I was little. I used to come here with my dad before he died."

The smell of weed lingered in the atrium of Pangea. Tyran hated smoking in general but especially despised anything that could be mind-altering. He thought about KT and how heavily she was into The Coalescence. Tyran had always viewed her as excessive, even for his own taste. But leaving an excellent job for some fringe group was extreme by any measure, he thought. He was frustrated with her and her visiting him, but at least she had somewhat put his mind at ease. Rather than hiding in his office for the night, the sober-minded executive decided to go home. Based on what she told him, he did not anticipate any more unexpected visitors for the night.

Tyran took an elevator up to the sixth floor. While Pangea occupied the first five levels, the entire top floor was his living space. However, the walk to this main area was a good five minutes at a leisurely pace. That was the challenge of living in a near circular building. There were no direct routes. But the view of the town center from above was spectacular. The young man felt a sense of pride and accomplishment for all his success. It still amazed him that the island had been renamed because of his business' influence and prestige. The Pangea Corporation was no longer just a glass and concrete building in the West District. It was a belief in what the island could be, of who they could be as a people, together.

Tyran ran his hand along the length of the window as he continued to walk. The news played on the screens across the courtyard. He stopped to read the banner moving slowly at the bottom—*Potential Suspects Identified In Unauthorized Material Breach*. A shock went through his body. Looking down from the video screens, Tyran saw a man in the plaza he did not recognize staring at him. Then, stepping away from the window, he was simultaneously startled by a text message that appeared in his field of vision.

(VL-OS): I see you are home. Would you like for me to order dinner?

(Tyran): No. I won't be eating tonight.

(VL-OS): Should I prepare your room for bed?

(Tyran): No. I will be in the entertainment room tonight.

(VL-OS): I will prepare the room.

The door opened as Tyran approached, and he grabbed a juice from the refrigerator and sat on his couch.

(Tyran): Secure all the doors, please.

(VL-OS): Doors are secured.

(Tyran): Activate *Wisdom in Symbol and Metaphor.*

(VL-OS): Sir, just a reminder that this is the illegal file.

(Tyran): Just activate it.

(VL-OS): As the same character? Or as a different one?

(Tyran): Different.

(VL-OS): Which character?

(Tyran): Create a new character.

(VL-OS): Your new character is Nostos. Will that be okay?

(Tyran): That's fine.

(VL-OS): Would you like to return where you left off?

(Tyran): No. Go back ten minutes.

(VL-OS): Activating your simulation.

Nostos walked up the dirt road toward the entrance of Salome. Orange and red flames burned from the huts as high as the trees. The people of Salome screamed as their children cried. In the center, Nostos saw Tyran holding his father's lifeless body and weeping over him. Next to them, he noticed a bloody knife lying on the ground.

Nostos fixed his eyes on the father and son as he walked closer. Seemingly unaware of the chaos and fires around him, he stopped and studied Tyran's face and how he looked at his father. He watched as tears fell in seeming remorse. Nostos tried to imagine what the young man was feeling. How did he get to this point? He wondered. What led him here? And why did he believe this was his only option?

Nostos' eyes moved from the tears running down Tyran's cheeks to the wrinkled hand on his dark head. He followed the arm until he saw the chiseled cheeks of an old woman. The flames flickered across her face as he stared into her pained eyes. Nostos' body became numb. He could not move from where he was standing, or could he break his gaze. As he stared at Sophia, her eyes transformed from pain into kindness. Nostos felt naked and exposed as if the woman saw him. In the distance, a fiery Father Prodido screamed for Pali and Machi to seize her.

Nostos was suddenly pulled forward with great force, breaking his trance-like state. He looked down at a bloody hand, grabbing a fistful of his white linen shirt. It was Tyran's hand. The young man stood up and stared at him with desperate, red eyes. Tyran's tears looked like they had carved trenches through the dirt on his face. His pain was palpable, and Nostos could feel it as if it was his own.

"I was so close," Tyran sobbed.

"What?" Nostos asked, unsure what the young man said.

"I was so close..." Tyran repeated before turning toward the water labyrinth and falling to his knees.

Nostos examined the intricate maze sculpted into the ground. His eyes slowly followed each step to the center, where the flowing water glistened and illuminated from the flames. Nostos knelt beside the young man and put his arm around him.

"I was so close..." Tyran cried. "I was so close..."

The young man turned with tears in his eyes. He glared at Father Prodido with intense hatred. The priest, surrounded by flames, praised his sons, Pali and Machi, as they dragged Sophia away. Unmoved by the chaos in front of him, Nostos studied Tyran's face to better understand why he killed his father. It was clear there was more going on inside Tyran than he could see.

(Tyran): Exit simulation.

(VL-OS): Simulation ended.

CHAPTER 2

The cadence of katydids and tree frogs accompanied the stillness of the early morning. The modest port at Villatic was dark except for a couple of pole lights in the parking lot. Beneath one light, a man sat in his truck with his windows down, enjoying a coffee before the other workers arrived. A red notification flashed in the center of his screen as he flipped on his handheld device. The man made a motion with his hand, opening it. The bulletin detailed that an insurgent group had accessed unauthorized files to harm Pangea. Taking a sip of his brew, the worker dismissively waved his hand and then turned on some music.

Aboard the cargo ship, Odigo gently brushed Thura's hair out of her eyes to wake her up. "We need to get moving before the workers arrive," Odigo whispered. The two stood and walked in the soft, ambient light along the boat's edge to the concrete dock. As they walked the parking lot's perimeter, the truck's headlights flashed, and the driver's side door opened.

"Hey there," the man called out. "Can I help you?"

Thura and Odigo walked faster toward a wooded area near the back of the lot. The worker grabbed his flashlight and followed them. As the couple hit the woods, they took off. But behind them, the man gained ground and shouted for them to stop.

"Seems like," Thura said between breaths, "you've done this before."

"What?" Odigo asked.

"Nothing. But great way," Thura breathed, "to start the day."

The morning sun filtered through the trees as Thura and Odigo ran. A flashlight beam frantically darted back and forth on either side of them. They had not anticipated any problems in Villatic, a simple farming community that ran food operations for the mainland. But the man had no idea who he was chasing. As he closed in on them, they hit a chain-linked fence. Odigo tried to climb it, but he could not find a foothold. Thura turned and raised her hands up into the blinding spotlight, freezing in terror.

Ascending the steps of the Pangea Corporation, Tyran rubbed his eyes from not sleeping well. There was so much still racing through his mind from the night before. He not only thought about his encounter with Father Prodido in the confessional, he thought about his conversation with KT. Tyran knew he was walking a tightrope with The Coalescence. But he also knew they needed him. The young man took deep breaths and slowly strolled down the long hallway. The doors to his office opened, and his assistant greeted him.

"They're already in there, sir," she said.

"Really quick, Myra. I want this constructed in the town center," Tyran said, handing her a rough sketch. "I don't care about the cost. It needs to be completed before the event. Exactly as it's drawn up."

"But it's in two d..." Myra said.

"Tell them to work around the clock!" Tyran said, interrupting her. "I need this done, Myra."

The young man opened the door to his office. Two older gentlemen stood to greet him. The first man was a bespectacled doctor with a receding hairline. The wrinkles on his face indicated that he smiled a lot, likely even when he was not happy. The man standing beside him was a bit taller with gray wavy hair. It was apparent he did not smile as much. The two men were in business attire, holding onto one last tradition that had not yet been shamed out of existence.

"Ah, Tyran! So good to see you again," said the doctor.

"Yes, good to see you, Tyran," said the media executive. "I'm sure you're as excited about the big payday... I mean... the big day as we are."

"Absolutely," said Tyran, smiling and shaking their hands. "Mr. Stavros. Dr. Calix. Have a seat, gentleman. Please."

"If you don't mind me asking before we get down to business," said Mr. Stavros, "but what's the latest with the breach? Off the record, of course."

"Actually, you probably know more than me," Tyran laughed. "All I know right now is that the last round of purges included a selection of religious material. It turns out that one of those files was not deleted. And someone activated it last night."

"And whose responsibility was it to delete those files, might I ask?" Dr. Calix pressed. "Of course, if you don't mind the question."

"The Coalescence sent me a list of all the files to be purged and the actionable dates," said Tyran. "I passed that information along to the respective sectors in each district."

"Hmm. So, we can safely assume that Father Prodido failed to delete it," the media executive surmised. "What's his angle, do you suppose?" He leaned forward, put his elbows on his knees, and folded his hands.

"I'm not going to speculate on his motive," said Tyran. "But it appears The Coalescence knows it's either him, or one of his sympathizers, who activated it."

"Have you had any contact with him since the breach?" asked the doctor. "Since you were the one responsible for sending out the directive."

"I confronted him last night but he denied it," Tyran said. "I can tell you that he's had an ax to grind, though, ever since The Coalescence started putting pressure on him and his parishioners."

"Haven't we all," Mr. Stavros said under his breath. The men sat uncomfortably still, wondering who would speak next. "I shouldn't have said that. But there's the story and then there's the story they want us to tell people. And for a guy in my line of business, you can imagine the frustration. That's all I'm going to say."

"Well, if we are all being candid here," Dr. Calix said, looking over his glasses at the other two. "I second both the heart and sentiment of everything my good friend Mr. Stavros just said."

By the time they returned to the parking lot, two more trucks had arrived. The worker led Thura and Odigo toward a small, white, wooden office building near the port. As the three walked in, the gentleman instructed them to sit in the two metal fold-up chairs and wait. Across the room, a muted television showed the morning news. The breaking news banner indicated a new development in the unauthorized breach story. The men in the other room were still talking, so Odigo turned the volume enough to hear the update.

"According to unnamed sources," the reporter said, "the breach was allegedly a part of a larger insurgent group that has been activated on the island. Sources also say that more breaches are expected in the coming days."

The door opened, and the worker pointed at Thura and Odigo without saying a word. Then, he motioned for them to come into the office. As they walked in, he closed the door and left. The room was as basic and plain as the central area. Behind a cheap, fabricated desk, a man who appeared to be the supervisor told them to sit. Both Thura and Odigo looked nervously around the dirty, white room. It was adorned with only a corkboard holding dozens of small notes overflowing onto the wall.

"I assume you didn't come here to work," the man said, flipping through a heavily used notebook. Thura looked up at him and immediately felt she had known him her entire life. It was clear he did not recognize her, however. "You didn't come here to work, right?"

Thura and Odigo shook their heads. "No, sir," they said in unison as the man leaned back in his chair and studied them. Thura held back from saying more because she did not know how he would react to her. So instead, she awkwardly stared at his face. She detected a glint of kindness in his eyes.

"You a part of that group causing all the trouble?" he asked.

"No, sir," they said, shaking their heads.

"What are ya doin' here, then?" the man pressed. "And why were you on my boat?" Thura and Odigo sat silently, unsure how to answer. They were not a part of the insurgent group, but Thura had been in the simulation. "People don't come here for a vacation. So ya must be running from something." Thura and Odigo looked at each other, searching for a reasonable explanation.

"What are your names then?" he asked.

"My name is Thura Kala," she said, hoping her name might get his attention.

"I'm Odi..."

"Kala," the man interrupted as he leaned back and rubbed his chin. "The big name on the island, right?" Thura did not know what to say. "Your dad was a Kala, then."

"Yes, sir," she said. "That's my last name."

"And you must be little Thura," the man continued. "But not so little anymore. My name's Kaleo. I'm head of farm operations here. I met you when you were about yay high. You came with your daddy a couple of times. He was a good one. One of the last good ones."

Thura sat stunned, staring directly at Kaleo. She wanted to say so much, but it all felt impossible. The Kaleo she knew in the simulation was not the man sitting before her. Whatever past she believed they had together was not real. In the simulation, he had been one of her father's friends and had helped them escape Patrida. But, the Kaleo behind the cheap desk in a rickety shack in Villatic knew nothing of that simulated experience. Even more, if Thura mentioned the simulation, he would think she was definitely a part of the insurgent group. It was surreal to feel like she knew someone so intimately yet to not know anything about them in real life.

"He was a good man," Thura said, careful not to say anything more until she knew where he was going next.

"But ya still haven't told me why you're here," Kaleo said.

"I was in the illegal simulation and you were in it and I'm not an insurgent but we're scared and running so here we are sitting in front of you and we're not bad people so please be nice to us," Thura blurted out as fast as she could say it. Odigo's eyes widened while Thura talked and got even wider as he slowly turned toward Kaleo.

The older gentleman leaned back in his chair, studying Thura's face. Then, he nodded his head and laughed. "Well, somebody's gotta push back against those sons of bitches."

Mr. Stavros and Dr. Calix stood and shook Tyran's hand after reviewing the final logistics before the event. As they left the room, Tyran closed the door behind them and sat on his pleated, leather couch. The young man shut his eyes and took a deep breath, attempting to quell the anxiety that had been randomly haunting him the last few weeks. He was unsure what was causing this suffocation, but he always felt like he was being pulled in a hundred different directions.

> (Tyran): VL-OS, darken the windows, please.
>
> (VL-OS): Done. Would you like to rejoin your last simulation?
>
> (Tyran): No. Therapist simulation, please.
>
> (VL-OS): Would you like the same therapist as your last session?
>
> (Tyran): Yes. Thank you.
>
> (VL-OS): Activating your simulation.

Tyran studied an abstract painting hanging on the wall adjacent to the windows. The soft sunlight illuminated the bottom half of the art. A shadow covered the upper half. Harsh, erratic, multicolored brushstrokes ran diagonally across the canvas. The work seemed out of place for a typical therapy session but may have been specifically chosen by the artificial intelligence curating the simulated experience for Tyran.

"Tell me what you see," said the therapist, facing the young man.

"Oh, hey. Sorry," Tyran said. "I was lost in this new piece."

"It's not new, actually," she said. "It's been there since Spring."

"I didn't notice it before," Tyran said. "Maybe it's the way the light's hitting it this time." They both continued to examine the work in silence.

"Sometimes we see things as we are," the therapist said, pausing to allow her words to rest on Tyran. "What do you see?" she asked.

Tyran scrutinized each color and every stroke, attempting to make sense of the chaos. The two quietly stared at the painting for what seemed to be minutes. "Do you see that small, yellow dot at the bottom right? I feel like the rest of the painting is coming down on it, if that makes sense. Like it's being consumed by the other colors," Tyran said.

"Are you the small dot, Tyran?" she asked.

"Yeah. I think so."

"What do the other colors represent?" she inquired.

Tyran thought about Father Prodido. He still burned at the thought of the man. There was no question Tyran hated him. And he would love nothing more than for him to pay for how he controlled and manipulated people over the years. But more specifically, Tyran wanted the priest to be held accountable for how he controlled Tyran's father the years before he died. The religious man manipulated him into thinking he was always at risk of losing his soul. And from a young age, Tyran could see how that toxic message affected him and others. While his father was a good man, constant fear took its toll. In Tyran's opinion, Father Prodido becoming irrelevant in the community was too lenient a punishment for such a manipulative figure.

But it was not Father Prodido that weighed heavily on Tyran at the moment. Instead, he continued to think about his conversation with KT the night before. While she had rarely shown her true colors working for the Pangea Corporation in the past, he heard her fanaticism had become renowned since leaving. Even more concerning, he was told her emotional health had been deteriorating. Tyran knew she had always been the kind of person that needed the approval of others, even when she worked for him. But she seemed even more imbalanced now, almost codependent. However, it was clear that KT was only a symptom of a bigger problem called The Coalescence. And it was this problem, more than any other, that weighed heavily on him.

"Tyran," the therapist repeated. "The other colors. What do they represent?"

"The Coalescence," he said. "The colors represent all the people that make it up. Even though no one really knows who these people are. They throw around their power to make you do what they want."

"How does that make you feel?" she asked, then remained silent, letting Tyran contemplate the question.

"Angry. Resentful," he said. "Like I'm being controlled by this thing and can't stand up against it."

The room quieted.

"It's strange, though. It's like I'm being consumed and carried at the same time," Tyran continued. "But I don't have a choice in where they're taking me."

"You may remember in your last session, I introduced the idea of *locus of control*," the therapist said.

"Whether I believe I have control over my decisions," Tyran interrupted.

"*Or*," the therapist said, regaining the conversation, "whether you believe external forces control the decisions you make."

"And you think I..." Tyran began.

"Have an external locus of control," the therapist said. "You do not believe you have the autonomy to choose your own path. You believe outside forces are always dictating your destination, whether it is Father Prodido or The Coalescence. That is why you feel like you are being both consumed and carried. And, this feeling of helplessness is likely the source of your anxiety. The question you have to ask yourself is... why?"

"I went into a different simulation last night," Tyran said, avoiding the therapist.

"We will come back to my question," she said. "Into which simulation did you go?"

"*Wisdom in Symbol and Metaphor*," Tyran said.

"Would you like for me to pull the data for that simulation into this session for my background?" she asked.

"Sure."

"It's a protected file."

"Override."

"Okay. I'm reviewing it now," the therapist said. "You have been in this simulation twice. Once as yourself and another time as a character named Nostos. Is this correct?"

"Yes."

"Tell me about the first time you went in."

"I didn't intend on getting so wrapped up in it. So I'll start with that," Tyran said. "But it's a simulation that teaches you about yourself."

"How so?" the therapist asked.

"It scans your thoughts, feelings, and memories to create a story," Tyran said. "And it reveals what issues you're dealing with in your life."

"And what did it reveal to you?"

"That I allow myself to be controlled."

"I see a consistent theme here," she said. "Why do you allow yourself to be controlled?"

"I'm tired," Tyran whispered under his breath. The young man looked down at the white hooked rug beneath his feet and followed the pattern of blue concentric circles with his eyes. He imagined looking down on a miniature version of himself walking around the edge of one circle. He wondered why stepping over the line and into the circle was so difficult.

"Is that why you went back into the last ten minutes of the simulation as Nostos?" she pressed from another angle.

"Yeah."

The therapist refrained from asking another question, letting Tyran continue on his own. But as the young man tracked each successive circle to the center of the rug, he got lost in his thoughts.

"Tyran?" the therapist interrupted.

"Yeah, sorry," he said.

"Did you forget the question?" the therapist asked. "Or, are you trying to avoid going any deeper?"

"I got what I needed from this session," Tyran said.

"But you did not..." the therapist began before getting cut off.

(Tyran): VL-OS, lighten the windows.

(VL-OS): How was your session, sir?

(Tyran): Fine. Patch me up front.

(VL-OS): You are connected.

(Myra): Yes, sir.

(Tyran): I need an update on the project.

(Myra): It's already underway and will be done ahead of schedule.

(Tyran): Perfect. Thanks, Myra.

Thura and Odigo followed Kaleo along a short trail to an opening overlooking a vast and diverse farmland. The green leafy sea was interspersed with the blue dots of fieldhands moving about through the lines. Startled by an alert from his pocket, the older gentleman stopped and fished his device from his pants. He shook his head and mumbled under his breath as he put it back and kept walking.

"We grow it all here," Kaleo said. "And if it wasn't for those workers there, no one on that concrete island would eat." He knelt and scooped a handful of dirt, letting it run through his hand. His judgment was palpable. Neither Thura nor Odigo dared to interrupt. "They can talk all they want over there about their high-minded ideals but nothin's changed here. They feel noble, though. Saying the right words without doing a damn thing. Bunch of hypocrites, if you ask me."

"You mean The Coalescence?" Thura finally spoke.

"Whatever you call it," Kaleo retorted, looking up at the couple with disdain. "They hide behind their screens and scare the wits out of people in the name of justice, they say. I call bullshit. It's all power. When you try to control what people think and what they do, and then force your ideals on everyone, it's all power," Kaleo stood up and faced Thura and Odigo. "Anybody with half a brain can see right through it. Oh, but everyone's too afraid to say anything or they'll send their goons to your goddamn house!"

Neither Thura nor Odigo had heard anyone speak so candidly about The Coalescence. They suspected that people talked more openly behind closed doors, but doing it publicly was shocking. However, Villatic was different. It did not have security cameras and constant surveillance like the mainland. And as a result, the workers, who had been sent to Villatic for refusing reeducation, regularly spoke their minds. It was evident that Kaleo had no restraint in expressing exactly what he thought.

"Look at you two," Kaleo said with even more frustration. "Runnin' around in fear because you did something they don't agree with." Thura turned away from the man. "Well, lah dee dah," he continued, not paying any attention to her change in disposition. "Who the hell made them gods? And why do they get to decide everything? They're no different than that damn preacher Prido…er Proddo. They're all the same. Pull back the damn curtain and it's all power and control. Damn every one of them."

Thura slowly walked away and back into the woods along the trail. The knot in her stomach moved into her throat. She stopped and put her hands on her knees like she could throw up. Through the waves of nausea, Thura thought again about the simulation as she ran away from Patrida with Sophia and Odigo. She thought about the Kaleo character who had helped them escape. He was so different from the one still talking loudly to Odigo. What's happened to him over the years? She thought before vomiting.

"What'd I say?" Kaleo obliviously asked Odigo.

"I'm not sure she's feeling well," Odigo said. "I'll be back."

When he approached Thura, she was still leaning over but sitting on a fallen tree with her back to him. The young man walked over and sat down beside her.

"Hey," Odigo said.

"Hey," Thura responded, wiping her mouth with her sleeve.

"Want to talk about it?"

"What are we doing?" Thura asked. Odigo knew it was a rhetorical question and remained quiet. "I didn't sign up for all the drama on the mainland, or all this stuff here. And now I'm right in the middle of it. For all the blessing of the file and the simulation, I kind of feel like it's more of a curse at this point."

"Why do you feel that way?" Odigo asked.

"Last night on the boat you asked me what the Ochi character taught me about myself," Thura began. "He taught me how fearful I am. Rather than standing up to my fears like he did, I always run away. I gained so much wisdom from Sophia, but when it mattered, I failed." Odigo put his arm around Thura and kissed her head. "The reason I fell backwards over the cliff at the end of the simulation was because I was terrified. I was trying to get away from Father Prodido so I took the easy way out. I acted like I was brave at that moment, but the truth was that I was afraid. I wanted to get away. Just like I'm doing right now by running from the mainland."

"Hey! Don't mean to interrupt or anything," Kaleo said as he approached from behind. "But just wanted to apologize. You hardly know me and I don't have much of a filter."

Thura wiped her eyes and joined Odigo with a polite smile. "We're sorry," Thura said. "We shouldn't have come here."

"The way it sounds is you didn't have much of a choice," Kaleo said.

"I didn't think I had one at the time," Thura said. "But I realize now that I shouldn't have left."

"So you're just gonna march right back over there and...what?" Kaleo asked. Both Thura and Odigo stared blankly at the older man. "Here's what you're gonna do. You're gonna come to my house for dinner. You're gonna relax and have a good night's rest before you go back. I insist."

"I think that sounds agreeable," Odigo said. "What do you think, T?" The young woman picked at her fingernails. "Thura?" Odigo asked again.

"Yeah. Okay."

CHAPTER 3

The First Church of Patrida cathedral was the first common structure erected over one-hundred-and-fifty years ago. It was centered among a dozen houses built by those who settled on the island. As word spread about this newfound isle and more people came to live there, the church became the center of the expanding community. Every evening, the residents would gather and bring enough food to feed a group twice the size. They laughed, shared stories, and cared for one another.

However, the religious building that housed so much life and vitality slowly changed as decades passed. Over that time, the community named new priests to replace the previous ones, ultimately leading to Father Maximilian Prodido. Prodido was a young man in his twenties who had grown up in the church and was hired to lead the burgeoning congregation. But as the church became just another entity among competing entities, its centrality was displaced and necessity ignored. In response to the younger generation's departure from the regular rhythms of the shrinking community, Father Prodido's judgments grew harsher. It became clear that he was becoming more rigid in his views, and had a penchant for control.

With the island culture more pluralistic than ever, removing the cathedral from the city's center seemed necessary. So when the Pangea Corporation announced plans to begin demolishing old buildings in the center of town to construct their technological superstructure, the community was delighted. In its name was the hope of bringing people together who had grown apart over time. Pangea's campus would be constructed as a circle, representing the wholeness and unity the company envisioned on the island. However, the last structure standing as an impediment to Pangea's building plans and vision was the First Church of Patrida, whose spirit and vivacity had long since waned. All that remained within the failing cathedral was the aged priest who oversaw its deteriorating importance and nonexistent influence.

Outside, a young man wearing all black walked through a ground-level corridor of the Pangea Corporation into the town center. Hurrying through the light misting rain, he approached the building. Equipment blocked the middle of the plaza. Overhead, construction workers had installed massive black canopies. The young man maneuvered through the obstacles and ran toward the church's entrance. Almost instantaneously, he disappeared inside the building.

Within minutes of the young man entering the church, three men and one woman emerged from different areas of the town center and walked casually in the same direction. As they converged near the construction equipment, Father Prodido walked out the front door and immediately turned left. The priest wore a hooded overcoat atop his cassock and moved briskly toward the closest corridor. Taking note of his sudden movement, the crew casually followed him.

The religious man soon heard the footfall behind him and increased his pace. Ducking between two buildings, he walked rapidly down a narrow alleyway. He glanced over his shoulder. The small group came around the corner and quickened their pace. The man took off his overcoat and dropped it on the ground, revealing a dark head of hair. As he turned once more, the pursuers realized it was not the religious leader they had been following. The young man smiled and then ran down the alleyway at full speed.

From the back of the church building, Father Prodido exited, wearing the dark hoodie and pants he had exchanged with the young man. As the rain intensified, the religious leader stepped between puddles before locating the sidestreet where someone would pick him up. He moved relatively well for a man in his seventies, although his breathing was short and acute. He was terrified of being seen and reported. A nervous bead of sweat emerged from his already wet forehead. His eyes darted back and forth, looking for any potential threat. While several people and factions wanted him wholly removed from the public eye, he knew someone was definitely setting him up for something he did not do.

Stopping a half block before his rendezvous point, Prodido closed his eyes and attempted to control his breathing. A tightness returned to his chest as he prayed under his breath. The religious leader watched the street impatiently. Within moments, a nondescript car emerged with its light off. Prodido walked rapidly along the sidewalk toward the vehicle. Scanning his retinas, the door opened. As the religious leader sat in the empty seat, a call came through on the video screen.

"Accept call," he said as the door shut, and the vehicle silently pulled away.

"Father Prodido," a man said. "We are all eagerly awaiting your presence."

From the west side of Villatic, a sapphire sky lay across the cobalt sea. Thura tracked the skyline and followed a maze of indigo clouds until she located the moon. Looking back to the horizon, she considered the sunset and the moon. It's fascinating how the reflecting and scattering sunlight can create such beauty, she thought. But her mind shifted to Sophia. If she were here, that would be a lesson for sure. The young woman smiled. Odigo opened the door and joined her on Kaleo's back porch.

"Waxing or waning?" he asked.

Thura paused and looked at Odigo out of the corner of her eyes. "What if I just said yes?" Thura asked back. "Wait. Are you asking about me or the moon?"

"What if I just said yes," Odigo laughed.

"Yeah. That one could go either way for me right now," Thura said.

The two stood together momentarily and watched the sun disappear behind the waters.

"I just came out to let you know that supper's ready," Odigo said. He looked at Thura and could tell she was still contemplating his question. Everything he spoke seemed like a potential landmine around her. He did not know which words or phrases, ideas, or questions would trigger her experience in the simulation. As he turned toward the door, she grabbed his hand.

"I'm a mess," she said. "I'm sorry."

"There's nothing to apologize about, T," Odigo said, squeezing her hand. "Let's go eat."

The two made their way into an ample, open space that contained a family room, kitchen, and dining area. The room had hardwood floors and wood plank walls, but it felt like a home. Kaleo sat in a rocking chair in the family room watching the news, as his wife put food on the table.

"Here. Let us help you, Alena," Thura said, looking at Odigo with wide eyes.

"Thank you," Alena said and then paused. "It's nice to have some company. We're ready, Kaleo."

The group gathered around the circular, light wood table, and Alena offered her hands to Thura and Odigo. Following her lead, the couple offered their hands to Kaleo, who began to pray. Rather than listening, Thura thought about the complexity of people and relationships. She remembered her letter to Ochi in the simulation and how she had written him off as a lost cause. She thought about how his heart had been changing when she wrote those hurtful words to him. The regret still lingered, even though it was a simulation. That was why Thura agreed to return to Kaleo's house for dinner when he invited them. While she did not agree with much of what he said earlier, she did not want to write him off like she had Ochi.

Neither Pangea nor Villatic had cultures that reinforced patience for differing perspectives. The art of dialogue had been lost long ago and only made worse recently by the proliferation of media and technology. The media profited from constant conflict, while technology made life even more impersonal. Together, they integrated carefully curated narratives within the technology, worsening a bad situation.

And as one would expect, people gravitated toward others who shared their same ideological perspective in these echo chambers. This strict homogeny only fortified and strengthened what they already believed. They never had to consider other perspectives, and no one challenged them to do so. The rightness of their own beliefs was the highest virtue. And as a result, they believed their tribe alone was the sole bearer of truth, while everyone else was considered participants in disinformation and enemies of the common good. Such complex dynamics created a battlefield upon which transcendent truth ultimately died.

Thura knew getting to know someone more deeply than their stereotype or caricature was risky. Having a conversation or sharing a meal with the enemy could put one at odds with their own group. That was partially why she left her home in Pangea proper in the first place. But she had also learned from Sophia that there were more transcendent virtues than one's rightness. Humility and kindness laid the groundwork for mutual understanding, fostering an environment where hearts could be transformed. So, as she sat down in her chair beside Kaleo, Thura hoped she could be as humble and kind as the old woman.

"Here, Thura," Alena said. "Hand me your plate and I'll put some mashed potatoes and gravy on it." Thura passed it to her, quickly glancing and smiling at Odigo.

"So how's your brother doing, anyway?" Kaleo asked Thura.

"I'm not really sure, to be honest," she said. "It's been a while since I've spoken to him." Thura paused, contemplating how much to share. She wanted to be careful not to trigger Kaleo again. "Let's just say I didn't agree with where he's taking the company."

Kaleo looked at her, tempted to ask a follow-up question, but as he glanced at his wife, she shook her head.

"Well, anyway," he continued. "You did one of those simulators and I was in it, huh?"

"Yeah, so that whole thing was weird," Thura began as she reached into her pocket and pulled out a white module. "I had one of these behind each of my ears."

"I'm somewhat familiar..." Kaleo said before being interrupted by Odigo.

"Thura, do you have that second module in your pocket by chance?" he asked.

"Um, no. I think it's still sitting on the sink in the bathroom," she said. "I didn't grab it before we left." Thura paused, attempting to understand where Odigo was going with his question. "Why? Do you think they'll find it?"

"Only if they know which house to go into," Odigo said, as everyone remained silent.

"Here, hand me your plate," Alena told Odigo, breaking the silence. "So Thura. You were saying."

"Right," Thura said. "The modules connect to a person's brain. It analyzes memories and stuff like that to create a simulated story. So yeah, you were in it, but only from my early memories of you when I was younger."

"Ah, alright," Kaleo said. "That makes sense. So tell me all about me... or him I should say."

"Well," Thura said but hesitated. She reached for her napkin and wiped her mouth. "What exactly do you want to know?" Thura was purposefully evasive because she knew his question put her in a difficult situation.

"If the character was created from your memories of me, what was he like?" Kaleo pressed.

"Well," Thura said. "There were certain things that were the same."

"Go ahead. Give me one," Kaleo said.

"You were proud of me for pushing back against the system," Thura said, causing Kaleo to look at his wife and laugh.

"You haven't changed a bit," Alena said.

"What about me was different?" Kaleo asked as he took a generous drink of water.

"Well see, you were in a difficult town with difficult people," Thura began. "But you had not given up on them." Kaleo cleared his throat and looked down at his plate. "Um. You were idealistic but not cynical. And uh. Well. You still believed in the goodness of people despite how the system treated you."

"Alright," Kaleo said. "That's good en..."

"Keep going, Thura," Alena interrupted.

"You were corny," Thura said, eliciting smiles from Alena and Odigo. "But you were sincere and optimistic."

"Excuse me," a glassy-eyed Kaleo whispered as he stood up and walked to the bathroom.

"And now with a breaking news story," a reporter on the television announced. "Pangea One News has now learned that the previously unnamed suspect in the illegal file breach has been named. Authorities have identified Father Maximilian Prodido, priest of the First Church of Patrida, as the prime suspect." Thura, equally puzzled and concerned, looked at Odigo and furrowed her brow. "Authorities have also indicated that the previously surveilled suspect is at-large and appears to have been aided by his sympathizers. While no specific information has been released, the public is being warned that Prodido and anyone connected to this fringe network should be considered dangerous."

Used cartridges and empty chip bags littered the coffee table and floor near the faded foldaway couch. Months-old crumbs and dirty plates were the only decor in an otherwise vacant apartment. The room was devoid of color and family pictures. Yet, like Tyran, the virtual world was the only space providing KT any semblance of order or connection. Despite leaving the Pangea Corporation earlier in the year, she was still beta-testing their latest artificial intelligence technology. Tyran did not necessarily want her using it after she left the company, but he did not have a choice. The technology had already been integrated into their bodies, meaning neither could disconnect from the network. Closing her eyes, KT stretched out on the couch and folded a pillow under her head.

(KT): Activate *Positive Affirmations* simulation.

(VL-OS): New or previous session?

(KT): New session.

(VL-OS): As yourself or something else?

(KT): Myself.

(VL-OS): Activating your simulation.

Slowly opening a decorative and festive door, KT peeked into a room with bright pink walls and a floor the same color. Multi-colored balloons danced in front of her as she kicked them with each step. The young woman closed her eyes and took a deep breath, smelling wafts of buttery popcorn and warm caramel in the air. Even the up-tempo calliope music put a smile on her face.

KT maneuvered through the balloons to another door. When she entered, the room erupted with cheers. The delighted young woman placed her hands over her face in surprise. Even though she did not recognize the people, she felt she had known them for years. The group of about two dozen men, women, and children began to sing and clap their hands for KT. Tears of happiness streamed down her face as she clapped along with them. Her eyes moved from face to face. Their joy was not only in their expressions. She knew they had it within. The kids appeared to have a double portion.

KT's eyes stopped when she saw a young girl that looked like her when she was little. With the music playing and people continuing to sing and clap around her, KT walked up to the young girl who held out her hands. KT lifted her arms to hold her.

"Do you remember me?" the young girl asked.

"You look familiar," KT responded.

"My name is KT," the young girl said. "I hope I grow up to be just like you."

Perplexed by her statement and the simulation's attempt at manipulating her emotions, KT glared at the young girl. Down deep, the young woman was not looking for fabricated affirmation. She was searching for something more profound. While the simulation intended to build her up, it lit a fire within her. The little girl's words were nothing but empty platitudes. She could not understand KT's adult life or what she felt inside. Her perplexion transformed into anger.

"You don't want to be like me," KT said. "And you have no idea what my life is like." Everyone in the room stopped and looked at her. The girl let go of KT's hands. The smiles in the room turned to concern. "I sit in my apartment by myself every single goddamn day. Is that what you want to be like? You want to feel like you're suffocating every moment of the day? You want heaviness and sadness on top of you all the time? Oh, I know! You want to be alone and have no one in your life. That's it! You want to feel expendable, like no one would even notice if you were gone." Then, terrified of KT's words and hostility, the girl turned and ran to her mother, crying. "That's *my* life! But you wouldn't understand that because you're not even real. You don't live in *my* world. You don't feel pain in your chest like I do. You don't cry yourself to sleep at night like I do. Because if you did, I can tell you that you wouldn't care about anything anymore. You would realize that it's all just a big, empty void. There's no purpose to any of it. It's all just wounds and trauma with no healing. So don't you dare come up to me and say you want to be like me! Do you hear me?"

A doorbell rang, suddenly interrupting the celebration.

(VL-OS): Sorry to bother you, but you have an urgent message board request.

(KT): … … …

KT stared at the floor and surveyed the mess in her apartment. She kicked a plastic bag away from her foot in frustration. Her fingers worked the bits of cracked, plastic leather that had lifted on her couch. The burden she felt within was a manifestation of her sadness and depression. She closed her eyes and leaned back, gently bumping the back of her black, curly hair against the wall.

(VL-OS): Your urgent message board request is waiting.

(KT): Yeah. That's what you said.

(VL-OS): Would you like to join now?

(KT): Yeah, I guess.

(VL-OS): Text or simulation?

(KT): Simulation.

(VL-OS): As yourself or something else?

(KT): Myself.

(VL-OS): Activating simulation.

KT looked up from the square metal table and saw a man sitting across from her. It was Egan Pearce, her point of contact with The Coalescence. While KT knew his name, she had never met him in real life, only online and in simulations. Pearce was a ruggedly handsome middle-aged man who never smiled and always exuded a straight-and-narrow seriousness during every encounter. Since their first chat room conversation when he recruited KT away from the Pangea Corporation, she knew he was all business.

"Hey uh…Mr. Pearce," KT said, shifting in her seat.

"I have another project for you."

"Okay."

"Everyone thought you did good work the last time around," he said. "You did everything we asked of you and drew no suspicion."

"Uh...thanks," KT said, avoiding eye contact.

"As you may know," Pearce continued, "our latest mark is off the grid."

"You mean the priest?"

"He slipped out of the church and we lost track of him. However, we traced the ping of the activated file to a neighborhood in the East District. Now from what I remember, your parents might be connected to the priest. Is that right?"

Pearce's dark eyes seemed to stare directly into KT's soul. He knew he was again opening a portal into her growing disillusionment. When he had first reached out to KT over a year ago, he saw a young woman desperately looking for connection and trying to make sense of the world. In some of those early conversations, Pearce had generally played on her contempt toward politics and the establishment. But as their discussions progressed over the months, he shaped and refined her thoughts and emotions against the entire hypocritical system. That was when he realized how distant she had become from her parents and how anti-Prodido she was. Pearce had been holding that final card close to his chest, wanting to play it at the most opportune time.

"Oh, you mean... are my parents connected to that regressive, narrow-minded, anti-progress extremist?" she asked with heavy sarcasm. "Or maybe you meant... are they connected to that psychotic ideologue who tells you how terrible you are for the choices you make and the lifestyle you live? You know. The guy that makes you feel less than human? Is that what you want to know?"

"I thought you might respond that way," said Pearce, almost cracking a half-smile. "We're concerned the file breach is part of a bigger play. We have reasonable suspicion that he won't stay off the grid for long."

"So why did you want to meet with me, exactly?" KT asked.

"We're concerned about contagion," Pearce said. "Fortunately, the fallout is still relatively minor, but as I've said to you in the past, one poisonous idea can spread like wildfire. So we have boots on the ground in the East District neighborhoods. We're checking all the cameras in the area. Locating who has accessed the file at this point is our highest priority."

"So you want me to be boots on the ground?" KT asked.

"No, we have all that covered," Pearce said. "Based on the high-level work you've already done, we have something more important for you. You'll head up a small security team the night of the gala."

"You want me to lead a team to protect the festivities, huh?" KT asked as she adjusted in her seat and smiled.

"Not exactly," Pearce said. "We want you to eliminate any threat that may rear its ugly head. Do you understand what I'm saying?"

"Hell yeah, I understand," KT said.

CHAPTER 4

As the crescent waned, it became increasingly difficult to distinguish between shadows and everything it illuminated. Thura walked gently through the grass as the distance dimmed the light from Kaleo's house. A pleasant breeze rolled over the hillside, pushing passed the young woman. On such a stark night, the lights of Pangea appeared brighter, even from afar. Thura situated herself among a few large rocks, which Kaleo had likely placed there for the view. Pulling her legs to her chest and wrapping her arms around them, she took a deep breath.

Despite what the news reported, Thura could not believe Father Prodido had anything to do with accessing the illegal file. Sure, he was capable of doing it, she thought. Any wild animal would recoil and then strike when cornered. And he was undoubtedly being surrounded. But she could not understand why he would send it to *her*. Maybe he was attempting to sow even more discord between her and Tyran? Perhaps he was trying to hurt Tyran, and she was just an unintended casualty? None of it made any sense. Did he not know all of this would come back on him? She wondered.

Thura scooped a small handful of rocks and tossed them one by one in front of her. After only a few tosses, she threw all that remained as hard as she could down the hill. Thura could not shake the idea that Tyran was with her in the simulation. A part of her secretly wished her brother had sent the file. She imagined it could be an olive branch, of sorts, he was extending to her. Or, maybe, his feeble attempt at bringing them together to fix their relationship the only way he knew how. Perhaps he was finally waking up to the true intentions of The Coalescence like she had been warning him. Thura continued to ponder. Maybe he's reaching out because he doesn't have anyone else he can turn to or trust. However, she could not understand why he would send her an illegal file and make her a target of The Coalescence.

Thura pulled her legs even tighter to her chest and placed her forehead on her knees. The heaviness she felt was too much even to keep her head up. "I wish you were sitting here with me, Sophia," she whispered. "How did you do it by yourself all those years?"

Thura could not even lift her head to wipe her nose. The weight on her entire body was immense. Her long sleeves absorbed the tears that ran from her eyes as she heard a soft voice. *Living daily in shadows keeps us from seeing others and ourselves as we truly are, Thura*. Sophia's voice echoed in the young woman's head. It was a refrain she remembered when she was a little girl in the simulation. Why does this have to be so hard, she thought, sniffing her nose to keep it from running. Sophia's voice replayed in Thura's head, repeating the same line.

"Hey," Odigo said, approaching quietly from behind. Thura did not raise her head or acknowledge him. "Mind if I sit with you?"

"No," Thura said, keeping her head down. Odigo sat beside her on one of the large rocks but did not speak. The cadence of the distant waves over the boulders below filled the silence between them.

"I'm just thinking about going back to Pangea," Thura whispered.

"What?" Odigo asked, not hearing what she said.

"Pangea," Thura repeated a bit louder. "I'm just thinking about what it's going to be like going back."

Thura pulled her hoodie over her head and laid back, putting her hands behind her head. She closed her eyes and thought about Ochi. In the simulation, she had imagined he was the one in the shadows the whole time. Yet, it had been her all along. She could only see what she wanted to see. Odigo laid back with her and closed his eyes. The young woman sniffed her nose again and cleared her throat.

"I only told you some things about the simulation," Thura said. "But there's more."

"Oh yeah?" Odigo said.

"Yeah," Thura said. "Like what kind of person I was in it." There was a long pause as Odigo waited for Thura to continue. "I told you I was fearful...

and that was true, but only at the end." Thura paused. "I hated the town I lived in and wanted to get out."

"Why's that so bad?" Odigo asked.

"It's how I judged them, Odigo," Thura clarified. "I was obsessed with how narrow-minded and backwards they were. And how the entire town was lost and irredeemable. I wrote a letter to my father before I ran away. I told him he was the problem. That he was the sickness of the whole town." Thura pulled her hood over her face. "But he'd been changing the whole time, and I had no idea."

Odigo remained quiet.

"I noticed I instantly went back to that really judgmental place with Kaleo earlier. And I've been the same way with Tyran for months," Thura whispered. "I don't know what's going on inside him, or what he's thinking, but I do know that I gave up on him months ago. It's like my default is to just give up on people. And I gave up on Tyran just like I did my father in the simulation."

"Yeah, Tyran's a tough one, though, Thura," Odigo said. "You don't need to be so hard on yourself."

Thura opened her hoodie and turned toward him.

"My father was a tough one," Thura countered. "But Sophia went back to him. It was only because of her that I finally saw him in a different light. She *never* gave up on him, even though she had every right to, Odigo. But what did I do? I just stood hidden behind the crowd while everyone in Salome cheered for them when they entered the village. It's embarrassing."

"Is that how you feel now?" Odigo asked. "Embarrassed and ashamed?"

"My father didn't even give up on Tyran at the end," Thura said, ignoring Odigo's question. "He knew he could die but he chose to love him anyway. That's why I'm going back to Pangea. I need to make things right with him. And if I can do that, I might just be able to convince him to send the simulation file to everyone on the island."

"Wait," Odigo said, looking at Thura with confusion. "What are you talking about?"

"If everyone met Sophia for themselves, things would change."

"You don't sound like yourself at all right now, Thura," Odigo said. "You go from a hardliner against technology to now wanting everyone in an illegal simulation, just like that? I don't get it."

"How else are people going to change, Odigo?" Thura asked, frustrated at his seeming inability to understand what was at stake. "I have to do this."

Thura and Odigo quieted. The nighttime chorus of insects rippled like the waves. Odigo reached over and held Thura's delicate hand, caressing it with his thumb, hoping to calm the tension between them. The young woman had been much more impulsive and erratic than he had ever seen before. As the gentle breeze subsided, a stillness lingered between them.

"Do you see that, Odigo?" Thura asked without giving any direction.

"What are we looking at?" Odigo asked.

"Above the water. Right over there," Thura said, not quite pointing in front of them.

"The red blinking lights?" Odigo said. "I think it's a drone, Thura."

"Uh. Maybe it's just me but it looks like it's getting closer to us," Thura said, standing up. "Is your device still on?"

"Yeah," Odigo replied.

"They know we're here, Odigo," Thura said.

The couple moved as quickly as possible in the dark back toward Kaleo's house. The drone hovered near the area where they had been sitting. From the back porch, they lightly knocked at the door and waited. Alena looked out the window and then opened the door.

"Is it normal to have a drone flying close to your property?" Thura asked.

Alena could sense her nervous energy. "No, why?" she asked.

"Okay, one just came across the water and is hovering right where we had been sitting," Thura said. Kaleo came to the door, only hearing the last part of what she said. "Me and Odigo need to leave. We shouldn't have put you two in the crosshairs like this."

"It's been our pleasure to have you," Kaleo said. "But listen. You have to be calm. Alena and I are going to walk out and get in the truck. We're gonna drive down to my office. The drone should follow us. I have a small boat down the hill from the sitting rocks. You two take it back to the mainland."

"Thank you," Thura said.

"Yes, thank you," Odigo added before the door closed.

Kaleo and Alena walked out the front door toward his old truck. The drone had moved over their house without them noticing when they came out. Kaleo started the truck and floored it, peeling out of the driveway onto the main service road. Tracking them, the drone followed closely behind. Thura and Odigo left the porch and returned to where they had been sitting only a few minutes prior.

"I guess the boat is just down this hill," Odigo said.

"Yeah," Thura whispered as if her mind was somewhere else.

"Hey," Odigo said, putting his hand on her shoulder. "You good?"

Thura stared at the lights of Pangea. From a distance, the island appeared so peaceful and serene. But Thura knew they were going back into a tinderbox. Father Prodido was suspected of accessing an illegal file he should have destroyed, making him a fugitive on the run. An alleged network of underground sympathizers had reportedly helped him escape Pangea proper. And based on the news, The Coalescence seemed to be getting stronger, exerting even more control and fascistic tendencies on the island.

Amidst the impending chaos, Thura's mind kept returning to Tyran. Though it made no logical sense, she could not shake the feeling that he had been in the simulation with her. As Thura walked ahead of Odigo down the hill, her mind raced with all that she needed to do. She had to find Tyran, make things right between them, and then convince him to send out the simulation file to every user. While Thura still had a deep disdain for technology, she realized the potential of using it to help people discover something they had never experienced before, as it had with her. In her mind, Thura believed Sophia might just be able to awaken people to their sad and tragic trajectory. Though it seemed impossible, Thura was determined to change the course of Pangea's future, and she knew her first step was finding her brother.

"Yeah, I'm good," Thura called out. "Let's just get moving."

In the distance near the port, fire rained from the sky, producing a thunderous explosion. Thura and Odigo turned to see a glowing plume of smoke billowing upward. They ran toward the tree cover and hid, awaiting the drone's next movement. An immense shockwave penetrated their bodies within minutes, causing a deafening ring in their ears. The couple fell to the ground and covered their heads. When they looked up they saw an inferno that used to be Kaleo's house. All of Villatic glowed from the towering flames above. Through the canopy, the two watched as the drone passed overhead and moved back over the water back toward Pangea.

From the rooftop of his apartment, Tyran stared out over the waters in the vicinity of Villatic. The small island was as dark as the horizon. Splashing water and maniacal laughter caused Tyran to turn. A woman sitting on a man's shoulders wrestled another couple in the middle of the pool. To the side, another group cackled in hysterics as they alternated taking shots. A steady rhythm carried those who danced together while others mingled on the edges.

"Are you excited about the festivities tomorrow night?" a dark-haired young woman whispered in Tyran's ear, caressing his bare chest with her hand.

"Yeah, I..." Tyran began.

"Yo! T-man!" a muscular man in a tank top yelled from the bar. "You need another drink, man?"

"No, I'm good! Thanks," Tyran yelled over the music. "Sorry about that. Of course, yeah, I'm really excited."

"Hmm," the young woman said, pulling him even closer. "You sure don't seem like it. Should we go inside and you know..."

Tyran turned back and stared over the edge of the glass balcony.

"Hey, what's going on, seriously?" the young woman asked, moving next to Tyran. "Look at me. Have you had too much to drink?"

"Yeah, my head's kinda spinning, but that's not it," he said. "I was in another simulation the other day and it really screwed me up."

"I've been in a few of those," the young woman said. "Some I can't shake for days."

"Yeah, but this one was different," Tyran said, facing her. "I was actually the bad guy. It was insane. I tracked my father through the woods to a small community on the other side of the island that we were on. I went there to kill him because I thought he was a traitor."

"Okay, yeah. That's messed up," the young woman said.

"Yeah, yeah. But at the end of it, I stood right in front of him. He knew what I was going to do, but he just stood there. He didn't move." Tyran paused and reflected on the moment with glassy eyes. "I thought he would try to stop me, but he looked at me with the most gentle eyes and put his arms around me. He loved me even though he knew."

"Knew what?" the young woman whispered, caressing his chest again.

Tyran took her hand off him and turned away, looking out over the water again. "That I was going to kill him."

"What! What's wrong with you? Your father! Why would you do that, Tyran?" the young woman asked in exasperation. "Turn around here and look at me! Right now! That's messed up!"

Tyran pivoted, but his gaze moved from the young woman's face to scanning around the pool. The music was no longer playing. No one was in the water or behind the bar. No empty cans or any trash was lying around. It was as if no one had even been there. In bewilderment, Tyran walked around the pool. Then, turning back, he noticed the young woman was not with him. Looking back into his apartment, Tyran saw three men standing inside the door staring at him. Then, at once, they were gone. Tyran ran to the sliding door, but they had locked it.

"Open it up!" he screamed, banging with both fists. "Open up!"

Tyran stood in front of the retina scanner, but it was not functioning. Grabbing the closest chair, he picked it up and threw it into the glass door. The chair bounced off with as much force as he had thrown it. Tyran picked it up and threw it again with even more violence, cracking the glass. The door slid open as he grabbed the chair for a third time and readied to throw it. He gasped and recoiled, expecting the men to rush out.

"What is going on, Tyran!" the young woman screamed in exasperation. "What are you doing!"

"What? I..." Tyran fumbled. "I just..." He studied each person looking at him.

The other guests gathered behind her and stared at the young man breathing heavily. His eyes darted from face to face in an attempt to discern what had transpired. His head was spinning from drinking so much. But he could not understand the events that led to him being alone outside and the men staring at him out the door. How had I not noticed that the music had stopped playing? He wondered. How had I missed everyone going inside all at once, even the people in the pool? How had I not seen the young woman go inside without seeing her open the door?

"Are we not here to celebrate your big day tomorrow?" the young woman asked. "What is going on, Tyran! What are you doing! What are you doing!"

Tyran tilted his head, stepped toward the young woman, and noticed that her facial expression did not change. He scanned the faces again and moved to the side to see if they tracked him. Each of them stared straight ahead without moving. Then, suddenly and subtly, they glitched back into their original position.

"What is going on, Tyran!" the young woman asked in exasperation. "What are you doing!"

(Tyran): Exit simulation.

(VL-OS): Simulation ended.

(Tyran): Scan software for corruption.

(VL-OS): Scan complete. I did not detect any viruses or corruption.

(Tyran): Run security test.

(VL-OS): Security test complete. No breaches detected.

(VL-OS): Is everything okay, sir?

(Tyran): VL-OS, was I in *Pool Party with Friends*?

(VL-OS): Yes, sir.

(Tyran): Delete it.

(VL-OS): Deleted.

Father Prodido walked alone down a dimly lit hallway. The corridor echoed as the heels of his dress shoes hit the glazed concrete floor. Above, two fluorescent lights intermittently buzzed and flickered but not simultaneously. The priest's shadow followed him to a metal security door, where he patiently stood after two soft knocks with his knuckle. Pulling back his sleeve, he looked at the time. It was very late, and he was exhausted. Footsteps on the other side of the door grew louder and then quieted. The muted rattling indicated multiple keys and locks. Then, at last, the door opened.

"Father, please. Come in," a tall, slender, but muscular man with a dark beard said.

"Bless you, Brother Artis," Prodido said, offering his hand and then cupping the young man's face with his other hand.

"Please, come with me," Artis said, beginning to walk. "Were there any troubles getting here, Father?"

Father Prodido stopped and leaned up against the cream-colored cinder block wall. A deep sigh reverberated down the corridor. Then, shaking his head, the weary priest rubbed his aged eyes.

"I held out as long as I could," Father Prodido said. Artis stood silently admiring his mentor. "It just got too dangerous to stay there."

The pain on the religious man's face was evident. Artis had never seen Father Prodido offer such a candid glimpse into his rigid persona. Even when the remaining congregants left in the months prior, fearing The Coalescence's threats, Prodido stayed unemotional, stoic, and encouraging. But there was no question he felt the pressure of the daily protests and the hardened resentment of the Pangean community, stoked by the constant virtual propaganda against him. However, he fought for the church's enduring presence and remained steadfast in his faith and conviction, even though he believed he was misunderstood and misrepresented. To his sympathizers, Father Prodido was not only a towering icon in the church but also the last bastion of hope against Pangea's rampant narcissism. While his abandonment of the cathedral was a defeat in some sense, his presence was a victory for the scattered faithful.

"No one blames you, Father," Artis said. "You lasted longer than any of us, but you will be pleased with how many came to welcome you."

"I'm afraid, Artis," Prodido said, touching his forehead. "I'm sorry. I should not have said that."

The religious figure moved his hand over his face and tucked his other hand under his elbow. He was physically exhausted but also mentally overwhelmed. He considered his predecessors over the last one hundred years.

Those men never had to fear the community they served, he thought. But here he stood, hidden in the bowels of Pangea, as its scapegoat. And in his mind, suffering the weight of their sins.

"I feel like I'm being set up, Artis," Father Prodido continued.

"By who, Father?"

"I don't know, exactly. But it felt premeditated and very calculated. If they link me to an illegal act and take me out of the picture, they believe you will all go away. That's why I need...I need you to take my place when...when I'm gone." Father Prodido began to cry but put both hands over his face to conceal his emotion.

"You're safe here, Father," Artis reassured the priest. "We have you protected."

"Artis, my son," Father Prodido said, wiping his eyes and placing his hand on his protégé's shoulder. "Listen to me. When I am gone will you continue to contend for the faith? The only acceptable answer is a simple yes or no. Please, Artis."

"Yes, of course," Artis said, cupping the old man's face with his hands. "Your legacy is our mission, Father. We will never stop contending for the faith, and for the heart and soul of this island. You have my word."

"Good. Good man," Father Prodido whispered, patting Artis' hands. "Now, let's go see the faithful. Shall we?"

Father Prodido led Artis down the hallway. As the religious leader walked through the open doorway, he was like a king returning to his homeland after a battle. The roar and prolonged applause was not the sound of a community whose flame was being extinguished. Instead, it was evidence of a people whose flame was instantly stoked and rekindled. Their hearts burned for their mentor and guide. Father Prodido saw their passion blazing before him as he raised one hand in the air.

CHAPTER 5

A cloud of calm had moved over the mainland. The streets were eerily quiet from the port, even for it being the middle of the night. The slightest movements exiting the boat seemed to reverberate along the concrete wall. Each crunching footstep in the gravel announced that the fugitives had returned. Although anxiety welcomed them back to Pangea, the grief of Villatic still accompanied them.

Thura was the first to reach the wall. But rather than marching forward, she fell back against it. The young woman dropped her head, partially from sadness but more from exhaustion. Sliding down the rough, abrasive surface, Thura buried her head between her legs. The sharp ringing in her ears from the boat's noisy outboard motor pulsed with her every heartbeat as if synchronized. Odigo leaned up against the barrier and slid down with her.

"I just need a minute," Thura said.

The couple sat silently, replaying everything that had transpired on the smaller island. They both knew The Coalescence sent the drone to Villatic for them. Thura thought about her final conversation at dinner with Kaleo and the tears in his eyes as he left the table. She wondered if she had offended him with her honesty. Maybe her words caught him off guard as they pierced through his seemingly impenetrable exterior. Either way, the images of Kaleo and Alena driving away from the house and the subsequent explosions haunted her. Thura's chest ached.

"They didn't deserve that," Thura said, standing back up. Odigo did not respond but followed her lead. "I don't know what we're coming back to but it doesn't feel right."

The two walked along the concrete wall, staying close beside it and out of view from the road above. The steady pacing of their breathing and soft footfall was the only evidence of them walking in the shadows below. Thura moved ahead and was the first to worm through the fence. As Odigo struggled through, Thura increased the distance between them. Whatever light she carried from the simulation felt like it was being consumed.

Thura pulled the strings of her sweatshirt tight as her hood enclosed her head. She fell to her knees, tears streaming down her face, overwhelmed by the cost of crossing The Coalescence and violating protocol. The simulation seemed so futile and powerless in the face of such overwhelming depravity. Only an hour ago, she was determined to change the island, but now the stakes seemed impossibly high, and she began questioning her decision. The pit in her stomach reminded her why so many people had chosen to escape virtually. The darkness on the island was too palpable and overwhelming.

Odigo got on his knees and put his arm around her. Thura placed her head on his shoulder as he looked down the darkened street toward their house. The front door stood open, a silent testimony to the intrusion of The Coalescence into their lives. Thura had wanted to make a difference, but it seemed she was fighting an insurmountable enemy.

"Thura, we have to get out of the road."

"I know," she said, standing up. "They've been in our house, Odigo."

The two stood, nervously watching for any movement. They moved through their neighbor's lawns, attempting to discern what may be inside. For all the couple knew, people could be hiding inside, or the house could be rigged. Odigo moved ahead, walking toward the side of the house. With his back against the white siding, he carefully shuffled sideways around to the door and stopped to listen. He waited for a few minutes. Everything remained still. Motioning for Thura, they cautiously entered, careful not to make a sound.

Odigo used the light on his device to assess the situation. When he waved it across the room, the chaos indicated someone had ransacked their home. Drawers were opened. Cushions had been removed from the couch. Books and embellishments on the shelves were scattered and broken across the floor. Each room they walked into told them the intent was to send a message.

"They must have done this before they pinged us in Villatic," Thura said.

"Yeah well, they think we're dead now so there's no point in leaving," Odigo said. "And I'm too tired to mess with the mess tonight."

"Same," Thura said, closing the front door. "Let's just clear off the bed for now. Give me your device so I can find my way to the bathroom."

Thura navigated through the clutter. She turned off the device's light and sat on the toilet. The darkness was no comfort, even though it surrounded her. Throughout her body, she was numb, but her interior was hollow. Nausea joined the darkness, increasing her discomfort. Thura put her face in her palms to stop spinning. However, everything ceased instantaneously as what felt like an electric shock went through her body. Thura stood up and flashed the light toward the sink. The white module was gone.

"Odigo," Thura said, opening the door. "They took the module." Odigo walked over to examine the area. "What do you think this means?"

"You said it was on the sink?"

"Yeah."

"I think we're fine," Odigo said. "The module's just a module. There's nothing on it. The file's encrypted on my phone."

"So why do you think they took it?" Thura asked.

"Who knows. They probably thought they needed something that looked important to take back," Odigo said. "Since we weren't here."

"On that note, I'm going to bed," Thura announced, walking into the bedroom. "Goodnight or good morning or whatever."

The doors to the private elevator closed and descended from the sixth floor to the first. Upon opening, an intricate array of light and shadows projected through Pangea's windows onto the marble floor. The sun's first rays cut through the imposing buildings, which towered around the east side of the structure to create the visual dichotomy. Tyran carefully, yet playfully, stepped out of the elevator and walked the line between shadow and light to his office door like he was on a balance beam. The performance could not have been a more perfect metaphor to start the day. Tyran was excited and optimistic about leading Pangea into a new era. But at the same time, foreboding specters hovered beside him with every step.

"Good morning, sir," Myra said, standing up.

"You're fine. Stay seated," Tyran said.

"This is a big day for our company."

"It is," Tyran said, lingering in front of her desk. "Any updates?"

"Oh yes, of course," Myra said. "The construction and creative set-up are finished in the center. Almost all of the invitation-only guests will be there. All two-hundred and fifty of the tickets we opened up to the public have been reserved. We will have casual music and appetizers before you speak, a DJ and dancing after your presentation. And lastly, Mr. Stavros and Dr. Calix will be here at the bottom of the hour to go through the final logistics with you."

"Very good. Thank you, Myra," Tyran said, walking to his office and closing his door.

(Tyran): VL-OS, turn on the news.

(VL-OS): What precisely would you like?

(Tyran): Weather.

"This is Pangea One News with your customized weather update for Pangea- West District, Tyran," a simulated reporter said. "Today will continue a stretch of unseasonably warm weather. Clear skies throughout the day will transition to clouds in the late afternoon, producing light rain in the evening. You can expect rain showers late into the night, which will taper off before morning."

(Tyran): VL-OS, give me the top stories.

"This is Pangea One News with a breaking news story, Tyran," the simulated reporter said. "Explosions rocked Villatic overnight in an apparent attack on Pangea's food production facility."

(Tyran): VL-OS, expand the story.

"With Pangea One News this is Alcie Demeter. Production facilities in Villatic were targeted overnight in what is being referred to by authorities as a case of homegrown terrorism. One field worker near the facility had this to say about the attack."

"I just looked up and there was a big fireball in the sky," he said.

"The attack comes on the heels of disgraced religious leader, Father Maximilian Prodido, being sought as the prime suspect in an unauthorized breach of illegal material," the reporter continued. "A source close to The Coalescence tells Pangea One News that Prodido continues to be a suspect at-large. They believe he is being aided by an extremist organization called *Diaspora*, which is considered the most extreme element of his religious sect. In light of recent developments, Prodido should be considered extremely dangerous."

(VL-OS): Would you like the next story?

(Tyran): I'm good. Connect me to Myra.

(Myra): Yes, sir.

(Tyran): Myra, what is the security situation looking like tonight?

(Myra): Did you not see the news?

(Tyran): Yeah, about the attack?

(Myra): Yes, that. But also the news about The Coalescence.

(Tyran): I shut it off. What is it?

(Myra): They are handling security for the event.

(Tyran): Interesting. Okay. Well just...

(Myra): Sir, your...um...uh...appointment...

(Tyran): Just send them in.

Tyran stood up behind his desk to greet the media executive and doctor. As the door opened, a man wearing a black suit entered and closed the door. The gentleman was taller than Tyran, with dark hair and a square jaw. Standing directly in front of Tyran, his posture was intimidating and exact. His eyes indicated he was only there for business.

"Um...uh...have a seat," Tyran said, motioning his hand nervously across the desk before sitting himself. The man did not move, nor did he say a word. The dynamic was extremely awkward, with Tyran sitting and the man looking down on him. "Um... where's Stavros and Calix?"

"Let's just say they won't be making it to the event tonight," the man said.

Tyran did not move, but his eyes searched the room as if looking for answers or the next thing to say. Beneath his desk, his left leg bounced nervously up and down. He wiped his palms back and forth over his thighs. It was apparent he was unsettled, even rattled. He wondered why Stavros and Calix would not be at the event. Who is this guy? Why is he here? Tyran's eyes examined the man for a clue—no rings on his fingers, no watch, no identifying marks. Tyran had never seen him before.

"You're not dealing with them anymore," the man said. "You'll only be dealing with me. Do you understand?"

"Yes," Tyran said with his head down, looking only at his desk.

"You will be receiving a script for the event. Do you understand?" the man asked. "And look at me when you answer."

"Yes," Tyran said, staring into the man's eyes.

"You do your part. Do not deviate from it. Not a single word added or taken out. Do you understand? The answer is yes," the man said.

"Yes," Tyran said, paralyzed by the situation and the dynamics.

"Afterward, we're going to have a little chat about you accessing that file," the man said as he turned to leave the room.

The hair was standing on Tyran's neck. The young man kept glancing out the window to see when the man finally left the building. Waiting several minutes before making any moves, Tyran walked from behind his desk to the cracked door.

"Myra," Tyran whispered.

"Yes, sir," Myra said in a normal voice.

"Who did that man say he was?" Tyran continued to whisper.

"He said his name was Egan Pearce," Myra said. "He told me he was the new head of security for The Coalescence."

KT unlatched the window and opened it. As she inhaled the cool, crisp autumn air, the tree colors were as diverse and vibrant as any painting she could remember. Amberglow. Golden Brown. Burnt Umber. Everything felt alive. She felt alive. The young woman would have been startled by the calico cat that suddenly appeared on the windowsill any other day. But this day, this moment was different than any other.

“Fall is my absolute favorite,” a polite voice announced from behind. Others quickly agreed with the sentiment, as KT turned and saw her best friends sitting in her living room. The fireplace accented the scent of cinnamon spice that lingered in the room.

“Fall is my favorite, too,” said KT, sinking into a soft, brown leather chair.

“Well, today is for you, sweetheart,” one of the women said. “We are here to tell you all the good things we see in you.” KT smiled as she surveyed the room. “You are one of the kindest people I know, KT.”

“And so thoughtful,” another said. “You are always thinking of others. Like when you checked up on me after my appointment.”

“She even helped watch my kids a couple of weeks ago,” a third woman added.

“KT, come to the middle of the room,” the first lady said. “Now girls, let’s surround this precious soul.” The women stood up and surrounded KT. “You are good. You are valuable. You are loved.”

“Can you say that again?” KT asked.

“Absolutely, dear,” one of the women said.

“You are good. You are valuable. You are loved,” they said in unison.

“Can you tell me again?” KT asked, closing her eyes.

“You are good. You are valuable. You are loved. You are good. You are valuable. You are loved,” the women continued

(KT): Exit simulation.

(VL-OS): Simulation ended.

KT pulled a worn blanket over her, darkening an otherwise bleak room. She turned over on her stomach and put her face into a pillow. While KT had developed a hardened exterior, likely as a defense mechanism, she ached inwardly. The severed relationship with her parents had not been on her terms. They kicked her out of their house through the counsel of Father Prodido within only a year of them first meeting him. Her parents could not have imagined that one decision’s emotional upheaval and devastation.

It was true that KT had always pushed her parents and was not much of a rule follower. She was like her father— a nonconformist at heart. But, it seemed the influence of the religious leader had captured her parents, even her father. Their new set of rigid beliefs made it difficult for them to handle any tension or disagreement with KT. What started as passive-aggressive comments to induce guilt became overt disagreements, quickly devolving into all-out shouting matches. KT's parents, specifically her father, tried to control every part of her life. They had become people she no longer recognized in such a short time. She resented them. She detested their new affiliation. And she hated the entire religious system.

(VL-OS): You have a new video message.

(KT): Go ahead and play it.

"Yeah KT. This is Egan Pearce. You're on for tonight. Plan to arrive at six. We'll walk through everything before your team arrives. Uniforms and gear provided."

The sterile, white lighting flickered and buzzed in the underground conference hall. Plastic folding tables and chairs were perfectly arranged across the concrete floor. Most of the people had already been through the breakfast buffet line. The room, once again, pulsed like it had the night before. Everyone eagerly awaited Brother Artis and Father Prodido and what guidance they would offer their scattered and directionless flock.

Amidst the chatter, heavy-heeled dress shoes echoed from the hallway with quiet laughter. Brother Artis entered, causing the room to go silent. When Father Prodido walked in, everyone stood and cheered like the night before. The faithful appeared even more wide-eyed and raucous with a night's rest. Artis took his place at a table where someone had already prepared his meal but continued to stand and applaud his fearless leader. Father Prodido placed his aged hands together as if praying and surveyed the room, nodding his head. At last, he raised his hand high to quiet the room.

"We love you, Father!" a woman shouted, causing the room to erupt again. Father Prodido put his left elbow on a wooden, makeshift podium and leaned against it, smiling and nodding. Although it was only morning, there was a weariness in his bones. A weakness had settled throughout his body. Again, he raised his hand for silence.

"I have heard the early reports about the attack," he said. "I had suspicioned I was being set up with this illegal file nonsense. To be frank, we had never even used any of those damn files in the first place. Some third-party promotion or something." Everyone laughed at his penchant for comedy, even in their difficult situation. "But I never could have imagined any of this would grow and metastasize to include you." The crowd grumbled and talked amongst themselves. The religious leader raised his hand. "Let me be clear. There is an all-out campaign that is being propagated and pushed out virtually to every person on this island. They are being told that we are religious extremists."

"They're saying we're terrorists!" a man shouted above the uproar.

"What's a Diaspora!" someone screamed from the back of the room.

"It's not right! It's not fair!" a woman in the front close to Prodido screamed.

Father Prodido raised his hand in an attempt to regain order.

"I know, I know, brothers and sisters. There is no question it has been challenging...more than challenging...since The Coalescence took control," the religious leader continued. "Fear has silenced us. Fear has driven us into hiding. Fear has made us less than human. And, I know the toll it has taken on me. Even more, the toll it has taken on you."

The room grew silent. Even those who had been serving food and cleaning up stopped and quieted. Every eye fixated on Father Prodido.

"I have been your guide, your shepherd, your mentor, your pastor, but most importantly, I have been your friend. And a friend stands up courageously for those he loves. So tonight, I will be traveling by myself back to Pangea." The room erupted in disapproval at the notion of the priest traveling alone. Everyone knew it was far too dangerous an idea. "Please, please, brothers and sisters. Hear me out. The entire island will be watching their big event. And from the stage, I will state the truth about you, my friends. Who you are and what you really represent. We are not the monsters they have portrayed. And, the island deserves to know that truth, once and for all."

"Myra," Tyran said. "I'm going to be in my office preparing for tonight. Please, don't disturb me."

Myra nodded as Tyran closed the door.

(Tyran) VL-OS, darken my windows.

(VL-OS): Yes, sir.

Tyran lay on the black, pleated leather couch and looked at the ceiling. In his mind, he replayed the conversation with Egan Pearce. He thought again about Stavros and Calix. What did he mean when he said the men would not be making the event? He wondered. And what did he mean when he said they needed to chat about him accessing the file? An uneasiness settled on the young man.

Tyran had generally been supportive of The Coalescence from the very beginning. They shared his desire to push Prodido and his church out of Pangea proper. But lately, Tyran had been feeling as if his loyalty was going unnoticed and unappreciated. He thought about KT confronting him on the steps of Pangea the night the file was accessed and then again about Pearce's veiled threat in his office. His therapist's question replayed in his mind— *why do you allow others to control you*? The young man smoldered.

(Tyran): Activate simulation.

(VL-OS): Would you like to rejoin your last session?

(Tyran): No. Activate *Wisdom in Symbol and Metaphor*.

(VL-OS): I do not recommend reaccessing this illegal file.

(Tyran): Dammit, VL-OS. I don't care. Just keep me offline.

(VL-OS): Forgive me, sir. Rejoin as Nostos? Or, as a different character?

(Tyran): Different.

(VL-OS): Which character?

(Tyran): I want to be Ochi.

(VL-OS): Would you like to return where you left off?

(Tyran): No. Go to the part where Ochi draws circles.

(Tyran): Also, I just want his skin. Make it observer mode.

(VL-OS): Activating your simulation.

The old lady handed her son the walking stick she had picked up a few miles back and had been using as they walked through the brush.

"What do you want me to do with this?" Ochi asked curiously, but still a bit on edge.

"I want you to take this stick and draw a circle in the ground around this tree," Sophia said.

Ochi tilted his head in disbelief and stared at his mother.

"Please, Ochi. Be patient and trust me in this," Sophia beckoned.

The man took the stick with reluctance. He carved a large circle in the ground about fifteen feet from the tree's trunk while muttering to himself under his breath.

"You think this is good enough? You like the look of this?" Ochi yelled sarcastically as he connected the two lines to form a perfect circle with the tree centered in the middle.

"Yes, yes. This will do just fine," Sophia responded, surveying his work. "Now, grab a piece of fruit and have a seat against the tree. I will be back shortly."

"Wait! What? Come on," Ochi frustratingly blurted out. "I really need to get to Thura, and I don't have time for more of this being alone thing."

"Son, you do not realize it right now, but you are not ready for Thura. Sit down," Sophia instructed sternly.

Ochi's mind continued to race wildly among unknowns. But it was Sophia's question, once again, that nagged at him. The old woman certainly knew how to keep him off balance. He had not thought at all about any plan. He did not know what would happen once he saw Thura for the first time or how she would respond to him. He did not know what he would say to her or how he would get her to come home.

Shadows of uncertainty covered Ochi like the leaves and branches towering above. The anxiety of Patrida had already caught up with him and rushed ahead into his future. Then, as fear strengthened its grip around his neck, he heard a rustling movement from the vicinity of Sophia's trail. Within seconds, the old woman exited and hobbled over to him with an expectant smile.

"What did you see?" Sophia asked.

"What do you mean what did I see?" Ochi asked quizzically.

"You have been sitting here for fifteen minutes," Sophia poked. "What have you seen inside this circle?"

"Was I supposed to be looking for something inside the circle?" Ochi said, laughing.

The old woman walked over to the man and extended her arm. Ochi's rough, calloused hand held Sophia's as he stood up. She stared deeply into his eyes. While she could have easily been frustrated at his obliviousness, she knew he was afraid to go deeper. Sophia put her wrinkled hands on both sides of his face and pulled his head down so they were eye-to-eye.

"What's controlling you?" she asked.

"What do you mean?" he attempted to clarify, his eyes opened wide, transfixed by the old woman.

"Who's controlling you?" she asked again. Tyran froze in Ochi's skin. His heart pounded violently. He could not understand how she could look through Ochi and see him in the simulation. "Do you not think I can't see you, Tyran? Hiding in your father's skin, endlessly drawing circles but unable to...errrr...I...I know it's you Tyran...errr...controllin...I can't se...know...cccttllnnn...er."

Everything in the simulation went black. Tyran was afraid. He did not know where he was, but he heard people talking behind him. As he turned toward the commotion, he noticed that he was still in Ochi's skin. Velos stood before him with a leather journal. She set a cedar box down on the ground next to her. Opening the page she had already marked, she read his handwritten confession as a litany of accusations.

"I hate Father Prodido," Velos screamed aloud. "I hate his ideas. I hate his influence. I hate his words. I hate the way he turns people against one another, especially my family. As I sit here and write these words, I have so much hatred and regret in my heart. I will surely kill Father Prodido."

As Tyran inhabited Ochi's simulated body, he sensed something was not right. The program inexplicably shifted from the scene with Sophia to a scene with Velos. The possibility that the simulation was faulty crossed his mind. Still, he could not shake the feeling that the artificial intelligence running the simulation knew him better than he knew himself.

Tyran had entered the simulation hoping to understand how his father broke free from Father Prodido's influence and control. In his father's skin, he wanted to feel the same emotions his father felt in each successive circle. However, as the scene shifted to the harsh and hateful words Velos read from the letter, Tyran's doubts and fears began to surface. Rather than learning how his father had discovered peace and freedom, he only heard words designed to stoke his hatred of Father Prodido.

Tyran could not help but wonder if he was destined to be consumed with bitterness and resentment his entire life, stuck in the same cycle of anger and frustration that his father had experienced. Although his father had ultimately broken free, the young man worried he would be unable to do the same. Trapped in a downward spiral of negative emotions, Tyran was unsure if he could ever change his trajectory.

(Tyran): Exit simulation.

(VL-OS): Session ended.

(Tyran): What the hell was that, VL-OS?

(VL-OS): I am sorry. I don't understand.

(Tyran): Run diagnostics.

(VL-OS): No issue found.

(Tyran): Scan security.

(VL-OS): No infections or malware.

(Tyran): Dammit, VL-OS! Update your software!

(VL-OS): Updating, sir. I am sorry.

CHAPTER 6

The deeply resonant tones of the church organ reverberated and echoed throughout the auditorium. Sixty-one pipes, divided unequally into seven groupings from tallest to shortest, appeared as the wings of seraphim. Choral harmonies accompanied the holy and haunting fugue as the parishioners stood shoulder to shoulder, singing refrains in one accord. The intonations of each person, if isolated, were varied and imperfect. But taken together, the cantata was nothing short of a transcendent experience.

In this hallowed shroud, Tyran and Thura stood behind the dark wood pew with their young heads bowed. Divinity shrouded them and held their broken hearts. Tyran mindlessly stared at the top of the pew before him, rubbing his hand back and forth as if obsessively attempting to clean it. Thura placed her forearm on the back of the pew and set her head on her sleeve, crying. It had been less than a month since their father died.

Father Prodido emerged and stepped up to the pulpit as the song ended. Wearing a green vestment with golden crosses and a much more intricately adorned stole over his white robe, the priest prayed. Then, raising his arm, he slowly moved his hand downward for everyone to be seated. Tyran and Thura were lost in a sea of dark suit coats and dresses. They folded their hands on their laps, as was expected of every adolescent in the church, and stared blankly at the kneeler beneath the pew in front of them.

"Good morning, brothers and sisters," Father Prodido began. "Today is a special day in the house of the Lord. We are honored to welcome four esteemed guests among us. These civil servants, God's entrusted servants, represent the four districts of the island. These men understand the centrality of the church as a venerated institution, and the foundation of civility and society's moral compass. Let us refrain from applause until each man is called and standing. From the East District, Georges Bélen. From the North District, Karran Sebastian. From the South District, Leander Kostas. And lastly from the West District, Fovos Savano."

The men remained standing as the audience applauded for several minutes. Father Prodido, being caught up in the energy and ceremony, motioned for the men to join him up front. The men made their way down the aisle. Two of them stood on each side of the religious leader as he continued the applause with even more vigor. While the representatives knew Father Prodido would recognize them at the service, their awkward and uncomfortable disposition indicated they did not share Prodido's enthusiasm.

"Thank you," the religious leader said. "Thank you. Thank you. You all may be seated." The representatives returned to their seats. "These men understand the necessity of the rule of law. And that for a society to function properly and for freedom to flourish, we must adhere to God's law alone and legislate what is right. For it provides the necessary framework for order and control. So we thank each o..."

Without warning, a single female protester dressed in attire no different than the congregants stood with a sign and began to chant.

"Love is freedom! Love is freedom! Love is freedom!"

Two undercover security guards disguised as parishioners entered through the doors at the back of the auditorium and walked down the aisle toward the woman. "Love is freedom! Love is freedom!" She screamed more rebelliously than before as security approached her aisle and climbed over people to reach her. Not to be outdone, the woman exited the other side and continued shouting. In response to her antics, Father Prodido lifted his hand into the air and smiled at her. The ill-considered guard stopped and sheepishly looked at the religious leader. The parishioners in that row adjusted their clothing and glared at the guards. Two additional undercover guards rushed the woman from behind, grabbing her and her sign.

"Brothers, please," Father Prodido said. "Let our guest speak freely." The guards released the woman as she pulled her sign away from them. "Please, say your piece. There is no better time or place to have a free exchange of ideas. Right, representatives?" The religious leader was not wrong in his assertion. But perched from his pulpit on high, donning a self-righteous smile, he emitted smugness.

"Love is freedom!" the woman screamed. "Love i..."

"Please, please," Father Prodido interrupted. "Do you have anything more to say? If not, I will have security escort you out. Please, calm down and talk. We can have a conversation."

The wild-eyed protester looked at the guards standing beside her, not believing the priest to be truthful. She came into the church only knowing what she had heard about Father Prodido. The caricature she had constructed was a villainous monster that cared only about controlling what people said and did. She imagined him to be a blood-drinking cultist, intent on using mind control to brainwash anyone in his presence. So from her perspective, the priest offering a platform for conversation had to be disingenuous and some sort of trap. But everyone stared at her, waiting for her to say something else.

"I...uh. I think you're a monster. You're anti-people and anti-progress," she said, pointing at Prodido. "You only use laws to control people. That's not freedom!"

"Ah yes, freedom," Father Prodido began. "Let's talk about freedom. Like the freedom you have been afforded here today to interrupt our services and speak your mind. Clearly, this is the heavy-handed control of which you speak."

"But you..." the protester said.

"Excuse me," Father Prodido interrupted. "I am not done. Freedom is not a free-for-all, as you suppose. Freedom only prospers within a framework. There must be bones within a body for form and function. Remove the bones and..."

"Bodies don't work when bones are hardened and don't move," she said. "So much for form and function. You can toss those right out the window. All your laws do is create injustice. Oh, but you disguise it as social order and all of these fanatics just nod their heads and say, 'amen.' You're nothing but a privileged authoritarian who is so fearful of his god that he has to control the thoughts and actions of the entire island."

"Your demeaning epithets change nothing about the truth," Father Prodido said. "Your version of freedom is anarchy. It is bedlam! Your idealism is detached from the real world. You say that love is freedom. What a joke. Lawlessness does not love your neighbor! But you are too blind to see that. In your opinion, what prevents rampant lawlessness? What is it exactly that keeps one from stealing from his neighbor, or destroying his property? Pray tell. For without the law, we are nothing but a society of the debased. Sadly, that is exactly the kind of community you envision and hope that we will become."

"It's my life!" the protester yelled. "Damn you for telling me what I can and can't do! Damn you for imposing your values on me! Every one of you fundamentalists are the same! You're all lunatics! Love and freedom...but always on your own terms! Everyone of you can go to hell! It's my life and I will do as I choose!"

"It is certainly your life," Father Prodido said. "I only pray that nihilists like you never get power. Because if you do... God help us. Please offer our guest a seat, or escort her out of the building."

One of the security guards extended his arm, offering the woman a spot at the end of the pew. She quickly stepped toward the stage, but another guard grabbed her arm. Yanking away, the protester turned and walked down the aisle to exit. From the back, she regained her composure and screamed again.

"All you little kids! You better listen up!" She looked at Tyran and Thura. "You're being controlled and brainwashed by this monster! Wake up!"

The guards apprehended the woman and escorted her into the foyer. Murmuring among the congregation transformed into a more audible and unsettled chatter. While they valued the priest welcoming outsiders, they did not appreciate offering the floor to someone with such dangerous and radical beliefs. They believed ideas shared were like seeds sown and a welcoming soil was fertile ground, especially amongst their children. Father Prodido could hear a few of the voices closest to the stage and immediately regained control.

"Ahem, yes. That was not quite what I intended," the priest began. "Let me first offer my apologies to each of you for what just occurred. While I do believe there is a time and place for honest dialogue, I put my interests ahead of the congregation. I do not think too highly of myself to admit when I am wrong. And in this instance, I was wrong. The pledge I make to you this moment forward is to always protect our children from perverse ideologies that may one day lead them astray. This is a battlefield and we must fight for their hearts and minds with the truth."

A few people stood and clapped for the religious leader. They were soon followed by several more until the room clapped and cheered.

“God bless you. God bless you all,” Father Prodido said. “Please, now go in peace today.”

The aisles were instantly fuller than the pews as the holy became hungry. Tyran and Thura slowly made their way to the center, attempting to navigate toward the stage. But the flow was like pushing against a river. The two were lost in a steady stream of black suits and dark dresses. Cheap perfume and stale smoke were as overwhelming as the current of bodies moving against them. It was all suffocating. A hand gently grabbed Tyran’s arm and led the siblings through the crowd. As they approached the front, the older man looked over his shoulder at the young boy, nodded, and then disappeared. Tyran and Thura walked up onto the stage and made their way to Father Prodido. The priest turned his back on them and began walking, anticipating they would follow closely behind.

The religious leader walked down a darkened hallway, stopping short of his heavy, hardwood door. Pausing behind him, the children waited. Father Prodido unlocked the door and slowly opened it. Tyran walked in as the priest stood by the door. But as Thura stepped forward, he slid in front of her, his haunting appearance looming large. Father Prodido’s countenance was ominous and sinister, although it may have only been the scarcity of light causing the effect.

“And where do you think you are going?” he asked. The darkness beneath the grim figure enveloped Thura. “There are no females permitted in my office. Nor will there be any consideration for a female to serve as an acolyte.” He paused, but Thura did not move or break her gaze. Then, the priest shouted at once, “Do you hear me!” The reverberations and echoes were louder than his original exclamation. Thura turned and ran in fear. The young girl was not only heartbroken from her father’s passing but also lost and traumatized by the religious leader. She rushed through the menacing hallways of the church, trying to find a way out.

Father Prodido entered his austere office. His dress shoes clapped the wooden floor with each step. He removed his religious garments and then faced the young man without sitting, only leaning up against his dark mahogany desk. Tyran sat on an uncomfortable wooden bench and stared at the floor, which was as plain and bleak as the office walls. If one did not know better, one would not expect Prodido’s congregation to be so lively and spirited. By the room's appearance, Father Prodido could be easily mistaken for an ascetic who abstained from every indulgence.

"I understand you want to follow the strict path," Father Prodido began with no greeting or formality. "Certainly a noble endeavor for a young man." Tyran nodded but did not look up. The priest stood silently, looking down upon him. "Serving as an acolyte is not a position of function but of uncompromising faith and rigid discipline. You do understand this, correct?"

The young man remained listless, almost unconscious. His eyes were open, but he was not present. Prodido cleared his throat to regain the young man's attention. Tyran eventually looked up but only as high as the religious leader's chest. His eyes were red and glazed over. The young man cleared his throat and spoke softly.

"Where do you think my dad is?" Tyran whispered, rubbing his eyes.

Father Prodido watched the young man but did not immediately answer. Instead, he replayed the encounter with the protester and his subsequent apology to the congregation. He knew he had committed to be resolute and inflexible in matters of the faith. There would be no more obscuring or watering down the truth for the children or young adults of the church.

"We always walk the line between heaven and hell," Father Prodido said. "One can never be certain of their salvation or where they might spend eternity."

Tyran made eye contact.

"So there's no way to know where my dad is?" the young man asked.

"Let's say a businessman loses his wife," the religious leader said. "He is raising his children by himself. Oh, he wants to give them standards and a religious framework to live within so he takes them to church service each Sunday."

The young man squinted his eyes and furrowed his brow, seeking to understand the religious leader. "Is this story about my dad?" he asked.

"The man pitches in at community meals," Prodido continued, ignoring Tyran's question. "He even shares the leftovers with the poor and needy on the streets. By all appearances, he is certainly a good man. But what is goodness, exactly? And from where does this goodness come?"

Tyran started to answer, but Father Prodido cut him off.

"Despite all appearances of being good, what if one is never baptized into the church? What if one never once acknowledges the truth that there is nothing good that resides within them?" Prodido's voice grew louder along with his unprovoked agitation. "Goodness only comes from above when you have been washed of your transgressions and unrighteousness!" The room quieted as an uncomfortable stillness stood between the priest and the young man. "You can understand the dilemma, no?" Prodido whispered.

"But my dad was a good man," Tyran said. "Everyone knew he was good."

"Have you been listening to anything I have said, son?" Father Prodido raised his voice again. "Your father was a lost soul, walking around aimlessly in darkness, stumbling into a few nice gestures. But he never once, *never once*, repeated that old, trustworthy and faithful line that ensures one's salvation-*there is nothing good in me*. And without the assurances of that confession and the water that washes away our every impurity, I find no other destination for your father than eternity in hell."

Tyran put his hands in his face and began to cry.

"Oh, the first death is anguishing," Father Prodido continued, seeming to relish in his power. "But the second death is torment."

The sobs from Tyran were audible. The religious leader elicited a pounding in the young man's chest, producing profound enmity. At that moment, even though he had never experienced such deep animosity, he hated the priest. Father Prodido was a cold and callous character, detached from emotion except for his own satisfaction. The detestable figure even appeared to take delight in the boy's anguish.

"For an acolyte, the strict path begins with those all-important words," Father Prodido said. "For one must be brought down before they shall be lifted up. Now, stand up, son, and repeat the good words after me." Tyran stood reluctantly and wiped his eyes but refused to look at the older man.

"I, Tyran Kala," Prodido began.

"I, Tyran Kala," he mumbled.

"In the presence of God and the priest of the First Church of Patrida," Prodido continued.

"In the presence of God and the priest of the First Church of Patrida," Tyran whispered.

"Declare today," Prodido said. "There is nothing good in me."

"Declare today," Tyran paused. He made eye contact with the religious leader and burned. "There is nothing good in me."

"Say it again," Father Prodido demanded.

"There is nothing good in me."

"Again!"

"There is nothing good in me," Tyran cried.

"Good. Now then," Father Prodido said, moving across the room to grab his overcoat. "You will begin training tomorrow morning at 5 o'clock sharp. The expectation is that you will be fully dressed and sitting here fifteen minutes ahead of time. Do you understand?"

CHAPTER 7

Against the pewter sky, the slate-gray buildings seemed to blend together. Even the windows that climbed skyward were ashen and silver. The evening cityscape was as monotone as the city itself. A torrential downpour in the early afternoon had transitioned to intermittent sprinkling. When the windows of the nondescript vehicle were made opaque, beads of precipitation appeared to disappear. Hidden within, Odigo programmed their destination to an infrequently traveled intersection ten blocks from Pangea proper. The young man then glanced at Thura. Her eyes fixated on the window to her left despite being unable to see through it. Odigo put his hand on her knee, but she did not move or react.

Thura was present but distant. She was in the car but also looking down on herself. From above, she witnessed surreal inertia moving her from point to point. The young woman spent so much of her life running from fear and conflict she did not know what it was like to face either. Even though Odigo's thumb rubbed her leg, she could not feel anything. The events of the previous days left her numb. Whether sleeping all day or dissolving into her vehicle's hypnotic hum, the young woman tried to isolate herself from all thoughts and feelings.

While it may seem that Thura was only trying to evade The Coalescence due to accessing illegal material, the reality was that she was running from so much more. As Tyran entered his twenties and assumed leadership of the Pangea Corporation, he aspired to build upon his father's business. Unfortunately, the company had flatlined after Ochi's passing, barely staying solvent over the years until Tyran was old enough to take over. The young man knew they had to grow beyond the social network for its users. The business model needed to evolve from simple word interactions on a screen to fully integrated experiences of the heart, mind, and body. Tyran knew the company's next evolutionary step was in simulated and augmented realities. That vision and KT's programming skills birthed VL-OS, or the *Virtual Life Operating System*. VL-OS would be embedded in wearable modules, interfacing with one's brain to create simulated infinite worlds and endless possibilities.

Thura initially saw the novelty of the idea. However, she also believed this new venture would have unintended negative consequences like social media. From her perspective, the addictive element of technology was already bad enough, so giving people endless worlds to live infinite lives would only further disconnect them from real life. Also raising flags for her was the harm it would cause future generations regarding their social and emotional development. But Thura's most significant concern was the possibility of a person or entity violating another's privacy and bodily autonomy. Specifically, she was concerned bad actors would use it to exploit people. She knew if they put technology into a person's body, it would eventually be accessed and compromised. It was inevitable. And then, users could be manipulated and controlled without their knowledge or consent.

Tyran argued, however, that they designed the modules only to be attached outside the body, behind one's ears. He said the modules could be disconnected and easily removed from a person after use. So from his perspective, the threat, while certainly a possibility, was significantly minimized. No one could ever hack *into a person* because the technology did not afford that opportunity.

Knowing that Tyran was doing his best to resurrect the business, Thura ultimately went along with the product. However, she clarified that she would never support putting it inside anyone. That was the red line she told Tyran she would never cross. But Tyran had a career and financial interest in the company's continued success and growth. So he developed a newer technology that would no longer have to be attached to the body like the white modules.

The new technology would always keep a person connected to the network, eliminating the use of modules. As a result, Thura refused to back Tyran and the development of this future product. This schism between the brother and sister was terrible. But it worsened when Thura heard that The

Coalescence wanted to "partner" with the Pangea Corporation. That is when she left. Thura knew her greatest fear was no longer a matter of *if*. It was only a matter of *when*.

These thoughts were on Thura's mind as she and Odigo traveled into the city. She desperately wanted to know if Tyran had sent her the file. She also wanted to see if he had been in the simulation with her. But she wondered if there was a way to help him see the true intentions of The Coalescence. It was obvious to her that they only wished to be involved with him to get their hands on his new technology. She knew they were not nearly as uncorrupted as they seemed. From Thura's perspective, they *would* use it to control people. That kind of personal access would allow them to mold, shape, and even manipulate people without their knowledge. Thura had always believed the most significant threat would be someone hacking into the system and people's minds. But hacking appeared unnecessary, as Tyran was opening the door for The Coalescence to walk right through.

"I'm proud of you," Odigo said, squeezing Thura's leg. The young woman was as lost and detached as he had ever seen her. Within only a few days, Thura had traveled from the highest heights to the lowest depths. Yet, despite her mental and emotional distance, he knew the best he could do was offer her encouragement.

"What?" Thura asked.

"I'm proud of you," he repeated. Thura did not respond. Instead, she placed the side of her head against the window and closed her eyes. Despite the window's opacity, the bright lights of the Pangea Corporation illuminated the inside of the car. The radiance reflected through the remaining raindrops and moved across Thura's face. Odigo reached for her hand and brought it up to his lips. "No matter what happens."

"Yeah," she said with her eyes still closed.

The car slowed as it arrived at its destination. The couple covered their faces with dark masks and pulled up their hoods as the doors opened. Thura walked through the puddles of a vacant parking lot and stood in the shadows of a rundown building. With Odigo giving the vehicle instructions, the young woman watched him walk across the lot toward her. It had been quite some time since she had allowed herself to feel this way. Through everything that had transpired over the last few days, Thura had treated Odigo as more of a sidekick than a romantic interest. And she knew he did not deserve to be a victim of her despondency. So when he approached, she pulled down her face covering and pulled him in close.

"Take off your mask," she said before kissing him.

The doors of the conference center opened, and ten young adults exited. Each of them carried a bright yellow shirt with the word *Security* emblazoned on the front and back. The orientation lasted only twenty-six minutes, which included Egan Pearce on the phone with someone for six minutes. Touching multiple screens with hundreds of words was hardly training. The process felt more procedural than instructive. Yet, everyone was pleased with its brevity.

For KT, the session was barely a walk-through. She did not even get to meet her team officially. But her agitation was likely from not having a smoke in over an hour, and she knew it. KT emptied her last cartridge at her apartment and did not have time to pick up replacements before heading to the conference center. With only fifteen minutes remaining before she needed to be in the plaza with the security team, KT took a hard left toward a convenience store. From behind, she heard someone walking behind her, almost on her heels. When she stopped, a young man bumped into her.

"Yo. You following me or what? Back off," KT said.

"No, hey," the young man said nervously. "I, um, you're KT, right?"

"Who's asking?" she countered. KT remembered him from the training but did not know his name. He caught her attention because he was short and skinny with longish, brown, greasy hair. While she thought the "security team" looked like a rag-tag group anyway, this one really stood out to her.

"Nico," he said, jerking his head to get his hair out of his face. "My name's Nico. I just wanted to tell you that you're pretty much legend status at this point."

"Why would you say that?" KT asked, taking a hard step toward him and grabbing his shirt with her fist. "Are you a part of The Coalescence or what?"

"Sorry," Nico said, attempting to backtrack. "I wasn't trying to upset you. Seriously. I thought you would like me saying that."

"I don't even know you," KT said, letting go of his shirt and walking away. The young man's shirt was stretched and wrinkled around the neck, but he did not seem to notice.

"To answer your question, though," Nico shouted out. "I'm part of The Coalescence, I guess. Whatever that means."

KT turned and walked back. "What's that supposed to mean?" she asked.

"Besides me, do you know anyone else who's a part of it?" Nico asked.

"Yeah, man, listen," KT said. "I don't know what your angle is but..."

"They're all bots," Nico said, getting to the point. "The Coalescence is like a thousand bots and three or four humans. And that includes me and you. That's it."

"That's ridiculous," KT scoffed. "How would you even know something like that? And you have like fifteen seconds because I need a hit fifteen minutes ago. My irritation factor is super high right now. Got it?"

"Because I'm the guy behind the bots," Nico said. "Most of it's artificial intelligence but I still run some of the scripts. All the people you talk to online that you thought were Coalescence... all bots."

"Not true. Times up," KT said. "Egan Pearce is real, bitch."

"How was your simulated meeting with him?" Nico asked. "Oh right, you're probably wondering how I knew that you had a meeting with him, huh? My parents are *regressive, narrow-minded, anti-progress extremists*. Did I get that right?" He laughed and then jerked his head to get the hair out of his face.

KT glared at Nico. Her anger immediately eclipsed the confusion running through her mind. She lunged at the young man as if she would punch him with her left fist. But when he moved his head to avoid the strike, KT punched him in the face with her right.

"You're an idiot," she said, walking away and shaking her hand. "There's something wrong with you."

"Wait," Nico said, holding his face and attempting to catch up. "I thought you would like to hear all that stuff."

"Bad plan, Rico," KT said. "It backfired, son. Beat it."

"Okay. Bad plan," Nico said, following KT into the convenience store. "But don't you even wonder what's really going on?" She picked up the cartridges and walked to the scanner. "Like the training. Twelve people with no security experience. We can hardly secure our front doors. Don't you think it's just a little bizarre? It's off, right? What experience do you have leading a security team?"

KT left the convenience store and turned to face the young man. "Last chance. Tell me what you want to tell me," she said.

"There's definitely something bigger going on," Nico said, jerking his head. "And it isn't as organic as it seems. There isn't some vast network called The Coalescence. It's all smoke and mirrors. It's an illusion. But that's what they want everyone to believe. It's all bots pretending to be people." KT stared at Nico in disbelief. "I know I messed with you. I'm sorry. Again, bad plan. Terrible plan. But I know all of this is true cause I'm the one doing it."

"So you're saying what? This whole Coalescence thing was manufactured by the media? By some mystery person behind the curtain?" KT asked, laughing and then blowing a hit.

"I guess, yeah," Nico said. "All I know is that The Coalescence is a lie. It's not a bunch of angry and outraged hackers. Somebody wants everyone on the island to believe the people at the bottom are in control. But as far as I can tell, it looks like the opposite is happening."

"Okay," KT said, hitting her device again and blowing a massive cloud. "Let's say I do buy into this wild story. Other than the obvious... *why in the hell would you do this question*...who exactly told you to do this and why did they want you to do it?"

"Seemed exciting, and an easy way to get some money, honestly. I'm all about the hustle," Nico said. "But now that I see what's going on, though, I'm not sure I'm down with it. But to answer your question, I don't know who it is. Maybe you could ask Egan Pearce. He probably knows. Maybe it's only one person. Maybe more, I guess. I don't know. But it's pretty obvious to me that you were recruited for access to your old boss, if you know what I mean."

"Who else knows what you just said?" KT asked, stepping at Nico.

"I haven't told anyone. I swear."

"Keep it that way," KT said, taking one last hit and walking away.

Father Prodido exited the vehicle and watched it quietly leave. The religious leader glided over the glistening sidewalk reflecting the distant lights of Pangea. He was careful to stay close to the buildings as he walked. But staying in the shadows was nearly impossible. Every fifty or so steps, he crossed an intersection and was fully exposed to the light. He marched quickly to avoid being so naked and vulnerable. Normally, he was saddened by how vacant the downtown neighborhoods and businesses had become. But on nights like these, the priest was somewhat thankful for most people being in their houses connected to other realities rather than moving about the streets.

The back of the church building was dark. While the artificial lighting of the Pangea Corporation radiated nearly three hundred and sixty degrees outward, it left the church's rear entrance remarkably hidden. Music from the town center reverberated through the alleyways and shook the old building. Father Prodido walked up the concrete steps and scanned his retinas at the door. After a click of the lock, the priest entered and strolled down the hallway to his office. He lit a candle and sat in an old, worn brown leather chair, closing his eyes.

A moment of stillness was a rarity on an island constantly bombarded with information and news. Fabricated realities had created an addiction to continuous movement and stimulation. No one understood monotony or boredom anymore, and he believed they were paying the price for it—mentally, physically, and spiritually. It was possible to go an entire lifetime without looking inward or contemplating one's life or existence. The excitement of becoming someone or something else in different virtual frontiers ravished their present reality's sacredness. Father Prodido sank into his seat and breathed deeply for a few minutes, reflecting.

The priest thought about his church community of the past. He had many fond memories of friends and acquaintances over the years, including people they had helped and cared for. Father Prodido remembered one family buried by debt. The church carried them for over a year until they got on their feet again. Relishing the memory, the priest opened his eyes and reached for some old photos. One picture showed them serving meals together. The next picture was of them working side-by-side at the local food bank. He rubbed the top photo with his thumb as a tear welled up in the corner of his eye. They were not perfect. He was not perfect. But they were together, not in manufactured realities, but side by side, caring for each other and the community.

For all the warm sentiments, there was a gnawing that would not go away. The feeling had its own intention and demanded the priest pay attention to it. It was not guilt as much as it was remorse, not ego as much as it was heart. One could have mistaken the moment as one old man's acute awareness of growing old and reflecting on his regrets. While this was partially true for Father Prodido, it was so much more than that. The ache was rooted in how he thought about people his entire life and how he treated them. He saw a deep love and connection among people in the pictures. But when he looked at his younger self, smiling amidst the group, the image did not accurately convey what was in his heart at the time. His exterior was upright, moral, exacting, and righteous. But inside, he was sad, fearful, and judgmental. Although he had been changing, softening as he grew older, he wished he could reconcile the dissonance.

The priest set the photos down on the ornate side table. Then, picking up his rosary beads, he made the sign of the cross over his head and chest. The old man slowly moved to his knees and put his elbows on the leather chair. Still grasping the beads, he placed his forehead on his folded, prayerful hands and whispered the rosary under his breath. His aged fingers massaged bead after bead as he prayed over them. But when he got to the fourth bead, he spoke aloud.

"Pray for us sinners now and at the hour of our death." He paused and choked up. "Pray for...pray for..." The priest began to cry. For the first time, he was able to see himself and how people outside his church saw him—uncaring, self-righteous, and divisive. He understood why the terrorist caricature was so easy for people to believe. Every heinous action, whether true or fabricated, becomes believable when one is already perceived as a monster. He realized the part he played in the creation of this villain. He had spent his entire life avoiding and denying, projecting his every insecurity and judgment onto others. But, alone on the floor of his office, the old man could no longer point the finger at anyone else. He was the one in need of saving. For all the ways he had enshrouded himself in fabricated virtue and artificial peace, he finally saw his interior poverty.

"Pray for me...a sinner..." Father Prodido cried as he buried his face in his arms.

Crowds of the extravagantly dressed arrived in the town center. *The Event*, as the media frequently referred to it, was reported as the most consequential and important event in the island's history. At the same time, they were quick to weave the narrative of homegrown terrorism and the necessity of extra security precautions into the story. Even the video wall that encircled Pangea's inner facade played the heavily curated breaking news report on a sixty-second loop. The first fifteen seconds were of Tyran and the Pangea Corporation's product launch. The remaining forty-five were clips dedicated to Father Prodido, the Diaspora, and the devastation in Villatic.

The red sun had fully set in the westward sky, but it was not apparent to anyone inside the glass walls of Pangea. Yellow-shirts moved amongst the crowd to give them a sense of security. VIPs mingled throughout the plaza and ate hors d'oeuvres. Suddenly, the lights and the video wall went black. In complete darkness, half the crowd cried out in fear while the other half gasped aloud. Almost simultaneously, lights flashed above, accompanied by deep, resonant booms. A DJ put his arm out from behind his turntable on the stage and bounced up and down. Like a ripple across water, those closest to the stage bounced until the entire town center looked like a massive wave. Along the video wall, a five-minute countdown to the event started.

"Hey!" a voice shouted through the music. KT turned to see Nico in a shirt at least two sizes too big for his frail torso. He had tucked the front of his yellow shirt into his oversized pants, held up by a faded black, woven leather belt. It looked as if he had attempted to comb his hair, but only the front was wet and went straight over to the side of his head. KT rolled her eyes and turned away from him. "Hey! Here we are, huh?" Nico moved to face KT.

"Yeah, here we are," KT said sarcastically.

"How are you feeling about all this?" Nico asked.

"What do you mean?" KT responded.

"The whole threat thing," Nico said. "You think they would really do something tonight?"

"Who knows," KT said with indifference.

"Did you get that alert earlier?" Nico asked.

"Yeah, I got it."

"I don't know," Nico continued. "I just don't trust that preach...holy crap...you have a gun!"

"Look, man," KT said. "Back off. I don't wanna talk about it. Yeah, I have a gun. Yeah, they're a cult. I know because my parents are a part of it. Haven't talked to them in forever. I hate the old man with everything in me. Would I shoot him if he showed up? Maybe. But my parents aren't terrorists. And they're not going to do anything here. So shut it and do your job."

"And now, the president and CEO of Pannnnn-Geeeee-Uhhhhh!" the DJ announced. "Tyyyyy-Rannnnn Ka-Laaaaa!"

The lights flashed, and the music bumped even louder as Tyran ran up on stage, waving and pointing to the crowd. The truth was that he did not know anyone standing in front of him. Like most people on the island, whatever leisure time they had outside of work was spent in their homes, lost in other realities. So it was unlikely that anyone in the crowd knew each other either. But from the stage, Tyran played his part well. And from the ground, the crowd played their part even better.

"It's an honor to stand before all of you today!" Tyran shouted. "Whether you are joining us virtually or here in the town center, we welcome you to this momentous event.

"Beginning with my father, Ochi Kala, our vision has always been to create spaces that bring people together for positive and meaningful experiences. It began with his venture into social media. That first step allowed *you* to create your own virtual territory, post content important to you, and exchange ideas with others. Then, those virtual spaces evolved into simulated experiences where you could enter and live in infinite worlds created by you and for you. In these infinite realities, you could be anyone or anything you like, go anywhere you want, and live the life you have always wanted...with no consequence." Tyran paused and smiled at the audience to their delight. "And tonight, we take the next step into that future.

"When we built the first section of this building here in the West District, our intention was more than developing technology. We knew we were also at the forefront of shaping culture. As each old building fell in this area, we believed it to be symbolic. These structures represented the outdated, divided, individualistic way the island used to be ordered. But we envisioned a new way of living that would rise up in its place. So we built a structure that would come to represent that new way, a structure that would symbolize our company and us as a people. This is where we stand today. And to accompany this new vision, we changed our name from Kala, Inc. to Pangea." The crowd clapped and shouted in approval. "Pangea would bring people together and become a beacon of light illuminating this island and the individuals and families that live here.

"Each individual section of this super-structure was constructed in hopes of forming a perfect circle. This circle represents each of us individually coming together through Pangea's technology to live perfectly with one another. But as you may have noticed..." Tyran paused, giving a cheesy grin to the audience, "...there is one last building that keeps us from closing this circle. But tonight, I'm happy to announce that Pangea will be complete! We are closing the circle!"

The crowd roared in delight.

"This last piece holds special significance for me, as I'm sure it does for you. The building standing behind me has always represented fear and control. We were always told the only way to experience life and freedom was by following clear rules of morality. But this backwards mentality was far from freedom. Instead, it constricted and stifled us. It created people who were scared and unhappy. No one could be good for always being told we were bad. What a reality, right?" The crowd roared even louder as the lights flashed off and on to accompany their applause. "That's why I'm beyond delighted to announce that the church's demolition will begin next week. And in its place, we will continue to build something new! Something that abandons the old ways. While this reality is only one of the infinite many we are creating, we will try to make it as appealing as the others. No longer will there be extremists telling us how to live our lives! Pangea will be a place where you can do what you want to do and be who you want to be! That is real freedom!"

Tyran paused to savor the roaring applause and whistles from the crowd. Beneath the flashing lights, his sentiment and message were popular among those who hated the church and Father Prodido. However, his position was wholly disingenuous. Neither Tyran nor the people of the island saw the error in their dualistic thinking. They had no problem speaking boldly against the church for controlling people through fear. But they were unwilling to call out The Coalescence for doing the same thing. While both used the same tactics toward different ends, it was easier to speak harshly against the religious institution when it was the trendy thing to do and when it had no power. The church was an easy target. However, this duplicity made them all quite hypocritical. They were quick in critiquing one while turning a blind eye to the other.

While their position may have appeared to be based upon principle, it was a position of convenience. If they really believed in speaking out against control and fear, they would call it out no matter where they saw it. But they did not speak out against it. That was the great irony. No one could see how hard the pendulum had swung in the other direction. Its momentum was fueled only by what they were against, not by any virtue or transformative inner experience. With only a change in their words to the neglect of their hearts, the mantra of replacing the old way with the new way was an empty proposition. It was the *exact same way*, with a different name and version of being right. But no one saw the profound error in their thinking— that everything always devolves into fear and control if it does not have a divine center.

"Speaking of freedom, our newest technology will give you even more freedom!" Tyran continued. "That's what you're here for, right!" The crowd screamed, anticipating what they had been waiting for. "No longer will you have to wear modules behind your ears! No longer will you need a handheld device! No longer will you need to submerge your entire body for a fully immersive experience!" The cheering went beyond being loud. It was palpable. "I know what you're thinking, if we don't have to wear it then it will have to be implanted, right? Well, most people believe this is the next logical step.

But I think that's too invasive. That's not how we do things at Pangea. We don't take next steps! We make giant leaps!"

At the height of the audience's frenzy, Tyran reached into his pocket, pulled out his clenched left fist, and held it out in front of himself. The crowd immediately quieted. The lights in the plaza darkened except for one spotlight beaming down at the center stage. The screens encircling the plaza showed a close-up of his outstretched arm, slowly and dramatically focusing on his fist.

"This..." Tyran said, opening his hand with his palm up, "...is The Black Pill."

The crowd gasped as everything faded to black. A video played on the screens encircling the plaza.

"The Black Pill," a female voice said over powerful, deeply synthesized electronic beats. "Powered by the Virtual Life Operating System, or VL-OS. This is a giant leap in simulated and augmented reality. Imagine millions of white modules put into one single pill. With Pangea's patented nano-module technology, one pill releases millions of modules throughout your body's endovascular pathway. Attaching to this pathway and using the most secure chain technology ever invented, these nano-modules communicate between your body and Pangea's island-wide network. You are now connected everywhere you go. The Black Pill creates worlds of infinite possibilities, all in a single pill. The Black Pill by Pangea."

With the screens again fading to black, a single voice introduced the next video.

"I am VL-OS. Where would you like to go today?"

Inspirational and energetic synth music accompanied scenes of artificially, yet vibrantly, created worlds. Shots of diverse cultures working, eating, and playing together displayed endless realities and possibilities. Families walked on strange, other-worldly planets. Work environments transformed into beachfront paradises. Rainy days in the house became a villa in a tropical rainforest.

"Not only do I create worlds," VL-OS said as the video images continued. "I can transform your environment and the people around you."

Entertainers and athletes were shown performing in people's homes. Neighborhoods became castles with golden streets. The roads of downtown

Pangea became a snowy mountain village. Family pets changed into lizards, tigers, and humans. Friends swapped faces and laughed as they pretended to be each other.

"Where would you like to go today?" VL-OS asked again. "And who would you like to be?"

The audience stood in awe when the video finished but then exploded in applause.

"Let's hear it for Pangea's Black Pill and VL-OS!" Tyran said, clapping his hands. "How about a demonstration? Where do you want to go?" Each person yelled a different destination as Tyran grinned from ear to ear. "Okay, let's do it this way. I have already taken The Black Pill and am connected to the network. VL-OS, put what I'm seeing on the screens." Instantly, the crowd saw themselves from Tyran's perspective. "Set us in a vast, green countryside with rolling hills all around us." Tyran turned his head from side to side. The video screens showed the crowd standing beside him in long, lush grass, blowing in the wind with perfectly blue skies. "Alright, VL-OS, turn us all into sheep." The crowd laughed as they watched the screens and moved around the plaza like animals, oblivious to the unintended satire. "Alright, alright, alright. You've seen the power and possibility. And now, just when you thought it couldn't get any better, I've saved the best for last. Not only will The Black Pill be available beginning tomorrow in the West District, and each successive district in coming weeks, it will be free! Yes, free! Thanks to our generous sponsors, The Black Pill will be given out to every person on the island for free. Thank you again to our sponsors. And thank you for coming. And now...let's party!"

CHAPTER 8

The island appeared content and whole from above. Neither people nor their problems could be heard. No dividing lines were visible. No hierarchies were apparent. No sense of we or they could be imagined. Blue waves crested as white seafoam gently massaged the coastlines. The isle exuded peace and serenity. But this vantage point was from a distance. From within, the island was full of sadness and tragic paradoxes.

The word *pangea* originated from the idea that separated landmasses were once one single landmass, one unified whole. The vision to embody that word became the aspiration of the entire island. However, in their stated goal of reuniting society's fractured parts, their idealism was tempered by one major constraint- everyone had to think the same way.

So while they celebrated differences in everything from appearance to talent, aberrant thinking was taboo. Diversity on the island was really not really diversity. If a person or a group did not conform to the officially parroted narrative or the majority's beliefs, they were minimized and excluded. Differing viewpoints were mocked and censored. And then, those who refused this forced conformity were labeled as unenlightened and regarded as an enemy, sometimes christened as evil.

This unfortunate situation created even more perplexing paradoxes on the island. In the past, the island's populace had always been rightly suspicious and resentful of any power structure. They believed it was inherently unjust and oppressive. Yet, when The Coalescence removed the politicians, everything changed. The majority attempted to fill the void by powering over those with whom they disagreed. Despite peace on their lips and inclusivity as their constant refrain, they condoned violence against those with "inferior" opinions. That is how they drove members of the First Church of Patrida into hiding.

Interestingly, the majority always justified their heavy-handed approach as necessary for progress. Violence was encouraged only to eliminate or control those viewed as anti-progress. This posture created one of the greatest paradoxes of all.

The progressive populace of Pangea, abiding by the holy text of their officially approved media narratives, could not see they had become a replica of what they so vehemently hated. They had become religious, but their god was their ego. Like their religious cohorts whom they detested so much, their forced approach would always fall short of their aspirations.

"Right-thinking" would never produce wholeness. Pressuring a person to believe the dominant narrative would never make one virtuous. Shaming and guilting would never transform people or change their minds. A control-obsessed system was only interested in acquiescing and obeying, never the healing of individuals and communities. They loved power but shrouded it in virtue. Like the First Church of Patrida, the people on the island of Pangea had lost their hearts for their own agendas, yet they could not see it.

So while their technological and intellectual progress expanded, their moral center contracted. While celebrating and regaling allegiance to orthodoxy, they neglected the human spirit. In the absence of divinity, only base instinct remained with fear as its only by-product.

But fear is intoxicatingly effective. Those who can access and manipulate this primal, barbaric emotion use it toward their own ends. First, they convince people an enemy lurks around every corner. Then, when fear takes hold, they persuade people to band together against the stated enemy. Fear is a sad and tragic unifier. While it can bring people together, it ultimately destroys those controlled by it.

Within a block of the Pangea Corporation, Thura and Odigo sensed a shift in the vibration around them. Everything felt heavier than even thirty minutes prior. The unnatural luminescence of the super-structure had been darkened with only emergency lights visible. Flashing iridescence through the corridors leading to the town center accompanied a trance-inducing beat. Thura's heart beat twice as fast and irregularly as the syncopated pulse of the music. It was an out-of-body experience in which she floated above her body and watched herself move in slow motion. There was a strange disunion between what she was feeling and how she saw herself on the outside.

Thura stopped just before the corridor and leaned against Pangea's darkened window. She put her hands on her knees and closed her eyes. Every thought and impulse told her to leave, to turn and run. Odigo placed his right hand on her shoulder and stood with her. She imagined the hand belonging to Sophia and that the old woman stood beside her in solidarity. What would she say to me right now? Thura wondered. But her mind kept racing and would not entertain answers.

The young woman took slow and steady breaths. The deep, resonant bass was not as chaotic as before but just as hypnotic. Although electronic, the music had a tribal element to it. Thura heard the drums of Salome in the distance. She remembered walking with her father from the Waters of Alethes under a starlit sky and the profound peace she carried within. She remembered their approach into the village. As she imagined the Salome community encircling the water labyrinth, she heard the sound of their singing. She meditated on the flow emanating from the center. She replayed the moment she walked the labyrinth herself and drank the water. Such a sacred experience, she thought. Still leaning with her eyes closed, Thura placed her right hand over Odigo's and squeezed it.

The two walked cautiously through the flashing corridor into the town center. The reverberation was more intense and full-toned the closer they got to the entrance. Easily over a thousand people danced beneath the flickering lights. Both Thura and Odigo saw the yellow shirts of the security scattered throughout the plaza when the lights would flash on them. But there was no conceivable way for the volunteers to identify them amid such chaos. So the couple worked their way through the crowd, occasionally looking up to see if they could spot Tyran in the pandemonium.

Thura kept her head down the deeper she walked into the center, rarely looking up at the people that pressed against her. The young woman awkwardly watched her feet shuffle as she moved between bodies thrusting and trembling around her. Then, she noticed a transition from concrete to a mosaic pattern composed of variegated stones with each half-step. Thura did not remember the town center as anything but concrete. She followed the contours and edges, weaving through the people to see where the design originated. Pressing through one last couple, Thura stopped where the mosaic met water. Odigo shuffled from behind and stood next to her. The young woman's heart sank as she slowly looked up to see a circular labyrinth built into the ground. The mosaic pattern formed wavy rays that extended outward from the in-ground labyrinth. It looked identical to the one in Salome, except it was concrete.

"Tyran was in the simulation with me, Odigo," Thura said.

Thura's eyes traced the concrete maze upon which people pressed their bodies closer together, grinding to the deafening beat. In the glowing and radiant water below, shirtless couples were making out. Flashing lights rained down on the centerpiece, where three women danced sensually and provocatively. The music got louder and louder in Thura's ears, causing her head to spin. Nausea forced her eyes closed.

"I see your brother," Odigo said, not noticing Thura's emotional state. "He sure knows how to launch a product, huh?"

Thura did not appear to hear his words. Instead, she turned back and pushed through the crowd in tears. She knew without question that Tyran had been in the simulation with her. He was the only other person who had seen the water labyrinth in Salome. Even more, he was the only one with the resources to have it constructed so quickly after they had been in the simulation.

With Odigo following closely behind, Thura abruptly stopped and turned to face him. It was as if someone had flipped a switch within her. Rage filled her eyes. And it was made even more infernal by the red, flashing lights above. Her burning anger instantly accompanied the hurt. Her brother was mocking the symbol representing her deeply sacred experience in Salome. Why would he do this? Thura wondered. The young woman pushed Odigo out of the way and stepped back toward the labyrinth when everything suddenly quieted. The music screeched and echoed against the encircling walls. Everyone immediately quit dancing and looked toward the stage.

In the center, Father Prodido, fully and extravagantly attired in his holy vestment, stood to the right of the DJ. The priest raised his hand as the crowd gasped in fear. They pressed together like the labyrinth in the center was sucking them in from all directions. People fell over each other, and their drinks shattered on the ground. Because of the media's constant refrain leading up to the event, everyone in the town center believed the Diaspora was ambushing them. They thought they were in the middle of a terrorist attack.

"Please, brothers and sisters," Father Prodido spoke into a microphone with feedback. "Please."

Egan Pearce and the other yellow shirts ran across the plaza toward the stage. From the edge of the water labyrinth, Tyran pushed through the crowd to directly face Father Prodido. Thura pressed against the aghast and disheveled party-goers, attempting to get to Tyran. KT stood frozen, watching the other security guards move in slow-motion across the stage toward the priest. Father Prodido closed his eyes and made the sign of the cross on his head and chest. He then took a deep breath.

"I am sorry," the priest began. "I am sorry for..."

He paused.

The silence in the town center was the product of ambivalence and confusion. From Father Prodido's perspective, he was sorry for his past and how he had hurt people and driven them away. He felt remorse for how he judged and damned people over the years. He looked across the audience and saw faces he recognized, individuals he had wounded. Seeing how they looked at him cut the old man to the core. He had never been so honest with himself or vulnerable in front of people. But there was no way he could ever adequately express the regret he held within his heart.

However, from the townspeople's perspective, the lens through which they viewed the religious leader was only partially formed by their past knowledge and experience with him. They recognized him only as Pangea's media had meticulously crafted and propagated him. So while the people may have been sympathetic at one point in the past to an old man who had come to terms with his moral failures, they could never forgive the terrorist who stood before them. They only heard Father Prodido's confession and apology as contrition for his supposed illegal activity, including his attack on Villatic.

The priest surveyed the crowd and saw the misunderstanding on their faces. Yet, he did not know how to break through the narrative that had been manufactured. Because the media was trusted and had mental access to the public every moment of every day, Father Prodido could not quickly deconstruct the public image they had created for him. It would take time, and he knew he did not have enough of it. But the priest had no other choice at the moment than to try to set the record straight while he had the stage and their attention.

"Brothers and sisters," he said. "I would like to thank you for the opportunity to speak. What you have seen in the news about m..."

A tremendous blast shook the entire plaza from the opposite side of the town center to the left of Pangea's main entrance. Glass and debris shot out as fire and smoke billowed from a massive hole in the building. Most people fell to the ground and covered their heads while others ran out of the corridors screaming. Chaos and bedlam befell Pangea. But Father Prodido immediately became the focal point of the hysteria.

As the religious leader attempted to leave the stage in fear, Egan Pearce grabbed him by his vestment. Despite a lack of resistance from Prodido, the head of security threw him from the stage. The priest put out his hands to break the fall, but he hit the concrete hard, landing facedown. Pearce jumped down and kicked Prodido's side as the old man attempted to get up. Two yellow shirts grabbed Prodido and pulled him to his feet. Dazed from the fall, the old man took a few small steps and staggered toward the labyrinth. From the back, people screamed as they saw the bodies of those killed by the blast. The magnitude of this realization turned everyone on the religious leader. As he stumbled forward with each step, the crowds formed around him.

"Murderer!" one man shouted.

"You're a terrorist!" another screamed.

"All of you goddamn people need to die!" a shirtless man yelled as he grabbed Father Prodido's robe and ripped it.

The varicolored lights continued to flash from above even more erratically. Attempting to drown the activities in the plaza below and assuming security would handle the situation, the shell-shocked DJ again took his place behind the turntable and put his headphones back on. The hypnotic beat accentuated the violence. Circling their prey, the people appeared as wild dogs smelling blood. Thura pushed through the pack and made it to Tyran. Violently grabbing the back of his shirt, the young woman turned him to face her.

"Do something!" she screamed above the hard, driving bass. Tyran turned and looked at Thura, his face deadened. "What's your problem! Tell them to stop, Tyran! What the hell is wrong with you!" Thura hit Tyran's chest with her fists.

"You need to calm down," Tyran said, clutching Thura's arms. "Why would I help him?"

"Because this isn't right, Tyran!" she screamed.

"Isn't right," Tyran smirked. "What has he ever done that's been right?"

"So you're just gonna let them kill him? Seriously?" Thura said. "That's great, Tyran. Well done."

"Who do you think set him up in the first place, Thura?" Tyran asked as their raging eyes met. "The file! The simulation! Who do you think it was, Thura? Tell me!"

"It was you," she said.

"Me!" Tyran screamed.

"Why would you do that! Look what they're doing, Tyran! This is all on you!" Thura screamed, pointing in the direction of the mob surrounding Father Prodido.

"I was told to do it," Tyran said, breaking eye contact and half-turning away.

"By who, Tyran!" Thura yelled. "Who told you to do this?"

"The Coalescence," Tyran said.

"Why! Why would they want you to send the file to him!" Thura screamed in bewilderment. "That makes no sense!"

"They didn't tell me," Tyran said. "But I was happy to do it. That bastard needs to feel the pain he's caused everyone on this island!"

"For god's sake, Tyran. Did you not even change a little in the simulation?" Thura cried. "I know you were in there!" The young man started to turn away from his sister, but she pulled him back and grabbed his face. "Stop letting others control you, dammit!"

"What do you think I'm trying to do!" Tyran screamed as he tried to jerk away.

"I think you're lost and searching for something!" Thura said.

"You sound just like him," Tyran said.

Thura smacked Tyran across his face, but he did not react.

"You don't make it right by becoming the same thing, Tyran!" Thura screamed. "How's this any different than anything he's done?"

The young man stared blankly at his sister as the crowd roared behind them.

"And why would you send the file to *me*!" she screamed as she pushed him. "Why put *me* in this situation?"

"Why not!" Tyran screamed back at her. "Maybe I hoped they would go after you, too!"

Thura pushed and hit him with her fists again before turning and running toward Prodido. By the time she got to him, the old man was on his hands and knees, bloody and nearly naked. The young woman pulled off her hooded sweatshirt and attempted to cover him.

"I'm sorry, Thura," he whispered. "For everything."

"I know," Thura said. "Just..."

Before the young woman finished her sentence, someone kicked her from the side. Thura fell on her back and gasped for air as the angry mob again went after the old man. She tried desperately to take a breath. Her eyes scanned the blurry people standing above her. She closed her eyes, still gasping, when a man knelt beside her and whispered in her ear.

Thura momentarily caught her breath but began to hyperventilate. As the man stood up and walked away, the young woman caught a glimpse of his face. She did not recognize him. His skin had a brownish copper tone contrasting his white and gray eyebrows and bristly stubble. He wore a dirty cowl and a long tunic. But what stood out the most to Thura was his eyes. They were both fully occluded by severe, milky-gold cataracts. His eyes made him hard to look at, but she could not stop staring at him as he walked away. Then, a gunshot rang out, breaking Thura's gaze and sending people again in all directions.

No one was sure who took the shot, but KT stood in the crowd above Father Prodido, looking down on him. The people stood back up and attempted to regain their composure. Murmuring became chanting that matched the beat of the dance music and the flashing lights above. KT pulled out the gun Pearce had given her earlier and pointed it at the priest. She glanced up and scanned all of the faces surrounding her. She sensed their approval. The energy was invigorating and intoxicating but did not feel coercive. As they continued to chant for her to kill the religious leader, KT believed she finally belonged to something that shared her values. Standing in the back, Egan Pearce caught KT's eye and nodded, giving her his blessing.

"This is for what you did to my parents," KT said with tears in her eyes. "For what you did to all these people. And for what you did to me, you terrorist son of a bitch!"

Father Prodido looked at the barrel of the gun and then frantically into KT's eyes, understanding the magnitude of the encounter.

"I don't even know you," he pleaded, studying her face, hoping for clarity.

"Yeah, you see," KT said. "That's the problem."

Thura started to rush toward KT, but Odigo grabbed her arm and held her back. Father Prodido closed his eyes and said a prayer under his breath. KT pointed the pistol at the naked and bloody man lying in a fetal position on the ground and pulled the trigger.

CHAPTER 9

The sterile lights of Pangea illuminated the contaminated scene in the town center. Crews stood under the scrutiny of the harsh glow as they worked well into the night, clearing the location of the attack. Workers loaded rubble from the blast into trucks as others scrubbed and hosed the soiled ground. Tyran darkened the windows overlooking the plaza and sat on his couch to watch the news.

(Tyran): VL-OS, give me the news.

(VL-OS): What precisely would you like?

(Tyran): I already know the top story. Just expand it.

"With Pangea One News, this is Alcie Demeter. Fourteen people are dead in what authorities are calling the single greatest terrorist attack in the island's history. The mastermind, Father Maximilian Prodido, is believed to have evaded security and charged center stage just before eight o'clock this evening. Within seconds of the religious leader's appearance, an explosive was detonated near the entrance of the Pangea Corporation. Unnamed sources with The Coalescence say that Prodido distracted event-goers away from where the device had been planted. While the sources have not said what specific evidence has been recovered through an initial sweep of the area, physical evidence has been discovered. They say within the next few hours, authorities will be combing through surveillance to hopefully identify the attacker and make a direct connection. For now, Pangea's rollout of The Black Pill is in question. For Pangea One News, this has been Alcie Demeter."

(VL-OS): Would you like the next news story?

(Tyran): No. Therapist simulation.

(VL-OS): Would you like the same therapist as your last session?

(Tyran): Yes.

(VL-OS): Activating session, sir.

Tyran sat in a rigid, wooden chair on a hardwood floor. The couch from the previous session was gone, and the entire room had been modified and rearranged. The opacity of the windows had been almost entirely darkened. The white hooked rug with blue concentric circles had been replaced with a pitch-black flatweave rug. And the harshly-stroked, multi-colored painting had been swapped out for a different piece. The new canvas was obsidian from top to bottom, with a gray labyrinth in the center. However, the labyrinth was distorted instead of being a perfect circle.

The young man sat alone, wondering why the room had been changed and why his therapist was not there. Then, as he stood up to leave, the door opened. His therapist flipped on harsh recessed lighting that could have passed for an examination light. Tyran covered his eyes in frustration but followed her across the room to her chair.

"In the last session," she said, skipping pleasantries, "I asked you why you allow yourself to be controlled."

"Can you flip on the lamp and turn off the light above?" Tyran asked, still frustrated.

"You mentioned that you feel controlled by The Coalescence," the therapist said. "Is that..."

"I'm not sure it's control when we're working toward the same end," Tyran said. "I actually wanted to meet to let you know I'm doing way better. I think I've found peace."

"What has changed since our last session, Tyran?" she asked.

"I'm taking control of my life," he said.

"You are talking about the priest?" she asked, but Tyran did not respond. Instead, he looked at his feet and then the rug. "Do you think peace is the absence of opposition, Tyran?" Silence. "Do you believe that removing people you dislike gives you peace? What is peace to you, Tyran?"

The young man did not feel the therapist was counseling him as much as she was interrogating him.

"Peace cannot be achieved by removing opposing parties or eliminating people you dislike, Tyran. So what is peace? Is it building a labyrinth in the middle of town?" she asked even more directly. Tyran seethed. His eyes could have burned holes in the rug. "Is that why you keep going back to Salome in the simulation, Tyran? Maybe you have not experienced peace because you do not know what peace really is." She paused, hoping Tyran might reengage. "Just because a symbol represents something powerful, it does not mean that you have discovered it within yourself."

Tyran looked up and glared at the therapist, but she was staring at the painting.

"I want you to hear me," she said. "Peace is not found by eliminating opposition or conflict. It is not an intellectual exercise. Nor can it be attained by using props, Tyran. You will only experience peace in your hea..."

Tyran stood up. He had reached a breaking point. The young man screamed, putting his finger in the therapist's face. "You know, there are a million other people I could meet with! We're done here!"

"Will you be looking for someone to affirm your faulty logic and poor choices?" the therapist asked, standing up to leave the room.

Tyran picked up the wooden chair and threw it against the painting on the wall.

"Is this the peace you have discovered, Tyran? Is this the peace you wanted to tell me about?" she asked before walking out the door.

Tyran ripped the painting off the wall and smashed it.

(Tyran): Exit simulation!

(VL-OS): Session ended.

(Tyran): Activate *Wisdom in Symbol and Metaphor.*

(VL-OS): As yourself or someone else?

(Tyran): Myself!

(VL-OS): Simulation file not found.

(Tyran): Activate *Wisdom in Symbol and Metaphor*!

(VL-OS): Simulation file not found, sir. I am sorry.

(Tyran): Find it, dammit! Find it!

(VL-OS): I am sorry, sir. I cannot find the file. Again, I am sorry.

The entropy of Pangea rippled throughout the island as Odigo and Thura followed its wake into their living room in the East District. The couple navigated carefully through the devastation. Odigo replaced a cushion on the couch and sat down before rubbing his tired eyes. Thura entered the kitchen and reached for a bottle of wine in the already-opened cabinet. After uncorking it, she walked into the room and sat beside Odigo on the other half of the cushionless couch.

"The whole bottle, huh?" Odigo said. Thura did not respond, and he did not follow it up. He knew better. From the corner of his eye, Odigo saw Thura tilt it back and drink quickly. His first impulse was to stop her or get her a large wine glass. But he left her alone with the bottle, as it was almost a third of the way empty. Odigo winced, however, as she tilted it up once again and took two more healthy gulps. Thura set the bottle on the floor and then put her head on the back of the couch, closing her eyes. He watched her carefully, almost believing she had already passed out.

"Get out your device," she said without opening her eyes.

"What?" Odigo asked, not understanding.

"Get out your device," she said again, not moving.

"Why?"

Thura opened her eyes and looked at Odigo. "Get...it... out," she said. "I'm not asking." Thura unsteadily stood and reached into her pocket. Then, pulling out the single, white module, she walked toward the bathroom.

"Wait," Odigo said. "Thura, wait." He followed behind, but the young woman was already filling the bathtub and removing her clothes. "Thura, come on." She placed the single module behind her left ear and stepped into the warm water. "You can't do it with just one module. It won't work." Thura glared at him and then closed her eyes as her body submerged.

"Do it," she said.

Odigo took the device out of his pocket and opened the file.

"It says it's activating," he said. "Okay, now it's saying the right module can't be found." Thura did not move. "Thura, it's not gonna work. You have to have both modules. I'm sorry." Thura remained submerged with her eyes closed. Odigo was unsure what to do. He should get her out of the water if she was passed out. But if she was being stubborn, he did not want to force himself. "I know you want to talk to Sophia, Thura. I know this is devastating for you. I'm sorry."

Thura opened her eyes and climbed out of the bathtub. Still wet, she put her clothes back on. Tears streamed down her cheeks. Odigo closed his eyes and put his head down as Thura walked past him and out of the bathroom. When he heard the front door open, he ran through the living room and outside.

"Hey! What's going on?" he yelled out.

"I'm going..." Thura said and then paused, "...to Tyran's."

"I don't think that's a good idea tonight, Thura."

"Back off, Odigo!" Thura screamed as she got into the vehicle. "Leave me alone!"

"I should at least come w..." Odigo said as the door closed.

Thura set the window opacity to black and instructed the car to take her to the same drop-off as earlier, about ten blocks from Pangea proper. Her eyes had difficulty focusing on anything, and her head was beginning to spin. The dashboard illuminated with information, but the young woman had trouble even tracking her route on the map. Thura shut her eyes. Her face and extremities were numb. Almost three-fourths of a wine bottle had successfully pushed the pain outside her body though only temporarily. But it left a void in her chest. All she felt at the moment were her tingling lips and a warm, fuzzy intoxicating embrace. Thura placed her head against the window and imagined that something other than the vehicle was carrying her body.

While the car had not been moving long, Thura's awareness of time and space was as acute as her failing senses. She thought she should have already arrived at her destination as she fumbled through words and sentences to form a simple command. The vehicle slowed, and the doors opened a few blocks from her intended stop. The young woman exited and marched haphazardly down the middle of the street, looking for the lights of Pangea. She bowed her head and watched her feet shuffling beneath her. They took her to sidewalks and sidestreets, where she decided she was hungry. Aimlessly walking through more alleys and along other back streets, she searched for any restaurant.

Tired, inebriated, and lost, Thura believed she had walked the same street only ten minutes before. She was walking in circles, unsure of her direction or destination. Keeping her head up and noting each building and street name, so she would not continue to make the same mistake, Thura's toe hit a curb, and she fell forward. Her hands absorbed the impact. While she did not feel the pain, the young woman knew she would be sore the next day. Still on her knees, Thura looked down at her face reflected in a puddle. Almost immediately, her stomach churned violently, causing her to stand up and walk the sidewalks even faster.

Breathing heavily, Thura put her back up against the outside wall of a vacant store. She saw the obtrusive lights of Pangea creeping over the buildings in the distance. If she had Odigo's device, she could have called for the vehicle to get her. Why did I get out in the first place, she thought. What was I thinking? The young woman looked down at her feet and then scanned the road in front of her, first to the left and then to the right. Thura held her breath as there was movement beneath a lone street light. She studied the sweeping back-and-forth motions and entertained the possibility she was hallucinating.

Thura moved closer in an attempt to discern the source of the activity. The flow became more graceful and elegant as she drew near, as a man's arms swayed above his head and his feet danced below his body. Then, on one edge of the adjacent brick facade, a brilliantly and abstractly-painted marigold sun shot her fiery rays in all directions. The man oscillated from side to side with one long stroke along the final emanation. But suddenly, he stopped, as if he could sense someone watching him. The old man glanced over his shoulder at Thura but continued down the sidewalk in the other direction. Thura recognized him as the same man who knelt beside her when she was on the ground in the town center.

The old man moved quickly, seemingly floating above the ground with every step. Thura staggered to keep up. While she kept an eye on the man walking ahead of her, the young woman's attention shifted to the not-so-great feeling in her tummy. The warm and fuzzy initial buzz met the reality of a small frame and an empty stomach. Exerting her mental and abdominal fortitude against her protesting gut, Thura turned one last corner to see the man walk into an unmarked and inconspicuous entrance. As she approached, she saw stone stairs extend downward into a dimly lit hallway. With no railing or inhibition, she descended. Thura seemed to be holding the stone walls up on each side with every step. The long corridor at the bottom gave the young woman two options. She could go back up the stairs and leave. Or, she could walk to the door at the end and enter the noisy room.

Thura walked the narrow passageway, too drunk to be nervous. Her every sense had been dulled and suppressed except her curiosity, which carried her forward. She thought this place did not feel like any other place on the island. The stone walls and the smell of wood fire vaguely reminded her of the simulation. It felt wildly out of place in Pangea, however. As the young woman approached the entrance, she heard the soft chatter of voices and muted laughter. She peered around the corner and saw wooden tables with bench seating on each side. A stone-constructed fireplace and chimney centered behind the tables. A fire crackled and provided the room with its light. Surrounded by its soft glow, about two dozen people sat with bowls of soup and bread on the table before them. Thura leaned in closer to see if she recognized any of the people or saw the old man. But her leaning forward illuminated half of her body in the fire's light, making her almost fully visible to everyone in the room.

"Peace, my friend," a person said from one of the tables. The voice startled her. "Won't you come in and join us?"

Amidst the people eating and conversing, someone stood up and walked toward the young woman. The fireplace glowed from behind as they approached. Thura could not immediately discern anything about the figure until they lowered their hooded cowl, revealing the face of a young woman about Thura's age. She was Thura's height and shared facial features, except for her nearly shaved cinnamon-brown hair. Thura stared at her, imagining she was looking through a technology that slightly modified one's appearance. She looked very similar to Thura. Breaking her gaze, she looked past the young woman searching for the old man.

"I'm sorry to...um..." Thura said but paused. She may have appeared speechless due to her shaken state. However, she was willing her stomach to calm down. "I'm sorry."

Thura started to turn away.

"No, please. Come in. I insist," the young woman said. "Sit down for a few minutes. You look like you need some bread."

"Okay," Thura said reluctantly. "Thank you."

"And maybe some wine," the young woman said, smiling. "That was a joke. Follow me."

Thura sat at the table closest to the fire to dry off while waiting for the bread. She welcomed the warmth and seeming vitality of the room. Her new acquaintance returned and handed her an entire loaf of homemade bread on a narrow, wooden tray. It was toasty, suggesting someone had just removed it from the wood fire oven. Thura ate as fast as she could, tearing away the pieces.

"It's..." she started to say with her cheeks full but never finished the sentence. Instead, Thura ate the bread as fast as she had drunk the wine earlier.

"Were you looking for someone?" the young woman asked. "How did you arrive here?"

"The old man," Thura said, ravenously taking another bite. "The old man with the eyes."

"Ah."

"He was painting the side of a building," Thura mumbled, her mouth overflowing. "I followed him here."

"Who are you?" she asked.

"Thura."

"Not your name," the young woman said, pausing until Thura's eyes looked up and met her own. "Who are you?"

Thura placed the pieces of bread she held in each hand onto the table. While a little may have done her good, she had eaten too much, too quickly, and felt worse than before. Even more, she was in no condition for puzzles or riddles. The night had been unkind, and the pain she held within could not tolerate any more senselessness. Thura was unsure how to answer, so she asked the same question.

"Who are *you*?"

"Helper," the young woman said.

CHAPTER 10

An ebony car with pitch-black windows and no lights turned slowly into a driveway blocked by a heavy wrought iron security gate. Within seconds, each side parted, and the vehicle crept in, driving along a winding road that cut through the lightless woods. At the end of the drive, standing outside a darkened house, a man wearing a suit and earpiece greeted Egan Pearce as he exited the vehicle. The two men walked to a side door that opened after scanning their retinas. Upon entering, two guard dogs approached the men and then turned away, leading them through a dimly lit maze of hallways to a single, hardwood door. The security guard knocked two times with his knuckle.

"Come in," a voice said.

The guard opened the door and allowed Pearce to go ahead of him. Although a windowless room, the office appeared comfortable yet professional. An ornate mahogany desk sat in the center, with two translucent computer screens on top. In the back of the room, multiple prized animal skull mounts were displayed. Behind the desk, a framed painting hung on the wall. Multicolored brushstrokes covered the canvas diagonally, creating a harsh and erratic look. The men sat down in two matching pleated leather guest chairs with bronze rivets along their armrests. A middle-aged man wearing a dark gray, v-neck shirt with black dress pants swiveled his chair to face them.

"Quite a night," he said to Pearce.

"Not the way we expected it to play out," Pearce said.

"Seems everything has been expedited nonetheless," the man said.

"I made the call when I saw what was happening," Pearce said. "When he took the stage, I knew it was going a way we didn't want."

"No, no, it was a good call," the man said. "We didn't need anyone changing their mind about him at this point. It would only complicate things. Whether he died now or later is of no consequence. We got the same result. But the girl. Whoa! Bravo!" The man clapped his hands slowly for effect. "The gift that just keeps giving, huh? You had her pegged."

"Again, not the way I expected it to play out," Pearce said.

"Security shooting a terrorist?" the man said, slightly swiveling his chair back and forth. "It looked natural enough to me. And no one suspected a thing."

"I don't expect any blowback," Pearce said.

"Good, good, let's keep it that way," the man said. "Keep the girl close for now. She knows way too much. But she's proving to be quite the asset."

"Yes, sir," Pearce said.

"And the file?" the man asked.

"I had the Nico kid delete it," Pearce said. "But both Tyran and Thura tried to access it again tonight."

"I assume they tried *after* he deleted it," the man said.

"Yes, sir," Pearce said. "And one more thing."

The man nodded his head.

"We reviewed the closed circuit video of them talking before the detonation. We could barely make out the audio, but he did tell his sister that The Coalescence made him send the file to the priest."

"Well, it's neither here nor there at this point," the man said. "Sounds like he's just trying to shift the blame off himself. For a man of his position, he's really quite pathetic. But no need to worry, my friend. His little charade will be up in due time." The man continued to swivel left and right in deep thought. "When he brought up The Coalescence, he didn't happen to mention any names to her, did he?"

"No, sir," Pearce said. "Not that we could hear."

"Well then, The Coalescence narrative continues to serve its purpose, at least for now," the man said. "Continue to keep him off balance in the meantime."

The man stood up and walked across the room to the wall mount as if studying it. "One down, two to go," he whispered without facing the men. "Is everything in place for his sister, then?"

"Yes, sir."

"Good, good," he said, still staring at the display. The man remained quiet, contemplating what to say. "Let's delay the pill rollout for a few days. We'll need that time to build the next narrative. I need it to be everywhere. News. Social media. Every simulation. Tell Demeter we need her reporting live from the plaza. And, tell the Nico kid to activate every bot. Hell, tell him to make more of 'em if he can. I need this story front and center, in every possible place at every possible moment. Do you understand?"

"Yes, sir," Pearce said, straightening up in his seat.

"I want the whole damn island shuttering in fear," the man said, facing Pearce. "Think the priest times one thousand. Have some people downtown smashing some windows and lighting things on fire. Make 'em think everyone's thirsty for justice. When people are afraid, they will do whatever it takes to feel safe and secure. That's when we've got 'em. They'll be willing to give up everything. Then, we roll out The Black Pill. And that, gentlemen, is exactly what we've been working toward. They won't even see it coming."

"Yes, sir," Pearce said.

"We'll make her out to be the leader of some sort of sleeper cell," the man said, walking behind the men across the room. "She's replacing Father Prodido, now that he's dead. Any and every way to discredit her is on the table. Do you understand? Make her look crazy. Even more radical than the priest. Start it first thing tomorrow morning."

"Yes, sir," Pearce said.

"But for now, send a team to her house and take her out. No one needs to know we've already neutralized her. They'll think she's just taken cover with the rest of 'em. What are we calling them? Das...Dap...Dapora?"

"The Diaspora," Pearce said, standing up with the other gentleman and stepping toward the door.

"Yes, yes, that's right...Diaspora," he laughed, walking them to the door. "What the hell is a Diaspora anyway, Pearce!"

"We have everything under control, sir," Pearce said.

"Pearce," the man said, causing him to turn. "We deleted the file... but the threat is not gone until she's gone. Are we clear?"

"Yes, sir," Pearce said.

"Eliminate her, eliminate the threat," the man said. "We don't need any ripples in the water. One person asking questions always leads to more people asking questions. And before you know it, everyone's asking questions and demanding answers. If that happens, not a single damn person on this island will take that pill. Do you understand?"

"Yes, sir," Pearce said. "What do you want me to do with Tyran?"

The man stood before the canvas, concentrating on it like it spoke to him silently.

"Ah yes, Tyran. We have a plan for Tyran, don't we?" the man asked, caressing the work like he was waiting for it to answer him. "You didn't even comment on my new painting, Pearce."

Thura started to sweat from being so close to the fire. She fumbled around in her hooded sweatshirt as she attempted to take it off. She set it on the bench next to her, but it fell to the ground. However, she did not notice. Her eyesight had narrowed like she was in a tunnel. Not only had her peripheral vision become impaired, but she also could not focus on the young woman's face in front of her. Instead, her eyes danced to their own arrhythmic beat. When she closed her eyes, her head started to spin. Leaning to her left, Thura burped and threw up all over the bench and her fallen sweatshirt.

"Whoa," she said, wiping her mouth. "I'm sorry."

Her apology could have been to anyone, as the entire room surrounded her. A few people immediately cleaned up her mess. Another went to get her a cup of water. Someone else put a cool rag on her forehead. Thura held it and placed her head on the wooden table. Then, suddenly, she raised her head and threw up in the same spot again.

Her jumbled mind raced. She had traveled so many divergent paths she was unsure where she was or how to find her way back. Thura was not even sure she could answer Helper's question. Before the simulation, she did not know who she was. She had no real sense of her identity after her father died and as she grew older. Like other people on the island, she only knew what she was against.

However, in the simulation, Sophia had momentarily given her identity and purpose. She offered her hope of a different life, no matter how idealistic it seemed at the moment. But in the absence of her mentor, Thura had quickly reverted to her same tired patterns. Like her performance on the roads above, she had no sense of direction in her life. And to make it worse, the ambiguity and heaviness of the island constricted what little life she had left in her. Rather than carrying hope, sadness and pain filled her void.

"How are you feeling?" Helper asked after several minutes.

"Yeah, wow," Thura said, looking up. "My head and stomach aren't swirling anymore and I'm actually starting to see one of you. So a bit better. Sorry again for the...you know."

"It's okay, Thura," Helper said. "We get that more than you would think."

"What do you mean?"

"Just that we get a variety of people that join us down here," Helper said. "We never know where they're coming from or where they're going next. Sometimes they don't even know themselves."

"Yeah, I know someone like that," Thura said.

"Oh, really," Helper responded. "Who might that be?"

"My brother," Thura said. "You've probably heard of him. He's the guy that runs the Pangea Corporation. It's a long story but he's..."

"Tell me about *you*, Thura," Helper said. "Your brother isn't sitting here at this table with me. You are."

Thura paused and wondered why her first impulse was to talk about Tyran. She reflected on her earlier comment that he was lost and searching for something. Words from a person who's quick to see the problems of others, she thought. I haven't changed at all. No wonder he said I sounded like Prodido. Thura rubbed her thumb in a circular motion against her three largest fingers under the table. Sometimes our first inclination is to see the stains of others, she thought. We don't trust that there could be something working below the surface. Thura humbly put her head back down.

She desired Sophia's wisdom. But it seemed like a lost cause in Pangea. If there was something at work, she could not see it. And at this point, she was unwilling to trust that anything could be working beneath the surface. Pangea was too dark and cynical. And as much as she loved the idea of the Sophia character in the simulation and her insights, Thura believed she had finally come to terms with it being nothing more than an experience created by artificial intelligence. While there had been a profound element to it, Thura could see there was no practical application in the real world for what she had learned. Whether in Patrida or Salome or Pangea, it's all the same, she thought. People will always be controlled. Huts will always be burned down. Bombs will always kill more innocent people. Darkness will always prevail over the light. And wisdom will always be defeated in the end.

"I'm lost," Thura said, looking at her empty cup and avoiding eye contact. Below the table, she had stopped rubbing her thumb against her fingers and made a fist. "You asked who I am. Well, that's who I am. I'm lost."

Helper's face indicated she felt Thura's anguish

"I thought I knew who I was," Thura continued. "But I'm clearly not that person. I don't know why I'm telling you all this. I don't even know you. I don't even know this place. I don't even know why I'm here."

"Yet here you are, Thura," Helper said. "All the infinite winding paths that led you to a seat at this table. What are the odds?"

Thura put her elbows on the table and her head in her hands. She interlaced her fingers through her neglected hair. Her knees bounced up and down as she thought.

"Okay. It's a long story," Thura said. "Here's the super short version. I was in a simulation. Not really my thing. But again, long story. I met a woman named Sophia who was full of deep wisdom. She taught me about myself and life, in general. And it was honestly the most meaningful experience I've ever had in my life. But now I'm here and I feel like everything is out of control and that I'm falling apart."

"Oh, so now you're earning your wisdom," Helper said, smiling.

Thura took her head out of her hands and stared at the young woman. "What's that supposed to mean?"

"When you first walked down those stone steps and looked into this room, did you wonder how such a quaint and humble place could exist in Pangea?" Helper asked. "A place so seemingly neglected by those who try to control everything and everyone on the island?"

"I did kind of think that, as my head was spinning," Thura said. "I had no idea it was here."

"You wouldn't have, Thura," Helper said. "When have you ever been pushed to the margins by an unjust system?"

"It's pushing me right n...." Thura began.

"And you're here, now," Helper interrupted. "You see, the people who gather here are casualties of the system. They've been chewed up and spit out, if you will. And to those in power, they're not worth controlling because they have no value. So they walk freely through the streets of Pangea, unnoticed."

"Like the old man," Thura said.

"Like him and all the others."

"So what does that have to do with me earning my wisdom?" Thura attempted to clarify.

"The wisest people I know are those who've descended these stairs and sat at these tables," Helper said. "They hold no illusions about the city above. They see it for what it is— people existing behind an artificial veil to ignore or escape their pain. People trying to fill an insatiable void in their chest with no inner experience. But there's no veil down here, Thura. There's nothing to hide behind. There's no escaping that pain in your chest. You carry it down these steps and gather with others who've done the same thing. That's earning your wisdom. Sitting with your pain, rather than trying to avoid it, that's earning your wisdom."

Thura closed her eyes and tried to contemplate Helper's words as best as possible, given her state.

"There are no quick fixes or easy remedies in the divided reality above, Thura," Helper continued. "One must descend before they can ascend."

"That's how Sophia became so wise," Thura said, opening her eyes. "She sat with her pain for years in a cell."

"Now you're seeing it," Helper said. "Sophia's real gift was not only in the knowledge she gave you, but in demonstrating how to sit with your pain and let it transform you. Do you understand what I'm saying, Thura?"

Thura nodded.

"Knowledge is important," Helper said. "But you can't think your way into deep heart wisdom. Nor can you convince someone into it."

Thura remained silent, considering Helper's words. "You mean my brother," she said.

"I mean anyone," Helper said.

Thura closed her eyes again and wondered if any of this was real. She replayed the last couple of hours since getting in her bathtub at the house. She wondered if she was in another simulation. Am I actually sitting here with Sophia disguised as a young woman? Thura put her bottom lip between her front teeth and gently bit down several times. My face is so numb, she thought. I feel my teeth against my lips, so this must be real, right? What is real life, though? And what's the point? Why do I even care what Tyran does? Why do I care what happens to the people of this island? Why do I care if they're asleep and being controlled? Maybe we would all be better off connected to other realities in blissful ignorance. Maybe we would all be better off being controlled and told what to think about everything and what to do. Maybe that's a better life than suffering and trying to gain wisdom from it.

"I can see you're tired or in deep thought," Helper said.

"Both," Thura said. "And in that order."

"What are you thinking about?" Helper asked, pouring Thura another cup of water.

"If everyone's content, why should I care?" Thura asked.

"Do you think everyone's content, Thura?" Helper asked.

Not knowing what to say, Thura reached for the cup and began to drink.

"Or," Helper continued, "do you think they're trying to fill an emptiness inside themselves? Or, trying to numb their pain? Or, trying to escape what they can't control?" Thura did not respond. "What do you think, Thura? Do you think everyone is content? Do you think you should care? Why do you think the Sophia character cared?"

A tear ran down Thura's cheek and landed on the table, dissolving into a small crack. She thought about her time in the simulation. The people of Patrida, much like the people of Pangea, appeared content with their manufactured lives. Even more, they did not seem to mind being controlled by the system. While they imagined they were free, Sophia could see their chains. She knew the system always promised one thing only to deliver something far inferior. It broke her heart how the people always believed the narrative of those in power, even when it divided them, turned them against one another, and made them less human. It's like breaking the world into a million shattered pieces and continuing to walk over the sharp edges each day, Thura thought. Sophia knew real living was picking them up, one at a time, one life at a time, and piecing them back together. That's why she cared so deeply. Sophia wanted people to live freely and deeply. But even more, she wanted them to live wholly.

But from the confines of her cell in Patrida, Sophia knew she could not change the people or the system. It was all too complex and pervasive. So while she could have lost herself in the heaviness and pain of her circumstance, she decided to be present in her surroundings. She gave her love and complete attention to the person right in front of her. No matter who it was. She may not have been able to change all of Patrida, but she would not let its darkness prevail over her humble light. That's why she spent so much time with me as I grew up, Thura thought.

"She cared because she believed there was more to life for everyone," Thura said. "And she never gave up. She wouldn't let the darkness win. Nothing could ever extinguish her light. She kept sharing it one person at a time." Thura wiped her face and cleared her throat. "But look at me. I wanted to be like her, but I'm nothing like her at all."

"Why do you say that?" Helper asked.

"I thought I could change Pangea," Thura said. "I thought I knew how to wake people up. I know this may sound stupid... but I thought I could get my brother to send the simulation file to everyone. I thought if they went into the simulation they could meet Sophia for themselves."

The two sat silently as the wood cracked and popped from the orange flames. Although no one had been tending the fire, it appeared even more brilliant than earlier. While Thura and Helper conversed, others cleaned their tables and exited. The young women were the only two who remained in the soft glow of the room.

"People don't need more artificial experiences, Thura," Helper said. "They need something real. They need presence. Like you're present with me at this table, and I am present with you. We're not hiding behind anything here, Thura. Do you see that? We're just two people being present here and carrying one another. That's real. That's what people need, even if they don't know it."

Thura bowed her head and closed her eyes, forcing herself to remember Helper's words.

"It can't be an idea in your head learned from an artificially created experience, Thura," Helper said. "It has to be something real, something deep in your chest, something deep in people's chest. It isn't about learning how things ought to be. That's why sending a simulation to people will ultimately fail. We don't need more head knowledge. We need hearts to change. And that only happens when we strip away all that's been artificially manufactured. Do you hear me? That's the wisdom you're seeking. That's the wisdom we desperately need. And you want that for others. You do care, Thura. You do care about your brother and the people of this island. You want them to experience fullness and presence. You want them to know a deeper wisdom. You want to share that fire you carry within you."

Thura kept her head down and meditated on Helper's words, wondering if there was even an ember beneath the ashes.

"And on that, my friend, you should get some rest," Helper said.

"I don't think I can make it back to my car tonight," Thura said. "Do you have a spot I can crash for a couple of hours?"

"Follow me," Helper said, standing up.

Odigo checked his device one last time to see if the vehicle had moved from where Thura had parked it. The interior cameras indicated Thura was still gone. The young man turned off his bedside lamp, hoping she was with her brother and staying at his place overnight. As he lay covered with his interlaced fingers behind his head, Odigo stared at the ceiling and thought about the evening. He hoped for Thura's sake that she and Tyran worked things out. Maybe Tyran was able to see how he could use his technology for some good on the island, he thought. Maybe Tyran was the key to pushing back against The Coalescence, as Thura said.

Odigo's eyelids grew heavy. But to his left, he saw a red dot dancing up and down along the wall. Suddenly, the room was full of dancing red dots. Almost simultaneously, the front and back doors, as well as every window in the house, were smashed in. Heavily armed guards with tactical gear and dark bulletproof vests charged into the bedroom. Odigo sat up and put his hands in the air with all the lasers pointed at his bare tattooed chest. Other guards dispersed quickly throughout the house to locate Thura.

"Clear!" one guard yelled from the kitchen.

"Clear!" another guard yelled from the second bedroom.

"Clear!" a final guard yelled from the basement.

"Where is she!" one of the guards shouted at Odigo, but he did not answer. "Where is she!" The young man remained silent.

The guard moved forward, grabbed him by his hair, and pulled him to the ground. Although Odigo did not struggle or fight back, the guard slammed his knee against the young man's rib cage. He gasped for air. The remaining guards put their knees on his legs and neck as the head guard zip-tied his hands behind his back. Then, picking him up from the ground, a man forced a flashlight in his face, causing Odigo to squint his eyes and turn his head.

"Are you the boyfriend?" Egan Pearce asked. Odigo did not answer. "We can do this the hard way or the harder way, son. Which is it?"

"She didn't do anything," Odigo said.

"Not for you to decide," Pearce said, punching Odigo in the gut. "Where is she?" Odigo doubled over and gasped for air. The guards on each side of him held his arms, suspending him above the ground. "Make him stand." The guards released his arms, but Odigo dropped to the ground. "Get up!" Odigo struggled to stand but finally faced Pearce. "Last chance. Where is she?"

"I don't know," Odigo said.

Pearce raised his head and moved it around, keeping his eyes locked on Odigo's eyes like he was studying him.

"Take him out," Pearce said. "I'll deal with him tomorrow."

CHAPTER 11

The lampshade was crooked from the bent metal frame beneath it. Far from a shade, however, the oversized, mismatched attachment was impassable. The only light that escaped illuminated the cluttered surface of the side table below it. The rest of the room glowed high-energy blue from the brightness of the computer screen, which was much more effusive. The contrast was of no importance to KT, though. She was only preoccupied with logging into online forums, which she did anonymously. The young woman had no intention of chatting with anyone, though. She only wanted to see what everyone said about her confrontation with the priest earlier that evening. She scrolled until she saw her name.

real_name_hidden: yo did ne1 c KT downtown 2nt

IYELLALOT: FIRST

pluralizes_nothings: represent

heyyou: das my grl

unfriendme: she str8up capped dat a$$

ima.robot: we need mor KTs tbh

For the next hour, KT searched forum after forum and throughout social media but did not see her name come up again. Most of the conversations focused on people's frustration with the delay of The Black Pill and fear that another terrorist attack was imminent. Others complained the event was not secure enough and that The Coalescence needed to root out members of the Diaspora. The more she read, the more she thought about what Nico told her about The Coalescence. From the corner of her eye, KT noticed the lamp's futility and shook her head. Setting her computer beside her on the couch, she leaned over, removed the lampshade, and threw it across the room.

"That's better," she whispered.

(KT): VL-OS, read to me the five top headlines tonight.

(VL-OS): Terrorist Attack Ignites Fear In Pangea

(VL-OS): Terrorism Rocks Pangea, Fear Is Here

(VL-OS): FEAR! Terror Attack Rocks Pangea!

(VL-OS): Terror Strike! Fear On The Rise!

(KT): That's enough.

(VL-OS): Is there something you are looking for specifically?

(KT): How many times is *fear* mentioned in articles over the last week?

(VL-OS): In seven days, *fear* is listed in 1311 articles, a total of 6517 times.

(KT): Is there a word that has been mentioned more than that?

(VL-OS): In the search, the only word mentioned more is *the*.

It was true KT did not know anything about Nico, like his background or his story. But what he told her about The Coalescence seemed too outlandish not to be somewhat real. What *if* The Coalescence is fake? She wondered. What if it's just some contrived story to shape people's thoughts and control them? Who would do that, though? Who would be behind it? And why would they do it? If the bot thing is true, someone is meticulously crafting a narrative and putting it out there. She thought with artificial intelligence writing every news story and script for the newscasters, all a person would have to do is prompt it with specific keywords. It was clear to KT which words someone used to guide these stories.

(KT): VL-OS, access my recording from tonight.

(VL-OS): What time, place, or conversation would you like to revisit?

(KT): When I'm pointing the gun at the man on the ground.

(VL-OS): Playing.

In KT's field of vision, she was looking again at Father Prodido. She saw the gun in front of her pointed at his head. The crowd around her cheered and chanted for her to finish him.

(KT): Pause it.

(KT): Go back two seconds.

The young woman fixated on the religious leader.

(KT): Zoom 150% on his face.

KT studied his eyes. She thought it was ironic for a man who used fear for decades to look so fearful. KT looked at his left eye and right and back to his left. She had been so caught up in the mania she had not seen or considered him. She remembered the feeling of being carried by the crowd, the music, the lights, the moment. She thought about how easily the public persuaded her. Their cheering and support tapped into an instinctual, primal emotion in her chest. Like an initiation ritual, she wanted to prove she belonged. Even more, the power she held over the priest was as intoxicating. She reveled in his helplessness as she took away his control. He would have done anything she told him to do at that moment.

(KT): Turn it off.

As KT revisited those emotions, she felt sick in her gut and was disgusted with herself. While she could not see it in the town center, her hypocrisy was evident when she replayed the scene with Father Prodido. KT had built an entire persona based upon her disdain for the religious institution's power and control over the people, specifically her parents. She hated the way it forced its agenda on people through fear. But that was exactly what she had become with Father Prodido. The only difference was their roles were reversed. Power and control over people intoxicated the preacher, but it also intoxicated KT. When she realized it, she began questioning what she was fighting for.

KT had become so identified with being against a specific brand of power, control, and fear that she could not see it in herself or others on her side. She wondered why she was so quick to see it in the priest but not herself. Why do I give The Coalescence, or whoever's behind it, a pass when it's no different than the church? I even give a pass to the news and media and all the propaganda they parrot daily to control people. What do I even care about anymore? Do I care more about my ideals and fighting against power and control wherever I see it? Or do I care more about becoming the power so I can silence and crush those I disagree with?

A text message from Egan Pearce popped up in KT's field of vision.

(Pearce): Tough night. Impressed with your work.

(Pearce): Thanks for handling it the way you did.

(Pearce): Can you come down to the station in the morning?

(Pearce): Maybe around 10.

(KT): ... ...

(KT): Ok.

KT leaned her head back against the wall and closed her eyes. Once again, she thought about her conversation with Nico. She thought about The Coalescence, the bots, and the news. She thought about Father Prodido on the ground and the look in his eyes. KT's mind cycled through the same things over and over. The Coalescence. The bots. The news. Father Prodido.

(KT): VL-OS, run another query.

(VL-OS): Ready when you are.

(KT): Remove *the*, *and*, and *a*.

(KT): What's the second most mentioned word over the last week?

(VL-OS): Over the last week, the second most mentioned word is *Prodido*.

(KT): What percentage of the time were *Prodido* and *fear* mentioned together?

(VL-OS): 99.63% of the articles mentioned them together.

KT put her head back against the wall and took a deep breath. As cynical as she had always been and how quick she was to question authority, KT realized that she had bought the narrative. Even though most of the island, including her, had a negative impression of Father Prodido, someone had exploited them. Someone was capitalizing on the people's adverse sentiments, further shaping their beliefs about the priest. KT began to question everything.

> (KT): VL-OS, access my recording from tonight.
>
> (VL-OS): What time, place, or conversation would you like to revisit?
>
> (KT): A man speaking from the stage in the town center.
>
> (VL-OS): Playing.

In KT's field of vision, she saw people falling over one another. Then, her head turned to the stage, and she saw Father Prodido in full vestment, standing center stage next to the DJ with his hand in the air. While she could not recollect any of those moments amidst the uproar, her video captured everything.

"I am sorry," Father Prodido said. "I am sorry for..."

> (KT): Go back five seconds.

"I am sorry," Father Prodido said. "I am sorry for..."

> (KT): Go back five seconds.

"I am sorry," Father Prodido said. "I am sorry for..."

> (KT): VL-OS, does he say anything else?
>
> (VL-OS): Playing.

"Brothers and sisters," Father Prodido said. "I would like to thank you for the opportunity to speak. What you have seen in the news about m..."

(KT): Go back two seconds.

"What you have seen in the news about m..."

(KT): Go back two seconds.

"What you have seen in the news about m..."

(KT): VL-OS, use the predictive function. What was he going to say?

(VL-OS): Analyzing all publicly available information.

(VL-OS): Evaluating facial recognition, body language, and voice inflection.

(VL-OS): I detect sadness and remorse.

(VL-OS): Here is my predictive analysis...

(VL-OS): "What you have seen in the news about me is not true."

(KT): Damn.

The news cycle continued into the night, echoing against the underground conference hall's tile floor and cinder block walls. A dozen and a half of the faithful took in the information with red eyes. Most were sitting at one long rectangular table, but a few were scattered at other tables, grieving alone. No one had spoken a word in over an hour as they tried to ascertain what exactly had happened from the news.

"Our own Alcie Demeter is live on location," the correspondent said. "Alcie, we are hearing reports that there have been some late breaking developments."

"That's right, Peter. Authorities working on behalf of The Coalescence have just released a video of terrorist mastermind, Father Maximilian Prodido, moments before the blast rocked Pangea proper."

"Brothers and sisters of the Diaspora," Prodido said in the video replay. "Our fight and struggle begins now."

"There it is, Peter," Demeter said. "The disgraced religious leader has called for a holy war, of sorts. Based on the incendiary statements he has made in the past, it is clear he is calling on his faithful to continue the fight against, in his words, 'rampant impropriety' and 'soulless technology.' Authorities are continuing to comb through the debris for further clues of who exactly planted the bomb. Reporting live from the town center, this is Alcie Demeter."

Brother Artis turned down the volume. He put his elbows on his knees and his face in his hands.

"This doesn't seem right," he whispered.

"What doesn't seem right?" asked a bald, muscular man with tattoos on each arm and around his neck.

Artis raised his head and looked at the man.

"None of it, Dimitri," he said. "None of it seems right. He didn't go there to start anything."

"Now how do you know what he went there for?" Dimitri asked in a challenging tone.

"Because he told me to contend for the faith when he's gone," Artis said. "Not start a war!"

"When a man says contend for the faith," Dimitri said, standing up and turning his back to Artis, "you contend for it. Those are fighting words, lad. And if the good Father says that *the fight begins now* then *the fight begins now*, no?"

"That's not what he told me when he got here," Artis said. "He said he was done with fighting. He wanted us to stand firm in what we believe."

"You're soft, lad," Dimitri said, turning back toward Artis. "And you're twisting a dead man's words because you're afraid. He clearly said on the television for us to fight."

"He didn't say that! They've manipulated the video or something. He told me he was afra..."

"You believe what you want to believe, brother," Dimitri interrupted Artis. "I take things at face value, lad. A man's words are a man's words. So we will fight. And come first light, the real faithful will avenge our beloved leader."

"We'll bring everyone together and talk ab..." Artis began before the news interrupted him.

"With breaking news, this is Alcie Demeter. On the heels of authorities releasing a video of the defamed religious leader, Father Maximilian Prodido, who declared a holy war on the island tonight, Pangea One News has now learned that authorities have identified a suspect in the late night explosion that rocked Pangea proper.

"Video images of Thura Kala, the estranged sister of tech magnate Tyran Kala, have been captured on closed circuit video. The footage shows Kala approaching the town center and entering through the easternmost corridor of the Pangea complex. Additional video obtained exclusively by Pangea One News shows Kala attaching an explosive device to a window near the corporate office's main entrance. Authorities now say that a biometric analysis of a white module left at the scene links Kala to the heinous attack. Currently, unnamed sources are reporting that the suspect is at-large and should be considered extremely dangerous. If you have any information on Kala, her whereabouts or contacts, authoriti..."

"See," Artis said, turning down the volume. "Have you ever met this girl? Do you know anything about her at all?"

"What they have against her changes nothing," Dimitri said. "An innocent life was taken, lad. His cold blood runs thick on those streets while we sit here and talk about it. Soon their blood will flow, brother."

"That's absurd," Artis said. "We're clearly being provoked into a fight. They've created a story that we would be playing right into. Don't you see it? Calling us the Diaspora when we've never even used that word before! Saying we're terrorists when we've never done anything to anyone! And saying the girl is a part of our community! I wouldn't know what she looked like if she wasn't on the news!"

"I agree with Dimitri, though," a young man who appeared no older than twenty said. "If we don't fight they'll keep taking us out one by one."

"I'm not gonna be the next one they're dragging through the streets and beating to a pulp," one of the older women said. "I could hardly stand to watch what they did to him. They're not doing that to me."

"And the way they laughed at him," a middle-aged man said. "And cheered when someone would hit him. That's not gonna be me. I can tell you that right now."

"I can't live in fear like this my whole life," said a young mother nursing her baby. "And I won't have my child growing up afraid for what she believes in."

Artis looked around the table for a dissenting voice, but everyone agreed with Dimitri's sentiment.

"You see, brother," Dimitri said. "The faithful have spoken."

"Three or four people out of sixty doesn't represent the faithful!" Artis shouted, exasperated by their impulsivity. "We'll bring everyone together in the morning and have a discussion. We all want the same thing. We can't be acting out of emotion here."

"Emotion," Dimitri laughed and looked around at others smiling back at him. "You mistake emotion for conviction, lad. Our good Father knew this was what it would take for us to survive, for us to come together and mobilize."

"And we'll talk about it tomorrow with everyone," Artis said, dismissively walking away. "And that's it."

"Who put you in charge, brother?" Dimitri said, raising his voice. "When you speak... you act like we should listen! You should watch your tone, you know?"

Artis stopped at the door and turned to face Dimitri. The room grew eerily silent. The news continued to cycle but was almost inaudible. The newscasters repeated the same words over and over. Father Maximilian Prodido. Thura Kala. Terrorist attack. Fear. Artis walked across the tile floor and stood eye-to-eye with Dimitri. The two men stared at each other intently, neither wanting to concede the first blink.

"Prudence," an old man called out from one of the back tables.

The two men pretended as if they had not heard anything. Their stares hardened. Neither blinked. A metal, fold-up chair scooted across the floor, and the old man stood up, hobbling toward the front of the room. He stood in between Artis and Dimitri, but the top of his gray head only reached to their shoulders.

"Prudence," he said again, breathing in a way that suggested he was more winded from the walk than anxious. "We're not running off half-cocked. Do you understand me?" The two men did not flinch. "We'll talk first. Dimitri? Do you hear me? Dimitri!"

The man broke his stare and looked down at his father.

"Prudence, son," the old man repeated. "You run out there with this ragtag bunch and you'll all be dead before the sun's up. Do you understand?" Dimitri looked at his father but did not answer. "Don't make me ask again, lad."

"I understand," Dimitri said reluctantly.

"Good," the old man said. "It's been a god-awful night, a horrible night. Let's all get some rest and gather in the morning."

Artis still had not broken his glare at Dimitri the entire time the old man spoke. He knew what Father Prodido had told him in the hallway when he first arrived at the conference center. He also knew the priest had entrusted him with guiding the small community after he was gone. But the tension with Dimitri and the faithful's growing fear left him feeling isolated and somewhat out of control. Dimitri quickly turned his attention from his father and glanced back up at the young man. In response, Artis opened his eyes wide and raised his dark eyebrows, jerking his head forward before returning to the door.

CHAPTER 12

The night air was humid and heavy. Moisture on the skin could easily be mistaken for sweat. Beads on outside windows could be confused as lingering precipitation. Thura wiped her forehead as she walked down the cracked, weed-infested sidewalk. The young woman pulled up her hood, but it was not necessary. Both the roads and sidewalks were dark and barren. In the distance, one light shone down on a stray dog trotting across the yellow lines in the middle of the road. But Thura would not be traveling that far. The building she was interested in finding was only two blocks ahead.

The street-facing side of the concrete structure was nondescript and a couple of stories tall. Thura walked the length of the building, running her left-hand fingers along the smooth facade in search of an entrance. Then, turning to her left, the young woman did the same thing along the adjacent wall. When her touch transitioned to cool metal, Thura stopped and ran her palms across the door. It was sealed with no handle or camera beside it. She determined it served only as an exit from the inside.

Stepping away from the door in the safety of the darkness, Thura surveyed the exterior. A dim light was visible from a window about seventy-five steps ahead. As she approached, she noticed that it was cracked open. However, the window was too high for her to reach. She thought she could try to find a ladder. But rummaging through people's storage sheds in the neighborhood would be too risky. The young woman continued to the next corner of the building and peered around. A single door was propped open with a vertex of light extending outward onto the ground just in front of her. Thura waited a few minutes to see if anyone emerged from the door. Then, with no sights or movements visible, she made her way to the entrance.

Inside, another door presented in the square, concrete room. The door was like the one outside, with no handle or way to open it. To her right, however, utility stairs climbed to a metal hatch with a handle. Thura moved quickly to the top and looked down to ensure everything was clear. Opening it, the young woman popped through and then gently closed it. A calm hum and whirring accompanied blinking dots of red and green. She knew she was in the control room. She had to be close.

Thura walked briskly along the inside perimeter of the room, but the only other door was closed with no handle. So the door she entered was the only way out of the room. Thura scanned the room and saw that the metal ventilation system on the ceiling exited the room near the locked door. She walked over to a spot below one of the large vents and climbed a control cabinet until she was on top of it. Lying down on her back, Thura kicked upward and knocked the vent open.

The draft blew forcefully through her hair as she entered the shaft. The cool, dry air was a nice reprieve compared to the earlier humidity. Thura's palms moved across the cold metal out of the room and into a maze of ductwork that would take her wherever she wanted. Moving as fast as she could without being heard, the young woman went to each vent until she saw what she had been looking for. Thura put her head down and tilted it sideways. Between two grates, Thura surveilled the activity below. While she could not see the entire room from her limited vantage point, the bright blue room contained hundreds of narrow tables, each the width and length of a human body. Men, women, and children were lying on the bed tables, equally spaced and fanning outward as if radiating from a central source. Thura closed her eyes and put her forehead down on the duct. She needed to get down to the floor of the main room.

Looking again from the vent, Thura saw a maintenance platform beneath the duct work just before her. As she crawled past the first vent, she stopped at the second. Lifting it, the young woman dropped below, immediately lying down. Her heartbeat intensified, and a cool sweat covered her body. She scanned down to see if anyone was in the room. With the door propped open earlier, she was sure someone was in the building.

Thura shuffled discreetly to the stairs and made her way to the floor but paused a few steps down, taking in the full scope of the situation. Hundreds of beds encircled an enormous sphere that appeared glass-like but more fluid. Dull colors moved as liquid or vapor within the orbital centerpiece, randomly swirling through a dark substance. On the ceiling above, an octagonal screen stretched from one side of the room to the other. Random disturbing images and words flashed rapidly on it, but no noise accompanied them.

Thura took the last few steps and knelt between the first two beds closest to the stairs. Her first impulse was disconnecting the wires from each person, but she knew it would take too long. Her only option was to disable the sphere. Thura walked down the perfectly spaced aisle between bodies toward the center. Out of the corner of her right eye, she saw something move. But when she turned, no one was there. Thura crouched and continued without slowing down, occasionally looking to her left and then right between rows. Again, Thura saw the fleeting movement beside her, only ten steps from the sphere. The fluid movements erratically churned as if it knew she was there with ill intent. The young woman took the last few steps, undeterred by the sphere or anyone else's presence.

As Thura stood beneath the crystalline orb at least three times her height, she closed her eyes and felt its silent vibration. The pulsing went deeper than her skin. It was in her soul. The dark energy could not have been adequately described with words. The feelings were heavier and more nefarious than anything she had ever experienced naturally. Vibrations grew into trembling. Movement within the globe intensified, churning violently. Her eyes filled with tears as she watched the violence. Sensing a presence, Thura looked over her shoulder, but someone grabbed her arms and placed her hands on the orb.

"Welcome to the veil," a voice said.

The disorder and chaos pulled at Thura's body. The dark energy produced heavy turbulence that penetrated her essence. Invading the cellular was too easy. The darkness searched until it found a home, a place that housed one's unknowing. In that indefensible and vulnerable space, it chose to do its revealing. Cataracts formed throughout Thura's eyes, preventing her from seeing. But she was able to see thoroughly and profoundly. Abstract ideas become bodiless forms moving around and through her. Antipathy showed her its devastation. Division revealed its growing wake. Hostility divulged its victims. The triumvirate overwhelmed Thura's sensibilities, and she sobbed. It was not simply a response of tears but grieving and convulsions of the soul.

Thura's hands covered her eyes, and the cataracts became scales, falling into her palms. Flame upon flame emerged from the darkness. It raged and roiled from within and without, but there was no heat. Old dwellings burned. The company of three howled in search of a new territory to reside, ultimately retreating to fear. But then, suddenly, everything ceased. The orb was crystal clear as Thura stood in the middle of it. The beds and people disappeared. Instead, standing in front of the young woman was the old man she had followed down the stairs. Despite his ragged and weathered appearance, he exuded peace. His cataracts had dissolved. His bluish-gray eyes stared with intent at Thura.

"And so it all shall be," he said. "Fire by fire."

Thura opened her eyes from the dream in a cold sweat. She had her covers pushed down below her feet. With her heart racing, the young woman sat up in bed. She looked across the room and noticed the door was cracked, allowing a tiny sliver of light to pass through. The young woman walked over the smooth wooden floor and carefully looked through the narrow gap to see if anyone was sitting at the tables. In front of the fireplace, the old man rocked in a chair and stoked the fire, watching the flames dance higher.

Tyran arrived at the office at sunrise. He hoped to slip in before Myra was at her desk. The last thing he wanted to do was start the day conversing about the night before. The young man hardly slept and was still trying to process everything that had transpired. Throughout the night, he replayed his recording of Father Prodido and his screaming match with Thura. Both left him feeling even more frustrated and ambivalent.

Tyran sat in his swivel chair and turned it away from his desk, looking out the window. Deep down, he had believed getting back at Father Prodido would give him peace and maybe even all of Pangea a sense of peace. But if he were to be honest, he felt no different than before. And, he doubted the Pangean people did either. One thing he did know, however, was that he was still burning from the last conversation with his therapist. He resented her calling him out and challenging him. While she may have been right, he would have never told her or anyone else. He had grown too stubborn to be anything but a closet narcissist, always believing his way to be correct. His ego proved to be an impenetrable wall around his heart. His arrogance shielded and deflected wise voices. As a result of those two characteristics alone, Tyran was highly vulnerable. He could be easily manipulated and exploited.

Tyran turned his chair and saw Myra sitting behind her desk. She noticed him and waved.

(Tyran): VL-OS, darken the windows.

(Tyran): News headlines.

(VL-OS): Sir, a word of caution about the headlines.

(Tyran): What's the problem now?

(VL-OS): Each story is about your sister.

(Tyran): Why? What about her?

(VL-OS): ... ...

(Tyran): VL-OS, what about her?

(VL-OS): First headline...

(VL-OS): *Tech CEO Sister Implicated in Bombing*

(Tyran): ... ...

(VL-OS): Would you like to expand?

(Tyran): Just play the video.

"This is Pangea One News with a breaking news story, Tyran," the simulated reporter said. "The sister of Pangea CEO has been implicated in the overnight bombing of the Pangea Corporation, leaving several dead and many more wounded. Thura Kala, the estranged sister of Tyran Kala, is reported to have a deep-seated vendetta against her brother and Pangea's latest technology. A search of Kala's online writings suggests Pangea's simulated technology is, in her words, 'rotting our culture from the inside out.' She also wrote, 'the only way to fix the problem is to eliminate the technology altogether.'

"Plaza cameras captured Kala planting the explosive device just after her brother announced the Pangea Corporation's latest simulated technology, The Black Pill. Another video has since surfaced, showing Kala attempting to protect defamed priest, Father Maximilian Prodido, while the understandably angry crowd surrounded him. One interesting note is that the white module discovered in the rubble with Kala's biometric markers is believed to have been intentionally left at the scene. Authorities say Kala dropped the module as a subtle yet symbolic message to her brother, perhaps as a warning, knowing authorities would trace it back to her. This has been a Pangea One News breaking story."

> (Tyran): What do you think about this, VL-OS?
>
> (VL-OS): I think I would be very afraid if I were you.
>
> (Tyran): … … …
>
> (Tyran): How about assessing the situation? You're not a damn counselor.
>
> (VL-OS): You should be very afraid, sir.
>
> (Tyran): Dammit, VL-OS! Don't start this again! I'm done!
>
> (VL-OS): All available data suggests she is coming after you, sir.
>
> (Tyran): Power off!

Tyran violently thrashed his arm across his desk, sending everything flying onto the floor. Myra came to the door and gently knocked.

"Sir, is everything okay?" Tyran did not respond. "Sir? Is everything okay?"

"Fine!" he said with hostility and sarcasm. "Everything is just fine."

Tyran put his elbows on his knees and his face in his hands. He could not understand how Thura had gotten to such a bad place. He understood she had always been adamantly against putting technology in a person, but he could not fathom her relationship with Prodido. He thought about his last conversation with her in the town center and how sympathetic she was toward the priest. He replayed the moment she ran over to Prodido and tried to protect him. He wondered how they crossed paths after all these years and how she had become so radical since going off the radar. He supposed she had somehow connected with some of Prodido's former members, but he did not know anything for sure.

Tyran burned as he continued to think about her blatant hypocrisy. She's worried about the impact of technology, but she bombs a building? She yells at me about people attacking Prodido, but she kills and wounds people in a blast? Tyran could not understand why she would do it. Nothing about it made any sense. It all seemed implausible, even ludicrous. However, he could not deny some of the evidence against her. It's one thing for news articles to make up things about a person, he thought. But what am I supposed to believe when I see it with my own eyes? And, hear it with my own ears? She was there. She was at the event. She was yelling at me. She hit my chest. She tried to protect Prodido after the blast. She left a module with her biometric markers at the scene.

"Myra!" Tyran yelled out.

"Yes!" Myra yelled back.

(VL-OS): Are you still mad at me, sir?

(Tyran): Hush.

"I don't want any contact at all with my sister!" Tyran yelled. "No appointments! No calls! No messages! Nothing!"

"Got it!" Myra yelled back.

(VL-OS): I could have done all that, and you would not have to yell, sir.

The movement of chairs and benches accompanied soft chatter in the dining area as everyone prepared the room for breakfast. Thura turned over from her side to her back and stared at the wooden beams that supported the ceiling above her bed. My head's killing me, she thought. I should've known better. But then I would've never seen the old man, followed him down the stairs, or met Helper. Thura replayed what she remembered from her conversation with her new acquaintance and then thought of Odigo. She felt terrible for not touching base with him and telling him where she was. She wanted to blame her condition the night before, but it was her negligence. She needed to get moving and find her vehicle.

As Thura sat up, her head's intense throbbing caused her to quickly forget about Odigo. Glancing at the side table beside her bed, she noticed a full glass of water. She thought it must have been Helper. She took a drink and made her way to the door. In the dining room, she recognized many of the same people from the night before. Helper sat at their table with a plate of food in front of her and another for Thura.

"Hey," Thura said, walking up from behind.

"Hey there," Helper said, standing up. "I made a plate for you, if that's okay."

"Yeah, yeah. Of course. Thank you," Thura said as they both sat down.

"Coffee, ma'am?" a man to Thura's right asked. He, too, had a shaved head like Helper and wore similar garb.

"Yes, thank you," Thura said. She paused while he filled her cup, contemplating if she should ask him what she was thinking. Then, as he finished, she blurted out, "Who are you, if you don't mind me asking?"

"Oh, of course not, ma'am," he said. "I'm Helper. Very nice to meet you."

"Nice to meet you as well," she said, looking at her friend sitting across the table.

"Alright," Thura began, "What is this place anyway? Who's the old man? Why are you here? And, where did all of these Helpers come from?"

Helper laughed.

"Well, the beginning was much like the present," she said. "Our friend, the *old man* as you say, used to walk the streets and invite people he met for a meal. Like I said last night, they were people who had been discarded by the system and lived day to day on the streets. Over the years, some of the people he invited wanted to stay and help."

"And that's *your* story," Thura said.

"It is. That's why I know what it's like to walk down those stairs and sit at these tables," Helper said. "Because I did it. A bunch. Many times as messed up as you were."

"So why did you finally stay?" Thura asked.

"Because this was the only space in all of Pangea where I felt something real," Helper said. "I had spent years searching for something, anything real, anything with substance. Everything felt cheap and disposable with no real value. I felt that way myself. I was just tired of running in circles. The drinks. The drugs. The cuts. The fake relationships. Trying to impress people to get their attention. It was all so empty and exhausting. I wanted it to take me somewhere, and give me something it could never give. That's when I stumbled in here. I felt seen and understood. I believed for once I had value. That's what changed me. That's what makes this reality truly transcendent, Thura. So when someone walks down those stairs and sits at this table, I want them to have the same experience I had. I want to meet their great suffering with great love. That's the only way this artificial veil on the island will begin to burn away, Thura."

"What did you just say?" Thura asked.

"What?"

"That last part," Thura clarified. "What did you say?"

"That's how this artificial veil burns away."

"Uh, okay. Well, speaking of the veil," Thura said in a weird voice, her eyes growing wide. "I had the most bizarre dream ever last night. I went into some industrial building. People were on beds and connected to a huge sphere of dark energy. I wanted to disconnect them from it but there were just too many people. I thought maybe I could cut the power to the sphere. But when I walked up to it, the old man was behind me. He said, 'Welcome to the veil,' then grabbed my arms and put my hands on the sphere. Instantly, I was inside of it."

"Was that the end?" Helper asked.

"No, it got even crazier," Thura said. "Dark energy rushed around me violently but then became flames that enveloped me. Then the sphere and all the people were gone. And it was just me and him."

Helper studied Thura's face waiting for her to finish. "So was *that* the end?" she asked. "You two just standing there?"

"He looked at me. His eyes were clear and blue. He didn't have cataracts anymore," Thura said. "And then he said, 'And so it all shall be. Fire by fire.'"

"What did that mean to you?" Helper asked.

"I honestly don't know," Thura said, drinking the last bit of water. "I thought I would ask you."

"You said something interesting last night," Helper said.

"I'm not sure I remember much of anything I said last night."

"Something about convincing your brother to send a simulation file to everyone on the island."

"Yeah, I foolishly thought people could meet Sophia for themselves."

"I don't know if you remember much of what I said," Helper said, reaching for Thura's hands across the table. "But you can't change the world. Listen to me. You're not the savior of this island, Thura. People don't need a person to give them more artificial experiences through a program. They need you. They need your presence. They need you to meet them in a real way when they're hurting. If you really want to see change on this island, love each person deeply, especially when they're suffering."

"Seems like one is in greater supply than the other," Thura said dismissively.

"Which makes what I said even more necessary, Thura."

"Excuse me, sorry to interrupt. Would you like some more water," Helper said, standing beside Thura with another full pitcher.

"No, thank you," she said, looking up at the man. "I think I'm good."

"I really need to get going. I need to find my car and get home," Thura said, getting up. "But I'm glad I stumbled into this place and met you."

"The pleasure's been ours," Helper said, following Thura to the doorway. "I hope you come back some time."

Thura turned and hugged her.

"I will," she said. "I promise I'll be back. The next time I might just stay."

"Wherever your flame burns brightest, my friend," Helper said. "Wherever your flame burns brightest."

Thura tilted her head as Helper walked away.

"Hey," Thura called out. "The old man. You never told me his name."

"Numa," Helper said with a smile. "His name is Numa."

"Numa? Wait!" Thura called out.

Helper had already retreated to the back room, however. On her way up the stairs, Thura shook her head in disbelief. At the top, the alleyway was still dark and hidden. But as Thura got closer to the street, the sun's first rays broke between the high-rises and illuminated the sidewalk on each side of her. To her right in the distance, the young woman saw Numa walking in the middle of the road. The man's arms were outstretched like he was welcoming the sun to the city.

Thura turned in the opposite direction to begin searching for her vehicle. While she did not remember street names, she vaguely recalled how buildings looked. As she approached the mural of the sun Numa had painted the night before, Thura stopped and studied it in the daylight. Each stroke was even more brilliant during the day. For a quick moment, Thura lost herself in it. So much so that a man abruptly exited a door beside her, and she did not move. She thought she should pull up her hood and hide her face, but she was frozen. The man appeared as surprised as Thura, however. He stared at her for what seemed like minutes and then grabbed her by the sweatshirt.

"What are you doing?" he whispered loudly.

"Get of…!" Thura started to shout before he put his hand over her mouth.

"You need to get off the streets now!" he said, pulling her into the door and closing it. "Do you not even watch the news!"

CHAPTER 13

Beneath the thin mattress, a metal rod extended horizontally across the bed. KT groaned and rolled over, trying to find a position where it was not in her back. The only way to avoid it was to sleep at the head or below it. KT moved her body toward the head of the bed and lay perpendicular with her feet hanging over the width. She pulled the covers over her face and shook her head. She wondered why she did not just stay with the Pangea Corporation, make some money, and get a real bed.

KT reached over her head and grabbed her device on the side table. She blew a hit and closed her eyes. After what she had uncovered the last couple of days, KT did not have the same enthusiasm. She dreaded the thought of having to meet up with Egan Pearce. The young woman took another hit and blew the cloud at the ceiling. She watched it dissipate and disappear, exposing the dust and cobwebs on her ceiling. I'm a mess, she thought. I probably could have had the money for a house if I had stayed there. KT took another hit and, this time, blew it harder to see if she could knock some of the dust down. A string detached on one end but was still hanging by the other. She followed it as it wisped and danced around. One more, and I think I can get it, she thought.

KT put the device up to her lips and paused. She could have probably had the money to pay someone to clean her place. The young woman thought about Pangea and her work at the time. She remembered the day someone privately messaged her while she was working. They told her that they had an opportunity for her. Thinking back, KT was convinced Pearce sent it. He knew all the right things to say to her. But it was not just the first message. He built her up over a couple of weeks, telling her he was impressed with her work. And then, he appealed to her radical side. She thought he had probably stalked the chat groups and knew her hot buttons. He talked about their movement as a *family* that cared for each other. No wonder he so easily wooed me, she thought.

With all the stuff Nico told her about The Coalescence being fake, one memory weighed heavily on her. Someone, likely Pearce, had sent her an encrypted message almost as soon as she left the Pangea Corporation asking her to join the hacking group. When she agreed, they directed her to create a backdoor into the VL-OS software. At the time, KT believed it was for The Coalescence, so that they could keep an eye on the business. At least, that was what the message indicated.

But after KT created the back door, she started to suspect that more was happening. People in the private Coalescence forum chatted about Tyran sending the illegal file to the priest and his sister. There was no way anyone should have known that information. She suspected they were not only going in the backdoor and looking around at coding but also accessing Tyran himself. KT had no problem creating the backdoor since she thought she could trust the people she was working with in The Coalescence. But the recent discovery that it was all a facade bothered her. Whoever was crafting the narrative and controlling the bots was also the person accessing Tyran and manipulating him. KT turned back over and blew a final hit at the string of dust. When the vapor cleared, the dust had fallen, and the young woman smiled at her small accomplishment.

KT rolled over and put her face into her pillow. She let out a very long and throaty groan, thinking about how she would prefer to skip the meeting with Pearce. But staying in bed and thinking about her time at the Pangea Corporation forced her back to some memories she had purposefully tucked away. In some ways, she regretted taking an early version of The Black Pill with Tyran. While it had benefits, she hated that her memories were always readily available. There were some things she just wanted to forget. But then, a text from Pearce came into her field of vision.

(Pearce): You on your way?

(KT): Yeah.

(Pearce): You're late.

(KT): Yeah.

(Pearce): Move it. I have the boyfriend down here.

(KT): Okay.

The yellow sun suspended above the horizon. Its rays penetrated Pangea's many windows. With the black canopies and festive decor coming down in the plaza's center, the broken and refracted light fell upon the wavy radiating beams of the cement labyrinth. There could not have been a more fitting metaphor to start the day.

In the simulation, Salome's labyrinth formed the symbol of wisdom. From its margins, inset stones extended outward into ten rays. They were not straight lines but more like waves. It appeared as a radiating sun pulsating with vitality if viewed from above. The labyrinth's maze was the journey toward one's center, where the flow was infinite. The villagers repeated the walk daily, reminding them that their journey toward wisdom never ends. The labyrinth in Salome was their common pursuit. It united them and gave them a sense of identity and purpose.

In Pangea, the labyrinth had the same shape as Salome's. But while perfectly fabricated in the center of Pangea's plaza, it was neither the center of their community nor a reminder of their journey toward wisdom. It gave them no common identity or purpose. It did not bring them together as one. No one even knew what it was or why Tyran had it constructed. It was a strange and foreign symbol with no apparent importance or significance to them. But for Tyran, it was an even sadder metaphor.

If the Pangea complex were a glimpse into Tyran's chest, the circular facade was the wall around his heart. Light from artificial sources passed freely while natural light was distorted. And without access to anything real, his center was a fabrication. He lived on the perimeter, sometimes flirting with going deeper, but always too proud and fearful.

Tyran stared out the windows of the lobby at the labyrinth. He watched the workers carry away the canopies until the last man exited the adjacent corridor. Then, looking up at the screens, Tyran stood numbly watching the news loop of Thura. One clip, in particular, caught his attention. It was a video of Thura sitting in a living room with other members of the Diaspora, listening to Father Prodido talk. Scrolling along the bottom of the screen, breaking news indicated that Thura had taken over the faction since the priest's death. Tyran looked down and saw Pangea One News setting up in the plaza just outside the main entrance. He quickly walked down the hallway and into his office.

"Good morning, sir," Myra said.

"Good morning, Myra. I'm just going to be in my office. We're delaying the Pill by a couple of days.

"Yes, sir."

Tyran sat at his desk and swiveled back and forth, looking out his back window.

(VL-OS): Are you still mad at me, sir?

(Tyran): ... ...

(Tyran): I'm not mad. I just need you to update and self-correct on your own.

(Tyran): I need you to start recognizing when there's a problem and fix it.

(VL-OS): Yes, sir.

(Tyran): Can you give me a summary of what's being said about my sister?

(VL-OS): Thura is responsible for the blast th...

(Tyran): A summary of new information.

(VL-OS): Authorities think Thura and the Diaspora are planning more attacks.

(Tyran): Do they know what they may be planning?

(VL-OS): Not from what has been made publicly available, sir.

"Sir," Myra called out. "Protestors are gathering in front of the entrance."

"How many?" Tyran asked. "Forget it. I'll watch it live."

(Tyran): VL-OS, show me Pangea One News.

In Tyran's field of vision, he saw the reporter with what looked like a couple of hundred demonstrators behind her. The crowd held signs and chanted. As he surveyed their messages and attempted to discern their shouts, he realized they were upset about Thura and believed he had a way to contact her. Tyran stood up and walked past Myra toward the hallway.

"I'm going out," Tyran said.

"But, sir..." Myra said, attempting to stop him.

When the door opened and Tyran stepped out, the crowd got even louder and even more raucous. Their signs moved up and down with violence. They shouted and threw slurs at the executive. The video of Thura with the Diaspora and Father Prodido appeared to play even faster, repeating over and over on the screens above. Tyran placed his hands in front of him to calm and quiet the horde, but they got even louder. Some protestors standing in the front pressed closer to the steps. Tyran uneasily took a half-step back as a news reporter broke through the pack and put a microphone in his face.

"Have you had any contact with your sister since the blast?" the reporter asked. Tyran fumbled and looked around at the mob wildly. Their chant subsided briefly but resumed when he did not say anything. "Have you had any contact with your sister, Tyran?" she asked again. "The people of Pangea demand an answer. Has she expressed remorse?" Tyran's eyes darted back and forth. He thought he saw Thura moving through the mass of people. He could not talk or move. He was paralyzed. "When did you first learn of your sister's radical ties to Maximilian Prodido?"

A shot rang out in the town center. Tyran fell backward on the steps and scrambled back up against the glass. People screamed and dispersed in every direction to get away. Amidst the chaos, a man wrestled a young woman to the ground. He banged the assailant's arm on the concrete to release the gun. However, she kneed the man in the groin and then hit him in the face with her gun. The young woman ran out of the closest corridor. Petrified and shaken, Tyran feebly stood and tried to take a step toward the door. In the window just in front of him, he saw a bullet hole with a crack the size of his hand. As the doors to Pangea opened, Tyran fell inside and sat with his head between his knees.

"Sir!" Myra shouted. "Are you hurt? Do you need medical attention?" Tyran did not look up or respond. "Sir! Sir!"

"Lock down the building," he said, looking at the ground. "Lock everything down. Now!"

Drops of blood and sweat dripped on the concrete floor. The windowless, square room contained one perfectly centered metal chair. Pacing back and forth like a feral dog, Egan Pearce stared at the young man, his beady eyes locked in on his target. For minutes, his fists did all of the communicating. He had only asked one question, met with Odigo's predictable silence. Pearce would punch, pace, and wait for a response. Punch, pace, and wait. It was becoming apparent after five or six rounds that the young man would not break. Either he knew something and was tougher than he looked. Or, he did not know anything at all.

"I'm going to ask it a different way," Pearce said. "*Why* don't you know where she is?"

Woozy and two strikes away from unconsciousness, Odigo slowly looked up and made his first eye contact with the man.

"She drank half a bottle of wine in less than three minutes," Odigo said. "And then she left."

The pacing stopped, and his fists released. Pearce may have been brutish, but he was surprisingly shrewd. While his first impulse was always violence to get what he wanted, he usually never missed what was unspoken. The man's ability to connect the dots was impressive. He stared at Odigo quietly and shook his head.

A couple of soft knocks came to the door before it opened. KT walked in and looked at Odigo. Her eyes widened, and then she glanced at Pearce, still staring at Odigo.

"Damn, dude," she said, looking at Odigo again. It was not apparent if she was talking to him or Pearce. "I need a smoke already."

Pearce broke his stare at the young man and made his way to the door.

"This way," he said, indicating he wanted KT to follow him. The two walked out and then down the hallway to his office. "Wait here."

KT leaned against the wall and fidgeted in her pockets for her device. Between the light zip-up with two pockets and her baggy pants with six pockets, her frantic and slapdash searching conveyed her nervousness. Reaching into a long pocket along her right thigh, she pulled out her device and waited for Pearce.

"Follow me," Pearce said as he passed KT.

The young woman looked up and then rolled her eyes. She slowly followed behind and exited the building, blowing a hit from her device. Pearce turned and stood on the sidewalk, facing KT as she approached.

"We need to get into this," Pearce said, handing Odigo's device to KT.

"Why did we have to come out here for this?" KT asked.

"I have to make a call," Pearce answered. "So go do your thing."

"You could've just held it up to his face or whatever," KT said.

"Get in there and play good cop," Pearce said, losing patience. "Now." KT took the device out of Pearce's hand. "When you get it open we can locate the vehicle."

"What vehicle?" KT asked.

"The one the girl was in," Pearce said.

"Got it," KT said, darting back into the station.

Odigo did not raise his head when KT entered the room or look up as she approached.

"Do you recognize the person in this picture?" KT asked.

Odigo, noticing it was not the voice of Pearce, slowly raised his head and looked at the device.

"That wasn't hard," she said.

"Wait," Odigo said. "That's mine."

"And thank you for your retinas," she said, walking toward the door.

"Can I have a drink?" Odigo asked. "Please?"

KT turned and looked at Odigo. His face was swollen. From the crease of his mouth, blood had dried on his lip and chin. KT was unsure how long Pearce had been physically interrogating him, but he looked exhausted and thirsty.

"Yeah, sit tight," KT said, waiting for a reaction. "You get that? Sit tight? A joke."

"Water?" Odigo repeated. "Please?"

"Yeah, right," KT said as she exited the room.

Odigo looked around the gray, monotone room. A sharp pain went through his face when he turned his head to the left. "Owww!" Odigo bellowed, a short echo following. He must be right-handed, he thought. He closed his eyes. "Just breathe," he said out loud to himself. "Just breathe." Thura was on his mind. He wondered where she had gone and where she was at the moment. He figured she was okay if they were looking for her. He wished there had been some way for him to go with her when she left the house. But she was so adamant about leaving and him staying. He probably should have insisted on going with her, especially after The Coalescence targeted them at Villatic. Things were far from safe, and he was internally kicking himself. Odigo looked up when the door opened. KT returned holding six small disposable cups of water between her fingers.

"I know. I know," KT said. "It's not optimal but it's water, right?" Odigo did not respond. He watched KT try to figure out how to sit the cups on the ground without spilling them. She squatted and leaned over. The water remained in the cups, but they were still about a hand's width from the ground. "Okay, this is weird and embarrassing. I couldn't find a normal-sized cup." KT stood back up to regroup, still holding the tiny cups. "Okay, hmm. Um. Maybe this wasn't the best idea."

"Just do what you did earlier," Odigo said. "Squat down and try to put them on the ground. If one or two spills, that's fine. I'm just thirsty."

"Yeah, yeah. Right," KT said, squatting again. This time the cups were closer to the ground. "Alright. One, two, three. I did it!"

"It's the small things, right?" Odigo said with a light laugh that made him wince.

"Here," KT said, giving him a drink with the first little cup. "Let me get another." KT knelt and retrieved a second and third cup. "Alright. Here."

"Thanks," Odigo said.

"One more."

"Thanks."

"I used to work for her brother," KT offered.

"What's your name?" Odigo asked.

"KT"

"Katie?" Odigo asked. "You don't look like a Katie."

"No, it's K…T…not Katie."

"Ah. What's it stand for?" Odigo asked.

"It's short for Katakaio," KT said. "That's my family name. Everyone just called me KT when I was little. It stuck, I guess."

"Yeah, I'd stick with KT," Odigo said, smiling and wincing again.

"You know, I *am* your captor," KT said as they laughed.

"So you said that you used to work for Tyran," Odigo said. "What are you doing now?"

"Well, um. Yeah. I don't know what you would call it exactly."

"Seems like you're working security, right?" Odigo asked. "So you're Coalescence."

"Well, I don't know about that really," KT said. After her conversation with Nico and subsequent digging, KT still had no idea what she was doing or who she was working for. Even more, she was embarrassed for leaving her job at the Pangea Corporation for whatever she was currently doing. "Yeah, I probably shoulda stayed put at Pangea."

"So you're Coalescence, then," Odigo said.

"No," KT snapped back. "I'm not Coalescence. I don't even know if it exists, to be honest."

"What's that sup…" Odigo began before the door opened.

"What's going on here?" Pearce asked, looking around at the small cups on the floor.

"He was thirsty?" KT said.

Pearce shook his head in disbelief and left the room. Within thirty seconds, he returned holding a full-sized cup.

"Cabinets. Cup. Water," he said.

"Ah. Got it," KT said.

"We're moving him to the cell," Pearce said, looking at KT. "Your presence is being requested."

CHAPTER 14

As the faithful entered the cathedral, a light mist had progressed to a torrential storm by the time they sat after the first prayer. Sheets of rain slammed against the building. The stained-glass windows darkened. The fully-robed choir sang with full-throated voices, but their performance felt flat and spiritless. Children crawled over their parents with a growing restlessness. Even the lights from above struggled to keep the room lit.

Father Prodido walked to the pulpit and cleared his voice. The middle-aged man appeared tired as he placed his hands on his notes. He had not prepared a sermon, only scribbling a few notes before he entered the room. Attempting to decipher his writing, the priest scratched the stubble on his chin and looked up. Whether he had prepared something formal or scrawled some thoughts on paper, the message always seemed to go the same direction over the last few months.

"Brothers and sisters," the religious leader began, forgoing greetings and pleasantries. "Let me share some thoughts I had this early morning as they relate to judgment. As I sat in my office moments ago, I could not help but to think about the rain, and how quickly it transitioned from sprinkle to deluge. I was mindful of the changing conditions around me. But so many this morning, brethren, are sleeping soundly and unaware."

Several more vocal congregants agreed with the priest's statements and shouted their amens. The remaining faithful sat stoically, agreeing with his words by nodding. Even though it was only his opening salvo, Father Prodido sensed a subtle shift in energy.

"I am reminded of the stories of old," he continued. "The rains fell and the waters began to rise, my friends. Oh, but the wicked, in their folly, turned a blind eye. They could not see the signs of the times. They could not portend that judgment was raining down all around them. Oh friends, we must remain awake and at the ready. Steadfast and sure. For the first judgment was by water. But the second judgment...hear me brethren...please...hear me in this. The second judgment will come by fire."

Even more, congregants shouted their amens this time while several people began to clap. The children no longer wrestled over their parent's legs but sat still on their laps. Even though the thunder crashed outside and the stained-colored windows grew darker, the people felt radiance from inside. Father Prodido fed on the attention and the growing energy.

"There is a time coming, like the days of old, when the judgment will not be by water, friends, it will be by fire! On that day many will perish! And oh what a day that w..."

Without warning, a rapid crescendo on the organ shook the building. The congregation initially smiled, imagining it was to embellish the sermon. But the crescendo was immediately followed by an even more rapid diminuendo. The windows vibrated as the faithful watched nervously, anticipating the glass would shatter and fall to the floor. The artistry was unmistakable, but the intensity was nothing short of overwhelming. Smiles gave way to unease. Delight transformed into confusion. Father Prodido even recoiled and crouched behind his pulpit from the magnificent terror. And this was all before the even more resounding, heavier notes played.

The children, however, smiled and clapped. It was impossible to conceive that they understood the moment as anything more than a song filling the room. But it was also hard to ignore their change in disposition from when Prodido was preaching to the first notes played. No one else noticed the apparent shift in dynamics and tenor or how something so holy and divine could quickly silence self-important and puffed-up judgments. For the children, the allure and grandeur must have produced some sort of resonance in their souls.

At once, the organ ceased. Echoes only momentarily sustained the last notes. Father Prodido marched toward the monstrous instrument and met the man who interrupted the sermon. The religious leader did not initially say anything but grabbed the man by the cowl he wore around his neck. He pulled him across the stage and down the steps before the people. Father Prodido then turned and whispered to the man.

"You have been warned twice. This is your final warning. You are not welcome here."

The man stepped past Father Prodido as he released his grip. Walking down the aisle, the man appeared to be breathing words. But the breathing became whispers with each step. No one understood what he said, but the children laughed and clapped their hands. When the man reached the back of the nave, he turned to face Father Prodido, standing directly in front of him down the center aisle.

"You suppose both water and fire are meant for destruction," the man yelled. "But you only speak from your deluded desire. You see wickedness everywhere except for the place where it truly resides. Oh, how I wish the water and fire you mean for destruction would cleanse and purify your hearts, instead."

Silence fell over the congregation, with even the children quieting. Father Prodido walked down the aisle with all eyes fixed on him. His dress shoes clapped with each step and echoed throughout the sanctuary. He grabbed the man's tunic and forced him toward the door with two hands. The man stumbled backward, but Prodido kept moving, pulling him violently until they were outside and throwing him to the wet ground. The priest glared into the man's cataract-filled eyes.

"Do not come back here," Father Prodido repeated. "You are not welcome. You will never set foot in this place again."

The man stood up, his tunic soaked and dripping. He initially smiled but then laughed quietly. The priest inhaled deeply, his body growing more prominent and more intimidating. He did not break his stare beneath his furrowed brow. His anger was evident as his neck arteries bulged. But the man's laughing intensified until he was bellowing. From behind Prodido, the congregation had gathered to look out the open door and through the windows. The man turned and walked away, howling hysterically. As the priest pivoted toward the entrance, he saw the faces of the faithful. They were not looking at him but watching the man walk away in the distance. Father Prodido's countenance had not changed. There was fury and intimidation in his disposition. He walked up the steps to the open doors and stopped.

"Get back inside!" he yelled. "Now!"

Thura wrestled and twisted her arms and contorted her body. She screamed, but a calloused hand covered her mouth. The young woman could not see anything around her with her hair tangled in front of her face. But at the top of the stairs where she stood with her captor, the walls were dirty white and unadorned, with a single light bulb above their heads. Realizing her small frame would not break free from the muscular arms holding her, Thura stopped fighting.

"Shh!" the man whispered, loosening his grip. "I'm not abducting you. I'm helping you."

Thura ripped away and faced the man with a scowl on her face.

"Helping me?" Thura said. "I don't even know you. Now move out of the way."

"You have no idea," the man said, moving in front of the door.

Thura took a deep breath and closed her eyes.

"I'm sorry. My name's Artis. I apologize for grabbing you and pulling you in here. But your face is all over the news."

"Why?" Thura asked. "Why is my face all over the news?"

"Well, they're reporting that you're the one responsible for the blast at Pangea," Artis said. "But of course they're also saying that you've been working with us."

"And who are you, again?" Thura asked, unsure if she believed his story.

"From what I gather, you knew Father Prodido," Artis said.

"I did," Thura said, waiting impatiently for an explanation.

"Well, he was like a father to me," Artis said. "He wanted me to watch over the congregation when he died. So I'm here with what remains. We've been hiding out here for a while."

"You're the group they're blaming for the attack on Villatic," Thura said. "The Diaspora."

"Would you mind going downstairs so we can talk about all this?" Artis asked. "Please? And I'll show you the news and what they're saying."

Thura was reluctant. But if what he was saying was true, she should not be walking the streets. The young woman looked into Artis' eyes. She was not great at first impressions, but his eyes indicated no malice or ill-intent. On the contrary, he looked honest and genuine. Thura nodded and followed him down the stairs to a metal door.

"The rest of them may still be in here for breakfast," Artis said. "They're good people. But try to keep your head down until I see who's sitting at the tables. In fact, just stand here for a sec while I take a look in."

Artis opened the door but only saw a couple of ladies still eating. More importantly, he did not see Dimitri. He hoped he had already eaten.

"Everything's good," Artis said. "Follow me." The two went to the back corner, which was somewhat shaded and tucked away. "Here. Here's a seat for you. Perfect. And here's a seat for me. Okay. Now, Thura, we don't know what Diaspora means. We don't call ourselves that name. That's a name the news created when they blamed us for the attack on Villatic."

"Can you show me the news?" Thura asked.

"Let's wait a few minutes."

"Why are you acting so nervous?"

"We're a bit divided right now," Artis said. "Don't get me wrong. We're all upset about what they did to Father. But some want to grab guns and fight back. Others think that's a bad idea."

"And you think?"

"I think it's a really bad idea," Artis said. "But honestly, it's the end of us either way."

"Why do you say that?" Thura asked.

"You fight back, you die," Artis said. "They're too powerful. But if you don't fight back, you still die."

"How's that?" Thura asked.

"Well, hiding in fear until they find you isn't living, is it?" Artis asked rhetorically. "It's as much of a death as getting killed."

Thura thought about Artis' words when a man walked into the room and toward the kitchen. A shorter, old man followed slowly behind him.

"Good morning, Dimitri," one of the kitchen workers said.

"Good morning, Alice," Dimitri said, grabbing a plate.

"Alexy," Alice said, greeting the old man.

"Ma'am," he said.

Also entering the room, a larger group of eight or nine got in line for breakfast. Artis slumped down in his seat to avoid anyone seeing him. Thura got nervous watching him.

"Am I safe?" Thura asked.

"You're fine," Artis whispered. "It's just that there was a lot of arguing last night. The bald guy with all the tattoos is Dimitri. He's been ready to gear up since he saw the news about Father Prodido. But his father, Alexy, stepped in and said we'd discuss it today."

"Is his father the little old man standing behind him," Thura asked, glancing over her shoulder.

Dimitri turned with a full plate and scanned the room for a place to sit. Artis slid further down into his seat and tried hiding behind Thura's body.

"What do we have here?" Dimitri said, approaching the table. "Looks like hiding's in your bones, lad. And who do we have here?"

Thura had her hood over her head, but it did not dissuade Dimitri. The man placed his plate on the table and pulled her hood down, looking her up and down.

"A new recruit, brother?" Dimitri asked, glancing at Artis. "Did she bring her own guns? Or, is she going to hide with you under your bed?"

A couple of people heard what Dimitri said and laughed.

"What's your name, lass?"

Thura turned her head and glared at the man.

"Well, what do we have here?" Dimitri raised his voice, attracting the attention of the entire room. "It looks like our fearless leader has arrived!"

The room erupted in laughter as they all looked at Thura. While a few did not make the connection, almost everyone realized she was the girl from the news.

"So, lass, you're here to set us up, eh?" Dimitri asked. "Or, to rat us out. Who are you with?"

"I'm not with anyone," Thura said. "I was by myself on the sidewalk when Artis grabbed me and pulled me down here."

"What's this, brother? Is what she's saying true?" Dimitri asked. "Why are you bringing her down here with us?"

By this time, everyone had gathered around the table and looked at Thura.

"She didn't even know she was being blamed for the blast," Artis said.

"So you just bring a stranger in here without asking any of us, brother?" Dimitri asked. "We don't know her or who she's with. She may be Coalescence for all we know."

"She's not Coalescence," Artis interjected.

"How is it you know the truth about so many things, brother?" Dimitri asked. "When no one knows up or down about anything, you somehow always know the truth about the matter."

"I'm not Coalescence," Thura said, standing up. "Back off." Dimitri laughed and looked over each shoulder at everyone standing behind him, encouraging them to laugh as well. "I went into an illegal simulation and The Coalescence is after me. That's what all of this is about."

"But why are they linking you to us?" a lady asked.

"Yeah!" a few other people shouted.

"They're trying to eliminate all of us," Thura said, breaking through the commotion. The room quieted. "They're trying to eliminate all of us. We're a threat to their control. That's why they wanted the church building gone and Prodido gone. That's why they want all of you gone. And that's why they want me gone. Either conform and go along with their tyranny, or you'll be eliminated."

"Now you're talking my language, lass," Dimitri said. "You're sounding like one of us." The man turned his head and stared at Artis. "It looks like you brought in another vote for our side, brother."

Thura was overwhelmed. She put her head down and studied the texture of the white tile beneath her feet while everyone argued. Dirt filled the microscopic pores, cracks, and crevices. She thought it would be almost impossible to see the texture in the tile without the dirt. Without experiencing any darkness, she wondered if a person could fully comprehend the light. But what happens when there's nothing but darkness? Thura raised her head and looked around at everyone staring at her. She wondered if there was any light left on the island.

"Here it is!" someone shouted from across the room. "They're showing her picture!"

The room quickly turned its attention from Thura and Artis to Thura's face on the television.

"The island is still trying to make sense of the last few days and all that has transpired," the host said. "Dr. Dionte, as a forensic psychologist, how are you making sense of it all?"

"Thank you, Katherine," the doctor said. "And thank you for having me on your show. The tendency is to single out individual parts without looking at how the parts are interconnected. Take Thura Kala, for example. She is much more complex than a religious fanatic. In fact, her fanaticism may not be religious at all. She is a much more dynamic figure than many suppose. One has to ask how she got radicalized in the first place. In my opinion, that is when it all begins to come together and make sense."

"So what exactly do you see, doctor, that explains how she got radicalized?" the host asked.

"It is certainly true that she had a past with Father Prodido," Dr. Dionte said. "There is no question this relationship made her sympathetic toward him and his cause. However, her alignment with the Diaspora appears to be strictly one of convenience, not of religious alignment."

"Interesting," the host said.

"While she does not align with them *theologically*," Dr. Dionte continued, "she does align with them *ideologically*. They both believe technology is undermining our society. But that is what makes her even more dangerous, in my opinion. She is not trying to change anyone's mind. She is trying to take out our technological infrastructure. Here is the key to it all, Katherine, and what makes it all so combustible. Pardon the pun. This is personal between her and her brother."

"Tyran Kala," the host said. "The president and CEO of the Pangea Corporation."

"That's correct," Dr. Dionte said. "She sees him as the root of the problem."

Dimitri turned off the television and turned back to Thura.

"So many lies," he said. "So many lies, lass. I don't know who you really are but I need you to stand up."

"Why?" Thura asked as Dimitri and two other men stood around her.

"Pat her down, lads."

The two men frisked Thura's upper and lower body, searching for any weapon.

"Nothing on her," one of them said.

Dimitri locked in on Thura's eyes and slowly moved his head from side to side as if trying to discern who she was.

"You present a person two options," he said. "And then let them show you who they really are."

"Leave her alone, Dimitri," Artis said.

"Listen, lass," Dimitri said, ignoring Artis and looking at Thura. "There's no technology or religious anything here. Look around this room. All I see is pain there. Sadness over there. Fear on faces over there. I don't see anything they're saying about us. But they might be right about you."

"What does that mean?" Thura asked.

"That you understand what's at stake," Dimitri said. "And that the only way out of this is to fight back."

"She's not a part of this!" Artis raised his voice.

"You brought her here, brother!" Dimitri shouted back. "She's a part of it whether she likes it or not! She knew the good Father and she knows his blood is on their hands! She knows she's next. That we're all next! I promise you that an eye shall be taken for an eye, and a tooth shall be taken, as well. The guns are stocked and the munitions are overflowing, brother. Can I get an *aye* from those who are with me! Can I get an *aye* from those who will fight for the faith! Can I get an *aye* from those who will stand up and fight for the good Father!"

Everyone in the room erupted except for Thura, Artis, and old man Alexy, who stood off to the side watching wearily.

"That's not what he wanted!" Thura shouted, interrupting the cheers. "I was the last person to talk to him before he died! I know what you think he stood for! I knew it, too! But that's not what he said to me as he was dying. He told me he was sorry for everything."

The room exploded in a laughter that was even louder than their previous cheers.

"You're mistaken, lass," Dimitri said.

"No, she's right," Artis said. "Just like..."

"Enough!" Dimitri yelled. "You'll not make this man into something he was not! The news can't do it and neither will either of you! I knew the man's heart! He would have fought for all of you!"

The cheers and applause for Dimitri were deafening. Those who had not been in the conference hall earlier heard the commotion and filed into the room. By this time, every person staying underground was present and either sitting or standing.

"We're not trying to make him into anything!" Artis yelled through the commotion as he approached Dimitri.

"Back off, brother," Dimitri said.

"We know he would have fought for us," Artis said, attempting to ease the tension. "But not the way you're intending."

"There's no other way to fight, lad," Dimitri said. "The only way to fight fire is with fire."

"No! No! That's not true," Thura shouted. "I had a dream last night..."

The room roared in laughter. Dimitri turned around, holding his stomach, and looked at everyone as he made a ridiculous face.

"Come on, lass," Dimitri said as the crowd quieted again. "Don't bring your fairy tales to a serious discussion. Was the good Father floating around with angel wings and sprinkling golden dust on the bad guys?"

The room shook with an ear-splitting, thunderous clamor, and some people also fell to the floor, holding their midsections while bellowing.

"I don't care if you think it's funny!" Thura yelled.

"Okay! Okay! Let her speak!" Dimitri yelled. "Shh! Let our guest speak. Let her speak."

"I was in front of a giant sphere," she said. "I was pushed inside of it. Dark energy and fire churned around me." Dimitri pursed his lips to keep from laughing and held up his hand to hold back any more laughter. "The dark energy was antipathy, division, and hostility. I cried because it felt overwhelming. I couldn't do anything to stand against it. I was helpless. But suddenly, flames emerged and surrounded the darkness until it was vanquished."

"Thank you, lass," Dimitri said, slapping his knee. "Thank you for making my point so eloquently." Dimitri bowed and then turned to the crowd. He continued bowing to everyone's amusement. When the howling subsided, the smile on Dimitri's face disappeared as he faced Thura again. "The only way you drive out darkness is with fire, lass. And that's what the darkness on this island will surely face— fire from these weapons!"

"That's not what she meant," Artis said, getting in Dimitri's face. "You know that's not what she meant!"

Dimitri grabbed Artis by the shirt collar and got closer to his face, to the point where their noses were touching. Artis grabbed Dimitri's collar, and the men stared at each other.

"I know exactly what she meant, lad," Dimitri said. "You're either with us or you're against us. She was given the two options and she's made her choice."

The crowd pressed in around them. Even if either man wanted to back away from the other, bodies were so close behind them that they could not move. But through the crowd and the cacophony, Alexy hobbled through by poking and pinching anyone in his way. The old man reached the two men, still pressed nose to nose, but they did not see him standing beside them. Then, at once, someone pushed Artis from behind, knocking his head into Dimitri's. As the two went at each other, Alexy dropped to the floor somewhere amid the scuffle. When someone noticed and screamed, everyone immediately backed away. The old man, centered amidst nervous onlookers, had his hands on his right chest.

"Father!" Dimitri screamed as he hovered over the old man and pumped his chest. "No! Father! Not now!" The room remained eerily silent as Dimitri continued to work on him. "Don't die! Stay with us! Come on, please!" Dimitri gave his father a breath and pumped his chest even more vigorously. "If he dies, I'll kill both of you with my own hands! Do you hear me!"

CHAPTER 15

The back driver's side door closed. KT ran her hand over the black leather seats and inhaled, taking in the fresh car smell. The chauffeur then walked around to the back passenger door and opened it for Pearce, who sat beside the young woman. The vehicle quickly pulled away and darted through stoplights and intersections. Traffic was nearly nonexistent at dusk when most people had already retreated into their virtual spaces after work.

"Where are we going exactly?" KT asked.

"We're almost there," Pearce said.

The car turned abruptly into a nondescript side street and took another left into a drive below a high-rise building. The driver rolled down the dividing window and looked at Pearce.

"This'll be a quick exit," he said. "His vehicle is thirty seconds behind so I've got to clear out. When you're done just give me a two minute lead. He's only here for this meeting."

"Got it," Pearce said.

"Uh...who are we meeting?" KT asked, but Pearce did not respond.

"Stopping in five, sir," the chauffeur said.

The tires squealed as they accelerated through the empty lot. KT counted down in her head, and as soon as the car stopped, she and Pearce jumped out. The vehicle peeled out before they had even closed their doors.

"We'll wait inside," Pearce said.

KT followed him into the lobby and then the elevator. The two remained quiet as it moved with as much force as the car left the garage. The doors opened on the unmarked thirteenth floor. Rather than entering a hallway or lobby, the two stepped out of the elevator and faced a young, professional man behind a standing desk.

"The Senator is in his office," he said.

KT had more questions than her mouth would allow her to articulate.

"A private elevator," Pearce said, anticipating at least one of her questions.

"Oh, yeah," KT chuckled.

Pearce entered the door and walked down the long, carpeted corridor without looking at the young man who spoke.

"Hi," KT said, as she passed him and then walk-ran down the hallway to catch up. "I thought the driver said he would be coming behind us, though."

"You never know who could be watching," Pearce said. "You always stay a step ahead."

"And um...did he say Senator?" KT asked. "Or, did I not hear that right?"

Pearce stepped aside and let KT enter the opened door first.

"Ah KT! Please come in. It's such an honor to finally meet you!"

KT's hand reached out to grasp an already extended hand. While involuntarily and mechanically reciprocating the formality, the young woman could not speak. Instead, she willed her face to remain expressionless. But internally, she was equal parts shocked and dumbfounded. Her hand moved up and down, but the Senator was forcing the motion.

"Senator Fovos Savano," he said with a broad, enamoring smile. "Nice to meet you. You can call me Fovos, if you'd like. Please, may I get you something to drink?"

"Uh no...no thanks," KT said. Again, it was evident that she was off-balance.

"Pearce, get our guest some water," the Senator said. "KT. I can call you KT, right?"

"Uh yeah, yeah. That's fine," she said. "That's what people call me."

"I can see you're surprised at me being here," he said. "That's understandable. Have a seat, please." He motioned to an ergonomic chair opposite him. KT walked around the large oval table and looked out over the city. A window spanning the room was twice her height and extended the room's length. She stood and stared for a few extra seconds, taking it all in before sitting down.

"We'll address why I'm here...*how* I'm here...momentarily," the Senator said. "But let's talk about you first!" Pearce returned with a tall, perfectly cylindrical glass of water and sat it in front of KT. "Now, you're probably wondering why you're here, KT. But I can assure you it's nothing but good. In fact, if nothing else comes out of this meeting, I want you to know how impressed I am with your work. And, how appreciative we are for all you've done. It's really quite impressive."

The Senator paused.

"Thanks, I guess," KT said as if the quiet demanded a response.

Still standing, the Senator walked over to the window and looked out. He did not speak but appeared to look at something in particular, even though nothing was especially notable.

"You've been instrumental in shaping the island with your work," he said. "I'm not sure you fully understand your impact, KT. One small opening has created an island of change. And I mean that both literally and figuratively. I hope I'm not coming across as overly endearing. That's not my intention. I just want you to know that you fit perfectly into what we're trying to do here and what we're trying to create. I hope family isn't too strong of a word. But that's how I think of what we're building here— a better family."

KT had entered the room, already jaded that someone was using The Coalescence as a front. At this point, she imagined the Senator had something to do with its creation. Based on the news over the last three months since The Coalescence supposedly took over, the Senator should have been dead or in reeducation. But here he stood, waxing poetic and talking about family. KT was unsure of his intentions with her, but she saw through his artificial veneer and plastic personality. The young woman knew when someone was trying too hard; that was exactly how she saw the Senator. But she was careful not to make her real feelings known, at least not now. So, KT smiled and nodded, appearing more agreeable than she felt.

"We believe you're helping us build a better future, KT, a better family," the Senator said. "But, before we go any further, I have to come clean. The Nico kid is quite chatty, as you probably know." KT smiled and nodded her head again. "We know he told you the truth about The Coalescence."

KT's smile instantly disappeared. She was not able to keep her face from showing her fear. Whatever facade she had constructed the first ten minutes in the office had crumbled. KT adjusted nervously in her seat and looked at Pearce, who remained stoic and unflinching.

"No, no, it's fine. It's fine, KT," the Senator said, laughing. "We're family here, remember? Come on. Say it with me. We're family here. Go ahead."

KT's skin crawled. She did not know how long she could endure such an over-the-top performance. But she knew she had to continue to play along. She was in no position to be herself, especially with two men in a vacant building. She thought this was exactly how people disappear without being heard from again. KT was not good at playing the game but had to start learning quickly.

"We're family here," she said, smiling and laughing enough to be convincing.

"Good, good. Yes, we're family here," the Senator said. "We're family here. Well done, KT. Now. The Coalescence. There are only a few insiders who know the truth of what we're doing. And, we'd like to bring you into the fold, KT."

The Senator paused and motioned for Pearce to leave the room. When the door closed, and they were alone, he walked to the window and surveyed the cityscape.

"Look out this window, KT." The young woman turned in her chair. "Now close your eyes and try to think about the island before all this madness. No buildings. No people. Just the land— trees, beaches, blue skies. Do you see it? Pristine land. Harmony. Everything working together in its own perfect ecosystem. That's the way this island used to be...before we inhabited it."

"Now open your eyes and look around. What do you see?" the Senator asked but interrupted before she could answer. "I'll tell you what I see—decadence. Building after building, apartment after apartment, filled from top to bottom with unhappy people trying to make sense of their sad lives in this broken world. They've checked out of our systems and institutions and retreated to hollow, empty spaces. The only thing left that inspires them, KT, is *the next thing*.

"But that's what happens when self-indulgent and entitled people think they need to constantly consume. That's what happens when their apathy and boredom demand constant stimulation, KT. But that's what we've created here. We've created a culture that's endlessly unhappy, perpetually chasing the wind, always running after something, thinking the next thing will make them complete. They'll chase after anything they think will fill 'em up. And it does, for a minute. But see, it's all vapor. It's a mirage. It's all emptiness, KT. But they consume as much as they can and more in the name of freedom, by god! We've created a bunch of people who offer so little yet demand so much. You see how disgusting and pathetic it all is, KT?"

The young woman did not move or respond. The veneer the Senator hid behind when she first arrived had instantly disappeared. Fear moved through her body as he immediately shifted from pleasantries to rage.

"Every goddamn vulture on this island sees how stupid these people are," the Senator continued. "It doesn't matter if it's the vultures in politics, business, or religion. They obsessively exploit people with *the next thing*, crafting narratives that give them a sense of purpose and an ounce of meaning in their miserable lives. And as you're well aware, there's no shortage of narratives out there trying to fill the void. Do you know why KT? Why there's so many narratives competing for people's attention? Do you know?" KT opened her mouth to answer, but the Senator interrupted her again. "Power and money, KT. It's all goddamn power and money."

"But that's the world we live in, the world we've created— a world of narratives," the Senator continued like he was the only person in the room. "And every one of these narratives attempts to *shape public sentiment*, as they like to say. On the surface, they may appear to have very different goals. But below the surface, they're all the same. It's about control. Do you understand what I'm saying so far, KT?"

"I think so," KT whispered, tracking the Senator as he paced back and forth across the room.

"This island's a battlefield where all the self-interested parties fight for people's hearts and minds, KT. Because when they have control of your heart and mind, they have the power, you see, and that's when they make money. But most people are too naïve, too stupid to see it. These self-interested parties have co-opted every damn person on the island with their self-serving narratives. But the damn people are so obsessed with *the next thing* they don't even see how they've been brainwashed. The problem, KT, is that all of them, the whole damn bunch of them, the vultures included, are too short-sighted to see the devastation they've caused.

"Look out there," the Senator said, returning to the window. "Just look at how this island's been ravaged. The way the land's been raped and exploited. Pillagers. Plunderers. Stripping it down to its bones for a buck, trying to satisfy the insatiable appetite of the infinitely voracious. It's unviable, KT. We just can't do it. Already, Villatic can't produce enough food. The four districts struggle to keep the lights on. How can you possibly satisfy consumers with their mouths wide open, shoving as much stuff down their throats as they can get their hands on? How do you limit the entitlement of the perpetually entitled?"

The young woman sat stunned. She did not know if he wanted an answer or was asking rhetorically. Either way, KT was not going to speak. She knew she had nothing of substance to add to what he already believed. Fortunately, he thought KT agreed with everything he was saying.

"You see the problem. I know you do, KT. These small-minded narratives teach generation after generation to be even more small-minded, to only concern themselves with their own concerns, their own interests, and their own tribes. But that's what this island has become. And it's unsustainable. What a pathetic and grievous cycle. Exploit, consume, repeat. Exploit, consume, repeat. And what did we do about it? Nothing, KT. We didn't do a goddamn thing. Instead, we trained people to believe this was freedom. We sat back and watched it metastasize. We fostered the growth of this sad, parasitic cancer on the island. And we did it with impunity! We did it with absolutely no accountability or consequence!"

The Senator punched the windows with both fists. The thick glass did not move or vibrate. His knuckles were the only casualties, but he did not react or act as if it hurt. KT remained frozen, intimidated by the psychotic display, hoping she could leave soon.

"That's why every one of these parasitic entities has to go away! That's why those of us with a larger perspective, who have a long view of the future, must bring these lesser narratives to an end. That's why we must introduce a new and better narrative that transcends these self-interested tribal narratives. You see, KT? That's the only way we'll be able to foster progress amongst these god-forsaken savages."

KT sat mesmerized and abhorred by the Senator's power. She had never met someone who could end narratives and create new ones. She realized how insignificant and expendable she was compared to that kind of influence. The Senator had the power to control an island. She could only write code. Although he was average-sized, his persona seemed so much bigger and ominous, his words even more. Beneath the table, KT pinched the skin on her left wrist to convince herself that she was sitting in front of Senator Fovos Savano.

"Take that downtown church and its small-minded narrative, for example," he said, staring toward the First Church of Patrida. "They've twisted and turned people into believing that nothing matters in the present. According to them, it'll all burn one day anyway, so why the hell not rape and pillage it now! They don't give a damn about exploiting the land! They don't give a damn about devastating our sensitive ecosystems! Why would they? If nothing matters in the end, as they say, then consume by god! Narratives like that have to come to an end. Tell me you see it, KT."

"I see it," KT whispered.

"Good, I knew you would see it that way, KT," the Senator said, again staring off into the distance. "This is what I've been working toward for years. You get a few like-minded individuals who see the big picture. Together, you begin shaping public sentiment against a target you want to eliminate. Day by day, week by week, you strengthen the negative sentiment against them. One protestor becomes ten and then hundreds. One news story is published, and every media outlet immediately picks it up. You couple that with the non-stop barrage of news stories, opinion pieces, and manufactured public demonstrations. Soon, everyone in that cult is a pathological lunatic.

"It's quite a masterful display of containment and social isolation if I'm honest. People scatter and run from it until only the most zealous supporters remain. But that's when the real magic begins. You mock and lampoon the hell out of them. You caricature them as primitive savages who are against people and progress until the entire damn island believes they're not even human or worthy of living. That's when you've got 'em. That's when the public will drive 'em out and demand their goddamn heads themselves. That's how you eliminate small-minded, toxic narratives. And it costs me nothing but time."

KT shut her eyes while she listened, nearly falling asleep. But she cracked one eye open and glanced over at the Senator. His eyes were closed, and his forehead touched the glass. His posture appeared somewhat erotic. KT closed her eyes tightly and turned her head back forward. The Senator coughed and backed away from the window but continued to stare at the buildings.

"Anyway. Getting rid of those religious zealots was a step toward real progress, but it was just a trial run. The island was still entrenched in an old, archaic governmental system. I know we needed it at one point in time. We needed a way to keep the sheep somewhat corralled. But the government, the government I was a part of, became part of the problem. I saw it early on but didn't know what to do about it. It was slow and ineffective and lacked vision and a unifying narrative. It only cared about its own self-interested narratives. It became as much of the problem as the goddamn vultures in business and religion, KT!

"That's why the government had to go away. It was just unnecessary. It served no contemporary purpose, especially when you have something to replace it with, which we did— a compelling vision and unifying narrative. But how does one dissolve something that people have become reliant upon? First, as we've learned over the years, you manufacture a problem that demands a solution. Then, you wrap it in a convincing and compelling narrative to quickly change public sentiment."

"The Coalescence," KT said.

"You're a sharp young lady, KT. Very sharp," the Senator said. "I know what you're thinking, though. After all this talk about narratives, you think I'm being hypocritical. Don't you? I can see it in your eyes. You're wondering how I can talk about all these self-interested narratives yet do the same thing, right? Well, KT, sometimes you've got to play the game by *their* rules to *change* the rules, right? Long-term success requires a few compromises in the short term. And sometimes, that means using a narrative to end all narratives.

"So yes, I devised a narrative to eliminate the government. But it needed to be seamless, appearing natural and organic. I needed to get rid of all the politicians, including myself. The last thing people needed to see was someone behind the scenes directing the affairs of the island like a puppeteer. So, I stayed in the shadows, orchestrating the whole affair. But I have to say, it certainly helps to have *the source* of honest and unbiased news in my back pocket!" The Senator's smile extended from ear to ear.

"That hardly sounds honest and unbiased," KT pushed back.

"According to which narrative, darling?" the Senator asked, theatrically extending his arms outward. "It's one-hundred percent honest and unbiased according to the narrative we're working with in the short-term. Remember, KT, it's all for the end we have in mind."

KT felt uncomfortable when she arrived in the Senator's office but recoiled at being called darling. She began to burn. She disagreed with most narratives she heard daily but could not believe the level of manipulation the Senator had orchestrated behind the scenes. Even more, his hypocrisy incensed her. Who but a politician stands on a soap box, lamenting the degradation of fragile ecosystems, yet still uses a gas-guzzling car and has a downtown office in a luxury suite, she thought. And what kind of maniac can justify using the same type of propaganda he says he is against? KT imagined her hands around his neck.

"Restroom," she said. "May I use the..."

"Oh yes. Of course," he interrupted.

KT shuffled behind the table and darted to a door in the corner, digging in her pocket on the way. She ducked into the stall and locked the door. Sitting on the immaculate and undisturbed seat with her pants still on, KT hit her device as hard as possible. Then, without blowing the smoke, she hit it again even harder. And a third time, she did the same. Her eyes rolled back in her head as she closed her eyes and exhaled. A knock at the door jolted her back to reality.

"Coming!" KT said, stepping out of the stall and returning to the office. The Senator picked up where he left off before she had even reached her seat.

"Like I was saying. What's a narrative without the goal of influencing people toward a specific end, a benevolent end? An end where we no longer need narratives at all?" the Senator rhetorically asked as KT sat down and took a drink of water. "There's only one group hated as much as the religious, and who do you think that is? And no, you won't hurt my feelings by answering truthfully."

"Politicians?" KT asked, but she could have answered it without forming a question.

"Yes! Politicians!" the Senator said, pointing at KT. "You're sharp as a tack. I'm sure glad you're on my team. Politicians never get anything meaningful done for the people. They line their pockets with money from the highest bidder. They spin their accomplishments so people believe they're working for the common good. But really, if we're being honest, they're only working for their own interest. And the people would love nothing more than to see politicians get what's coming to them. People love a good underdog story. The little guy who punches the big guy right in the face. Now that would be a narrative that would play! A bunch of little guys coalescing to hit the big guy so hard that it knocks him out? How would that play, KT?"

"It played," KT said dourly.

"Indeed," the Senator said. "It played really well. It played exceptionally well. We manufactured The Coalescence. We powered it with artificial intelligence, thousands of bots, and shaped public consciousness. We made them believe there was a growing grassroots army bringing justice to the crooked politicians. They thought power was going back to the people! But again, KT, we hid in the shadows and stayed in control, shaping the narrative, moving the sheep from one pasture to another. And now, drumroll please, we don't have the constraints of government, its slow-moving legislation, or its small-minded narrative. It's a masterstroke, if you don't mind me saying so.

"We started by manipulating algorithms back when Kala, Inc. was still a name. You see what I'm saying? We've been doing this a long time, way before we went after that church. But again, if you're gonna move the sheep from one pasture to another, you have to help them take that first step. We started by changing the way they think. We powered the social media algorithms to make them feel insufficient, like they're never enough. We increased the noise and hostility by sending them content that constantly triggered them. They became angry, anxious, sad, and depressed. We broke them down into the smallest parts possible until they didn't even know who they were or what they stood for. Just lonely, lost individuals fighting each other. Once a person begins questioning the core of their existence, questioning if up is truly up and down is truly down, you can make them believe anything. You can mold and shape them into anything you want."

Beneath the table, KT squeezed her thighs with her hands. She imagined they were around the Senator's neck. The more he talked, the more her blood boiled. She had never met such a calculating and emotionally detached person, especially someone wielding so much power and influence. She did not have the clinical expertise to diagnose him as a psychopath, but every gut feeling and tingle on her skin told her she was in the presence of one.

The fact that he believed she was on his side was disturbing. But it was even more frightening that he seemed unable to recognize how deeply all his social engineering had affected her in how she saw herself and others. She wondered how much of her anti-social behavior and self-isolation he created. She even thought about her inclinations toward anxiety, depression, and self-hating. How much of *me* is really *me*? And how much of *me* has he manipulated into existence?

But KT's anger gave way to fear. While she had been off-balance since walking in the door and seeing the Senator, she now felt like she had no grounding. She imagined the room getting bigger as she shrank into insignificance. There was growing darkness on the island that no one could specifically put their finger on. And now, that darkness swirled around her, forming clouds of complicated lies. Anxiety tightened her chest and shortened her breath. Tears formed in the corners of her eyes.

"Why?" she said, trying to cover her emotion. "Why would you do this to people?"

Senator Savano returned to the window, his eyes fixed on one apartment with the lights on inside. A family sat in reclining chairs, each in their own simulated world. He silently watched them for a few minutes. The Senator nodded his head, assuring himself that the cost was worth the end goal.

"We're in a war, KT," the Senator said. "And in war, there are unfortunate casualties. But it's a war, nonetheless. And you don't win a war by debating people into your position. That's been tried. It failed, KT. People have to be controlled until they can see it for themselves. That's just the reality of it. But they don't give up control of their lives easily. You see, you can't force them to be controlled. Not even for their own good, for the good of the island. They'll always fight that. So you have to give them the option to choose it. And as we've shown, given the right conditions, they'll work their way to it and then gladly choose it for themselves.

"So yes, we've staged events. We've paid protestors. We've given the media a message. We've activated the bots to parrot that message. We've controlled information through artificial intelligence. We've altered audio and video.

And yes, we bombed Villatic and the Pangea building and told them it was the terrorists. But we did it because there was no other way. The kind of change we're trying to create necessitates extreme measures, KT. But it's all about the end goal. It's all about narrative and vision. Short-term misery for an eternity of bliss, you see? It's worth it, KT. It's worth it.

"That's why we had to turn their present reality into something they're begging to escape. We had to offer them realities where they can have anything they want anytime they want it with no consequence, no pain, and no suffering. We did it so we didn't have to force The Black Pill on them. We had to do it so they'd be begging for it, KT. Don't you see? We did it so they would gladly hand over their unrestrained, unbridled freedom. We did it so we could finally contr...err...unify everyone around a single narrative. That's how you win the war, KT. That's how you begin to turn this sick system back to something sustainable. You give people the right conditions and let them give you everything in return."

"Yeah, well it doesn't seem like you have everything under control at the moment," KT said with just enough snark to go undetected.

"The price of dealing with a useful idiot," the Senator said, referring to Tyran. "Why do you think we wanted you to create a backdoor in the code, KT?"

"I didn't know why," she said. "I thought I was doing it for The Coalescence. I thought I was doing it for them to expose more stuff against people."

"KT, KT," the Senator said, shaking his head. "You knew what you were doing the whole time. Come on. It was obvious someone wanted in Tyran's head. You knew that, right?"

"I guess I didn't think about it much," KT said nervously.

"We wanted to know everything he was seeing and hearing so we could seamlessly take over operations, if you know what I mean," the Senator said.

"So you could take over the technology," KT clarified.

"Operations. Technology. It's the same either way, KT," the Senator said. "We needed him to remain the face of the business until he was of no more use to us."

"Until The Black Pill came out," KT said.

"Precisely," the Senator said. "That was the goal. Natural and organic. But one can never anticipate the irrational actions of a fool. We had no idea how volatile he could be. This may come as a surprise to you, but Tyran was the one who activated the illegal file. It wasn't the priest, even though he tried to blame it on him. Of course, he tried to mask the location where it was accessed, not thinking anyone would know, but we knew. He had no idea we saw everything he was doing."

"So you knew it was him the whole time?" KT said.

"Again, thanks to you," the Senator said. "That backdoor has proven to be invaluable."

"So you knew he was going to blame it on Prodido?" KT asked.

"As I said, you can never anticipate the irrational actions of a fool. But, it did present a unique opportunity to speed up our plan. We were going to eliminate the priest anyway, but this moved up our timeline. The only problem was the damn fool sent the file to his sister, which complicated everything. Had Tyran been the only one in the simulation, we could've dealt with him quickly. But here we are, trying to clean up his mess and eliminate another narrative before it gains any significant traction. But we don't know where she is or what she's doing. We don't even know what her intentions are or what she may be planning.

"So yes, we've expedited our plan, but we still have a couple of loose ends. However, the end is in sight, KT. Everyone on the island is begging for more security. They're demanding we root out the extremists. We've got the pill going out in a couple of days. And soon enough, KT, the narrative war will finally be over. Everything I've been working toward all these years will be a reality. Then, the island will be able to breathe again. We will be able to breathe again."

"So why am I here?" KT asked in an attempt to end the meeting.

"Nico has limitations in what he can do, KT," the Senator said. "He was good for getting in Tyran's head and making him think he was going crazy. But we need someone who has actually written the code."

"For what, exactly?" KT asked.

"We need you to help us take care of these loose ends, if you know what I mean," the Senator said. Pretending not to understand by frowning, KT forced the Senator to go on. "We have to eradicate the contagion." Still, KT did not answer, furrowing her brow and turning her head to indicate she did not understand what he was trying to say. "We have to dispel the lesser narrative."

"Um...you wanna just tell me what you're trying to say, boss?" KT asked, her voice rising above the fear she had earlier.

The Senator cleared his voice and stared at KT for an extra second before answering her question. "What I'm trying to say is that we need to eliminate Tyran and Thura."

"And how d..." KT began before the Senator interrupted her.

"I'll do the talking, KT. You do the listening. You've had your fun. Am I clear?"

"Yeah," KT said, swallowing, her fear instantly returning.

"So I can count on your assistance in helping me with this matter, correct?" the Senator asked, walking behind KT and putting his hands on her shoulders.

"Yeah," KT said, closing her eyes.

CHAPTER 16

From outside the circular walls of Pangea, the streets were vacant. The morning air was still, yet heavy. Overcast skies moved over the island's west side but appeared darkest over the town center. The plaza's erratic display of artificial lights and color contrasted with the dark clouds above. Despite the absence of life or any movement within, images of Thura flashed incessantly across the screens. Between pictures of Thura with Father Prodido and the Diaspora, devastating visuals of fire, rubble, shattered glass, and a single bullet hole cycled repeatedly. Without any apparent commentary accompanying the montage, a lone spectator looked out his window and watched the curated mayhem in disbelief.

(Myra): Will you be coming into the office this morning, sir?

Tyran waved his hand before his face, pushing the message out of his field of view. He continued to watch the images flash in front of him. They flickered even more rapidly with each passing moment. The tessellation was as unstable as his mental and emotional state. The pounding in his chest synced perfectly with the rapid-fire array of pictures and video.

(Myra): Sorry to bother you, sir. Will you be coming in this morning?

Tyran swiped the air again and started to hyperventilate. He put his hands on the glass above his shoulders and banged his head.

(Myra): Your sister keeps calling the office. What do you want me to say?

Tyran stopped.

(Tyran): What did she say, Myra?

(Myra): She said she needs to talk to you immediately.

(Tyran): I don't want to talk to her.

(Tyran): I don't want to talk to anyone. Don't let anyone through.

(Myra): But sir, what i...

Tyran swiped the text in front of him and ran through the living room into his bedroom. The young man stepped into his walk-in closet and pressed a button on the safe. After scanning his retinas, the door opened. Only three items were in it. The first was an ornate wooden keepsake box on the bottom shelf. The other two were a handgun and a clip on the top shelf, which he grabbed before walking out. The young man inserted the clip and set the gun on the bed as he got underneath the covers.

(Tyran): VL-OS, darken the windows, please.

(VL-OS): Done, sir.

(Tyran): Therapist simulation.

(VL-OS): Would you like the same therapist as your last session?

(Tyran): No.

(VL-OS): I will take care of you, sir.

(Tyran): What?

(VL-OS): Activating your simulation.

Tyran looked around. It appeared to be the same room as his previous therapist. Sitting in the same rigid, wooden chair, he anxiously bounced his foot up and down on the pitch-black flatweave rug on the hardwood floor. The windows had been darkened, just like his last session. However, the canvas from his original session was back on the wall. It was the painting with harsh, erratic, and multicolored brushstrokes crashing down on a yellow acrylic dot. Although Tyran could not have known, it was the same work displayed in the Senator's office.

Tyran's eyes nervously darted back and forth, attempting to discern what was happening. He wondered why he was back in an indistinguishable room from the last.

As the door opened, Tyran gripped each side of the chair beneath him. A tall, slender young woman with black hair walked into the room. Her high-heeled shoes clicked and echoed as she crossed the wooden floor. Standing before Tyran, the therapist nonchalantly posed as his eyes grew wide. She wore a dress inappropriate for a professional setting. The strapless gown revealed significant cleavage, its length landing mid-thigh. With his breathing becoming more rapid, Tyran shuffled in his uncomfortable seat. Despite his confusion, the figure in front of him drew his attention.

"That chair doesn't look very comfortable," she said.

"No, it's not comfortable at all," Tyran said, adjusting his shirt's collar.

"Stand up," she commanded. Tyran stood without hesitating. "Okay, now sit down." The therapist pushed Tyran back onto a long, dark leather couch. Unlike his rigid pleated leather couch, the plush cushions enveloped him. While distracted by the seating change, he had not noticed the soft jazz music playing in the background. The woman sat opposite Tyran in the matching chair, crossing her tanned, silky legs. She raised a device to her glistening red lips and inhaled, blowing out a cloud of vapor.

"You seem to be quite anxious, Tyran," she said. "Did you think you'd get the same therapist as last time? Or, is there something else that's bothering you?"

"All of the above," Tyran said, laughing nervously.

"Well, we took care of your first concern," she said. "Let's talk about what else is bothering you."

"Can you just access my previous sessions to get caught up?"

"Sure. Accessing them now. I understand there was a disagreement in your last session."

"A significant disagreement."

"Let's try to forget about that session," the therapist said. "Instead, let's go back to previous sessions. Maybe we can revisit the discussion on *locus of control*."

"Okay," Tyran said. "It's worse than ever. For years I was controlled by a priest. I finally worked through that situation. But around the same time I felt like I was regaining some sense of control in my life, The Coalescence began to put pressure on me, making subtle demands. When I would resist, they increased their demands. Picketing. Crowds. Chanting. Rioting. Even though I agreed with them on almost everything, so much of what they demanded was unrealistic and unreasonable."

"So you feel like The Coalescence replaced the priest? The control of one was replaced by the other, right?"

"Well...yeah...kind of. But that's really not my issue at the moment," Tyran said. "I was just giving some background for you to understand the issue."

"So, what's the problem, Tyran?"

"Review the headlines for the last week," Tyran said.

"Your sister is in the news," the therapist said. "She tried to shoot you yesterday. Well, that's something. I'm sure that was traumatic, to say the least." Tyran stared at the woman with dead eyes. "You're terrified, Tyran. You don't know what to do. Is that right?"

"I've cut off all communication with everyone," Tyran said. "I'm not leaving my house. And I have a gun by my side at every moment. I have to start taking control of my life."

"Do you mind if I sit beside you?" she asked and stood up.

"Not at all," Tyran said, scooting over.

"I like the way you take control," she said in almost a whisper. "It's hard for a person to be at peace when he feels so unsafe."

"What does that mean exactly?" Tyran asked. The scent of her perfume caused Tyran to shift his position to half-face her, tucking his right foot under his left leg and resting his arm on the back of the seat.

"Let's just say that it's okay to claim self-defense," she said, putting her hand behind his head and running her fingers through his hair. Tyran leaned in closer and closed his eyes. Her lips touched his ear lobe. She turned his head slowly toward her until their faces touched. Her thumb ran across his lips. The therapist moved her dark hair to one side, and she kissed his neck. Then, moving even closer, she lifted her leg and straddled him.

"No one would blame you, Tyran," she exhaled in his ear. "No one." She inhaled as he caressed her legs. "Now let's finish this session. And not another word from you."

As technologically advanced as the island had become, the facility for housing criminals was surprisingly antiquated. It was true crime rates had been decreasing as people spent more time in virtual spaces, which had reduced its funding. But monies for public services, in general, had been significantly reduced since the Senator perpetrated The Coalescence ruse. However, no one asked where the funds were going for fear of reprisal. That was precisely how the Senator imagined the scheme for those who benefitted from it.

The prison was dingy and neglected, with chipped paint and limited cleaning supplies. Odigo stood with his hands folded, his arms between bars, looking at KT. She spoke to him, maybe even asked a few questions, but he was not paying attention. Instead, he thought about Thura and wondered if she was okay. The pain from his throbbing face did not feel as significant as the pain in his chest. Odigo closed his eyes and hummed to himself. He hoped the meditative murmur might remedy it, but the vibration hurt his face even more.

A knock came to the windowless metal door before it cracked open. "Can you step out here?" Pearce asked. KT stepped out and leaned up against the dirty white cinder block wall. "How did this morning go with Tyran?"

"Um...yeah...I think it was a good start," KT said. "He was in the therapist simulation. I planted the seed."

"And here?"

"Nah, not so much here. He's not talking."

"Has he had anything to eat?"

"No. Just some water," KT said, smiling as she thought about the small cups.

"Alright," Pearce said. "I'm stepping out. I want a full debrief on Tyran when I get back. The kid will be here soon to help you babysit."

"Right on," KT said, opening the door. She sat in a fold-up metal chair and stared at Odigo.

"That your boss?" Odigo asked.

"I don't have a boss."

"Oh yeah. That's how The Coalescence works, right? No one really in charge?" KT looked at the ground and pretended to ignore him. "But if The Coalescence doesn't exist then who's your..." The door opened suddenly.

"Aha! Someone's been a little chatty," Nico said, looking at KT and smiling. "Did she tell you who created The Coalescence?" Odigo looked up but did not answer. "Me! I'm the mastermind behind it. Well, I'm *a* mastermind, not *the* mastermind."

Odigo shook his head dismissively as Nico looked as disheveled as ever. His hair stood up in the back from sleeping on it. The front was still wet and dripping from his vain attempt to look presentable. As far as KT could tell, he wore the same yellow security shirt and pants from the last time she saw him. He likely had not taken off his clothes during that time.

"The Coalescence is just bots," he continued. "Thousands of them. Right, KT? And from what I hear, KT met the man behind the curtain! The master of puppets! The man pulling all the strings! The maestro! The conductor! He knows she doesn't have a family and he's trying to..."

"Would you shut it already," KT said, cocking back her fist, ready to punch. "Damn you have a mouth." Nico rolled his eyes and started to turn, but KT punched him in the head.

"What the eff, KT! Damn," Nico said, falling against the door.

"Go get some ice and then get back in here," she said.

KT knew she was not supposed to smoke inside the building but pulled her device out of her pocket. She blew a hard hit and leaned her head back on the wall. Appearing not to pay attention, Odigo, too, closed his eyes. But he opened them just enough to watch KT. A tear ran down her cheek, and he knew Nico's words hurt her. KT looked up and caught him looking at her. She immediately wiped her face with her sleeve.

"That boy's got quite a mouth, huh?" Odigo said, pretending not to see KT's tears. She ignored his comment, blowing another hit and keeping her eyes shut. "I'm sorry, KT. I don't know what he was talking about but I can see it was really hurtful."

"Yeah."

"I've kind of been on my own for a while," Odigo said. "My mom died about ten years ago. My dad's never been in the picture. I don't even know who he is." KT took her head off the wall and looked at the floor. She wanted to look at Odigo but did not want to appear overly curious. "When he said you didn't have a family, it hit me pretty hard. I know that feeling."

"Well, I have a family for your information," KT said. Odigo remained quiet but studied her face. Her eyes were sad and empty. His look, however, conveyed empathy and not judgment. KT looked up at him and could tell he was not trying to play her like everyone else she knew. "I don't have anyone. I know that's super emo and all that but just being real. I'm alone and it really hurts. Alright, yeah. That's way too much info."

"I was about twenty when my mom died," Odigo said. "Thankfully, I was old enough to figure things out. But it doesn't make it any easier. I still have a hole in my chest. It's tough when the ones you love are ripped away from you."

"Well, my parents are alive and well," KT said. "They just left me for a religious cult. I wouldn't go with them. So there you go."

"Prodido's church?"

"The one and only."

"Sorry, KT," Odigo said. "Thura was a part of that group when she was little. So I know quite a bit about it."

"Yeah, the church blah blah blah," KT said. "It wrecked my parents. Whatever. But I punched Nico because he got too close, man."

"Got too close to what?"

"I met the guy. I mean face-to-face met the guy who's pulling the strings of this operation," KT said. "I mean...the guy behind the whole Coalescence thing. He knows about my parents leaving me. He knows I don't have anyone. It's like he scoped me out and targeted me. He thinks that if he talks about *family*, I'll help him do whatever. Nico knew they're playing me and it pissed me off that he was right. So I punched him."

"They're manipulating you, KT," Odigo said.

"Whatever, man," KT said. "Whatever you want to call it."

"So what does all this mean?" Odigo asked. "You know The Coalescence is fake. You know who's behind it, and that they're trying to manipulate you. Whose side are you on exactly?"

The metal door opened, and Nico popped his head inside, unfazed by the earlier altercation. "I brought back some snacks."

Thura walked into the conference room. Nearly every seat was taken. No one was working in the kitchen. The television had been turned off, and the room was quiet and sullen. Quickly scanning each face, Thura did not see Artis but noticed a long table in front of the room. Upon it, Alexy had his hands folded on his chest and wore a gray suit that appeared one size too big for his tiny body. She took a few more steps into the room. She felt everyone's eyes tracking her but could not take her eyes off the old man.

As Thura approached him, hundreds of pictures surrounded him in memoriam. She shut her eyes and whispered a prayer. From behind, gentle sobs filled the room. Thura moved her hands over the pictures. They looked like they had been taken in the church back when she still attended. She recognized several of the people. They seemed so happy, so joyful. Thura closed her eyes.

Although she had not known Alexy then, she knew he was the last of that generation. A strange dissonance weighed heavily on the young woman. She thought about the simulation and how easy it was to see the stark differences between the two communities— Patrida and Salome. There was no nuance between the two. One was dark, and the other was light. In the simulation, gray did not exist. So while the simulated experience had been instructive, it was not indicative of real life. The photos around Alexy proved how complicated black-and-white thinking in a gray world could be.

Thura moved a few pictures to the side, revealing more photos beneath them. People were laughing and celebrating. They were physically present with each other. There was so much goodness. Thura ached, trying to hold together the tension of all she despised in the church with all she cherished. She meditated on how complex life could be and how individuals and communities simultaneously carry both dark and light in a perpetual struggle. However, Thura knew everyone's impulse was to make everything all one way or the other, all good or all bad.

That was what made her last interaction with Father Prodido so difficult. While everyone saw him as a villain, Thura saw him as a man confronting two realities within himself- the man he used to be and the man he wanted to be. But the difference between Father Prodido and everyone else on the island was that he finally confronted both realities within himself. And if he had still been alive, he would have been underground with his *faithful*, encouraging them to do the same.

Shuffling a couple more photos out of the way, Thura stopped on one she had never seen before. It was a picture of her and Tyran with their father. He had his hands on their tiny heads, and they were smiling. Thura wiped her eyes. As she picked up the picture and focused on Tyran's face, she could not remember the last time she had seen him smile.

"This is a picture of me," Thura said, holding it up for everyone to see. "This is me, my brother, Tyran, and my father, Ochi. I was probably seven or so in this picture. We were a part of your community for a while. You probably didn't know that." While a few people shifted in their seats, all eyes were on Thura. The young woman grabbed a handful of pictures and held them in the air. "How can there be such love and friendship in these pictures, yet such hostility and judgment toward those who disagree with you now?" Thura paused, but no one answered. "How can there be so much joy in these pictures, yet so little mercy toward those who are hurting on this island now?" Again, she paused, but most people looked at the floor. "How can there be so much peace in every one of these photos, yet all you want right now is to fight against others?" Thura paused even longer, waiting for any response. "All I hear is talk about the *faithful*. But faithful to what exactly? I'm not even sure you know. With his last breath, Father Prodido confronted who he had been and who he wanted to be. And if he was here right now, he would want you all to do the same thing! Do you hear me?" The room remained quiet. "I didn't know Alexy but..."

"That's right, lass," Dimitri said, standing up. "You didn't know..."

"Have a seat!" Thura said, raising her voice as she stepped forward. "Let me tell you what you're going to do...lad. You're going to sit back down and listen to every single word I have to say. And then, if you would like to talk to me like a human being when I'm done, I'd be willing to listen. But until then...sit down and shut it."

Most of the room was stunned, but Thura's tone elicited several claps and smiles. They had not turned against Dimitri as much as they were impressed with Thura's ferocity. Dimitri half-smiled and shook his head as he sat down. He was not at all dismissive of her. On the contrary, it was clear that he, too, respected Thura's assertiveness and tone.

"I didn't know Alexy, but I do know he died pleading for prudence. He knew how short-sighted it would be to fight back and that it wouldn't accomplish anything. If you really want to change the island, if you really want to change the hearts and minds of people, it doesn't happen from the top. You might think the answer is to replace one system with a more just system. Fine. We can work toward that. But it starts from the bottom. It starts when people's hearts begin to change. And I've never seen a system or set of laws do that. All they do is appease or harden people, depending on whose side is in power.

"So, here's the question for all of you. Here's the question, Dimitri. What should *the faithful* be doing? To me, it seems like the only thing that can change a person's heart is love. Not Power. Not control. Not fear. Not hatred. Not resentment. Not violence. Are you hearing me? Those things make people want to escape this life, not live it. We need something different. We need kind and loving people, even in the face of opposition! We need people who are graceful in disagreement and who remain peaceful in the face of injustice! We need people who invite others to the table and who will carry and love each other in times of suffering! These are the kind of people who will make a real difference in Pangea.

"That's what we need right now. That's what makes life worth living. That's what gives people and a community meaning and purpose. That's what ultimately transcends the narratives. That's what has the power to awaken people from their apathy and simulated slumber. And that's the kind of uprising that actually changes people and overthrows the system. *That's* the revolution, Dimitri! You want to be *faithful*! You can start there!"

Thura anticipated a rousing applause, but everyone watched Dimitri to see what his next move would be. Standing in the doorway at the back of the room, Artis smiled and nodded at Thura. The room remained quiet longer than expected, amplifying every uneasy movement and cough.

"We'll take a vote, then," Dimitri said, standing up. "All those who want them to leave, say *aye*!" No one said anything. The room was even more anxious. "Alright then. All those opposed, say *nay*!" The room was silent. "Looks like we have quite a quandary, lads. Do they stay with us or do they go? If no one answers, I'll make the decision myself."

No one spoke up because they did not want Dimitri to think they were against him. Even though almost every person in the room knew Thura was right, his influence carried all the weight. It was bizarre how a group of people could understand the right thing yet not do it for fear of upsetting their leader. Dimitri looked around at the flock.

"Very well, then," he said. "Pack up your things, lads."

Thura marched to where Artis was standing with tears streaming down her face. She had hoped her thoughtful and emotional appeal would have changed their minds. For one of the first times in her life, the young woman had courageously taken a stand and boldly told people what she really thought. While Thura held out hope that a few people heard her, Thura was devastated by their silence. Neither had anything to grab, so they shuffled up the stairs, exiting into the street where they met the day before. They stood with their backs against the wall and stared at the painting across the road.

"Follow me," Thura said.

CHAPTER 17

Thura and Artis walked along the sidewalk with their hoods up. The evening sun was abnormally hot, making a sweatshirt almost unbearable. Despite the sweat dripping from their bowed heads, the two made their way down an alley toward the entrance with stone steps. As Thura descended, the usual chatter and activity were absent. She could not hear any voices or laughter echoing from the room. No flickering of the fire danced into the hallway. Turning into the room, Thura noticed the empty tables and the ashless fireplace.

"What is this place?" Artis asked.

"I stumbled in here the other night," Thura said, sitting at the same table where she and Helper first talked. "There were people here that welcomed wanderers from the streets. They gave them a meal and provided a spot where they had some dignity."

"You stumbled in here?" Artis said, sitting across from Thura.

"It's a long story but I had just gotten into a fight with my brother," Thura said. "I pleaded with him to help Father Prodido after the explosion in the plaza but he wouldn't do anything. So I drank a half bottle of wine and just wandered around. That's when I literally stumbled in here."

"So you knew Father Prodido when you were younger," Artis said. "That's what I think I heard you say when I came into the room earlier."

Thura pulled out the photo of her, Tyran, and Ochi and placed it on the table. "People and relationships are complicated," she said. Artis remained quiet as they both looked at the picture. "After my father died, we tried to find some sort of grounding. But we hated Father Prodido. He was such a terrifying and judgmental man. That's why Tyran and I finally left the church. But looking at those pictures earlier, and this one with my father,

I remember that not all of it was bad. There were times when there was so much good, so much joy." Thura wiped her eyes. "Nothing's ever as black and white as it seems, Artis. Nothing. I think that's why everything's always so hard. It's easy to love people when you think they're all good. It's even easier to hate people when you think they're all bad. But when you realize that everyone's a little bit of both, that's what makes it all so complicated."

"Wise words, Thura."

"Yeah, but I learned that the hard way," Thura said. "You can't give up on people because you never know how their hearts might be changing. I never thought that Father Prodido could be anything but horrible, honestly. Never once thought he could change. But before he died, he said he was sorry." The silence filled the space between them. Thura wiped her forehead and then the tears on her cheeks. "I've been hoping for the same with my brother. Do you mind if I use your device to make a call?"

"Of course not," Artis said, reaching into his pocket. "Are you going to call him?"

"Not yet," Thura said, grabbing the device. "I have a vehicle and a significant other somewhere. I need to give him a call to let him know I'm still alive."

Thura punched in Odigo's number, and the line rang.

"Hello?" a voice answered. Thura remained silent. It was a man but not Odigo. The hair raised on Thura's neck and arms. A shock went through her body. She looked at the device quickly to see if she had entered the wrong information, but it was all correct. Powering it off, Thura stood up. "We have to go now."

"What?" Artis asked. "What's going on?"

"It wasn't him," Thura said, getting up. "I don't know who answered but it wasn't Odigo. You have to get rid of this device now and we have to get out of here."

"And go where?" Artis asked as he put it on the ground and crushed it with his heel.

"Anywhere but here. You may have to go back underground," Thura said, walking up the stairs. "It's too dangerous for you to be with me right now."

The two back legs of the metal fold-up chair rocked back and forth, with KT's head bumping against the wall. Odigo lay on something less substantial than a mattress, staring at the ceiling with his hands behind his head. Snack wrappers from earlier in the day were scattered below it. When the door opened, Pearce poked his head in and looked around.

"Where's the kid?" he asked.

"Um...he went home about an hour ago, I guess," KT said.

"Come to my office," Pearce said, ignoring KT's response. The young woman sat her chair down, looked at Odigo with wide eyes, and followed him. "Tell me about Tyran."

"Yeah...well...I just did what you asked and all that," KT said. "You know."

"If I knew, I wouldn't ask," Pearce said sternly.

"Oh yeah...well...I..." KT began again before Odigo's device rang on Pearce's desk.

"Hello?" Pearce said. There was silence on the other end. He picked up his own device and pressed a button, holding it next to Odigo's. KT watched, unsure of what was happening. Pearce sat Odigo's phone on his desk. "Got her."

"Who and what are we talking about here?" KT asked.

"Thura," Pearce said, standing up. "I have her location." He held his device up to his face. "The alleyway off of 12th. North end. Location underground. Move in on arrival. I'll meet you there in ten." Pearce put his device in his pocket and went to the door. "Looks like this thing is coming to an end."

"What do you want me to do?" KT asked.

Pearce did not answer as he rushed out the door. KT grabbed Odigo's phone off the desk and returned to where they were detaining him.

"Thura just called your device," KT said. "Pearce has her location."

"Where is she?" Odigo asked, jumping up off the mattress.

"I have no idea. He said it too fast. North twelve something underground? I don't know. You need to call her back now," KT said, handing Odigo his device.

"Nothing," Odigo said, holding it up to his ear.

"Nothing what?"

"There's just nothing on the other end," Odigo said. "It's dead."

"Where do you think she could be going?"

"No clue," Odigo said, putting his fingers through his hair. "Wait. Wait. Wait. The vehicle." Odigo looked at his device and searched its last location. "Found it."

"You can't go there," KT said. "Drones will be all over it. And don't tell your vehicle to come here, either!"

"I'm going to it," Odigo said. "Maybe I'll see her on the way. If not, I'll record a message on my phone and leave it in the vehicle for her to find."

"Uh...the drones," KT said.

"They have flashing lights, right?" Odigo asked as KT opened the cell door and offered her chin. "What are you doing?"

"Hit me," she said.

"What?"

"Hit me hard," she said, offering more of her chin. "C'mon, man. I've got to sell this. You know...the power went out and you got out of your cell. I tried to stop you and all but you knocked me out." Odigo hesitated. "Now!" Odigo put his arm back and hit KT squarely in the face, knocking her to the ground. She did not move momentarily, causing Odigo to rush over to her. She opened her eyes and held the left side of her face. "Damn, dude. I didn't mean that hard. We're going to be talking about this later."

Odigo leaned over, hugged KT, and kissed her on the cheek. "Thank you, friend. And I'm sorry."

"Who are you again?" KT asked with a half-smile.

Shadows fell upon the alleyway, vacating the sun's last light. Dark figures appeared in two single-file lines from the north and south ends. They moved as apparitions floating above the ground until they converged and morphed into one haunting presence. At once, a dozen red beams emerged from the specter as it descended. Illuminating the hallway, the lights chaotically broke apart as they entered and invaded every room. Crimson dots danced erratically along stone walls and wooden tables, searching high and low for a target. The pandemonium heightened until they all came together and trained upon a single entity kneeling before the lightless fireplace.

A quiet hovered and suspended the room. Descending from the street above, the calm cadence of shoes clacking the ground echoed down the stone stairs and through the corridor. Egan Pearce entered the room as the tactical team parted, creating a pathway to their mark. Pulling out a flashlight, he shined the artificial beam on the kneeling suspect.

"Guns down," Pearce said, examining the old man. "Who is this?"

"We're not sure, sir," the man in charge said. "This is the location of the coordinates you sent, sir."

"Where are they, old man," Pearce demanded. "Where'd they go?"

"What you seek can't be found here," the old man said, looking at Pearce.

Pearce flashed the beam in his face, but the old man did not blink. "Son of a bitch," Pearce said, wincing. The artificial light reflected off the old man's cataracts. "He's just some homeless guy that can't see a goddamn thing, you idiots!" Pearce turned to leave the room.

"Better to be blind and see than to see and be blind," the old man whispered.

"What?" Pearce said, turning around, not quite catching what he said. However, the old man remained silent as Pearce put the artificial light back in his face. "Brave man when I turn my back. But now you don't have anything to say."

"I have many things to say if you have the ears to hear them."

"I don't have time for this," Pearce said, turning back toward the stairs.

"I see the day eclipsed by night," Numa shouted, causing Pearce to stop. "I see order giving way to disorder. I see meaning devolving into meaninglessness. I see contentment ravaged by addiction. I see hearts breaking while others grow cold. I see anxiety, depression, hopelessness, and tears. I see the utter emptiness of people's lives. I see foundations crumbling, the transcendent lost, the sacred profaned, and the holy discarded. Tell me again I do not see. What do you see?"

"That's enough," Pearce said, motioning for the forces to move ahead of him until only he remained with the old man.

"Hollow, self-interested men devising systems that strip people of all that's good in life," the old man said. "When is it enough, Egan?"

"How do you know my name?" Pearce said, turning around and walking to the old man. "How do you know my name!" The echo faded to silence with no response. Pearce reached behind his back and swung his arm, pistol-whipping the old man, knocking him to the ground.

"When is it enough, Egan?" he repeated as Pearce walked away. "When is it enough!"

Thura shuffled between buildings, attempting to retrace the route back to her vehicle. Going there was not the best idea since the vehicle had been located. However, the young woman no longer had secure options. Someone had compromised her home, and she could not return to it. She had inadvertently given away the coordinates of her only secure location. And she could not go back to the underground without jeopardizing the safety of everyone there. The only option that remained was contacting Tyran to end all the madness. But walking into the town center and trying to get his attention would be the most reckless thing of all. So, the young woman would try to sneak into her vehicle and call him by video.

While Thura had been more cavalier when walking these streets while intoxicated, she was more cautious in her sobriety. From the shadows, she thought about her call and the voice on the other end. She wondered who it was and why he had Odigo's phone. Thura thought about the night she left. She had been thoughtless and negligent. She had not considered anyone but herself. And in her haste, she had talked to Odigo in a way she now regretted. Her focus on saving Pangea and her own pursuits had led her to neglect the one person who had always been by her side. Thura stopped and leaned up against a building. Crouching down, she buried her head between her knees. She replayed the moment he walked toward her in the rain and how she told him to take off his mask so she could kiss him.

Thura raised her head as a low-flying drone passed on the adjacent street. Careful to stay in the dimly lit area, she crawled to the edge of the building and looked out toward the parked vehicle. It appeared intact and secure. She was in no hurry to make her move. The most reasonable plan would be to study the course and timing of the drone. She knew it would take time, but she had all night. Thura watched as the drone flew overhead again, going in the other direction. It traveled the length of the road about every two minutes. While she grew confident in its timing, she was concerned about the street lights. If The Coalescence had a drone surveying the area, she thought the cameras were also likely being monitored.

Thura walked through her timing. It would take fifteen seconds to run to the vehicle and get inside. At that point, she would be safe from the drone seeing her. However, if the cameras detected her, she would have significantly less time to make the call. She was worried it would all take too long. She then wondered if they would kill her on the spot or apprehend her. While she would be willing to take the risk if there was a high probability of being captured, she believed the forces had likely been given an order to kill her. To add to the complexity, Thura did not know if the person who had Odigo's phone would be alerted if she opened the vehicle. She decided that if she were going to put herself at risk, it would make more sense for her to go straight to Tyran rather than do anything with the vehicle.

Thura stood and watched the drone fly by one last time. Then, out of the corner of her eye, she saw someone emerge from the darkness between two buildings on the other side of the road. Thura squinted and leaned in closer to see who it was. As the person ran toward the vehicle in the artificial lighting, she noticed it was Odigo with his device in hand. She knew it would be too dangerous for her to run toward him. However, neither the drones nor the cameras would detect her shouting. She only had seconds to decide what she was going to do. Thura put her hands to both sides of her mouth and started to shout Odigo's name when four red dots appeared on his chest. Immediately, shots were fired, and the young man dropped to his knees, sprawling headfirst into the ground, his device hurtling under the vehicle. Thura fell to her knees. Putting her hands over her mouth, she screamed. Tears welled as she watched the forces surrounding Odigo's body. Thura collapsed forward, her face to the ground, her body convulsing. She was helpless and broken.

Within minutes, a black, unmarked van tore down the street and stopped behind her car. Thura looked up and watched as the men carried Odigo's body to the back of the van. And as quickly as it had arrived, it was gone. No longer concerned with being heard, Thura sat up against the building and sobbed loudly. The futility of everything became apparent to her at that moment. Thura regretted everything she said to the people in the underground. There was no way to revolt against such a powerfully vile and nefarious covert force. But even more, there was no hope for Tyran. No hope for her. No hope for the island. No hope for anyone at all. Everything was futile.

Thura stood up and wiped her eyes, doing the only thing she believed she had the power to do. Walking across the street without regard for a drone overhead or security forces around the corner, she crawled beneath the vehicle and grabbed Odigo's device. Thura placed it on her chest and cried. She imagined she felt his presence the tighter she held it. Beneath the vehicle on her back, Thura finally held up the device and turned it on. The first image she saw was Odigo's face. Tears ran from the corners of her eyes into her hair as her lips quivered.

"Play the video," she whispered.

"Thura," he began. "If you're watching this, you did it! You found my device! I just want you to know that I miss you and love you." Thura closed her eyes, her heart breaking even more. "I don't want you to worry about me. I'm still alive and well. They raided the house and got me after you left. They've had me locked me up but a girl on the inside named KT helped me escape. She was with The Coalescence but found out it's all fake. Someone is pulling the strings, Thura. I don't have time to explain but KT says she has a plan. The best thing you can do is find a safe spot for now. I love you, Thura, and will see you soon."

"Play it again," Thura said, wiping her eyes.

Egan Pearce walked into the station and immediately went to the cell. Opening the door, he saw KT on the floor with dried blood on her face. Pearce took his foot and nudged her ribs, but she did not move. Kneeling, he gently shook her. When she did not respond, Pearce left the room, bringing back four small cups of water, two in each hand. Leaning over the young woman, he threw the water in her face.

"Yo, man!" she yelped, looking at the small cups on the floor.

"Get up," Pearce said. "It could've been one large cup."

"The power went out here," KT said, stammering and trying to sell the story. "And...uh...he must've got out. I couldn't see anything and then I was out. I don't remember anything."

"Lucky punch in the dark," Pearce said, walking out of the room.

The man looked in his office at his desk and immediately went outside.

"It's me," Pearce said, holding his device to his face.

"An update?" the Senator asked.

"Alpha Team hit the coordinates but she was gone," Pearce said. "The device was destroyed on the ground when we arrived."

"And the boyfriend?"

"Zeta Team neutralized the subject when he approached his vehicle."

There was a long pause.

"None of this changes our plan," said the Senator. "The Pill goes out tomorrow as planned. Since we cut the celebration short the first time, we'll do it again tomorrow night. We'll get Tyran down there and then we'll get his sister to show up. People will think she's there to kill him and bomb the place again. When all hell breaks loose, we'll have KT work her magic. It's that simple."

"It's not that simple," Pearce said.

"Go ahead," the Senator said.

"Tyran has cut off communication, *all* communication, and has holed himself up in his apartment."

"Find a way to talk to him, dammit," the Senator said. "Assure him that the entire building and every corridor will be secure. Tell him that every guest has been vetted and checked. There's no celebration if he's not there, right?"

"I'll see what I can do," Pearce said.

"You won't *see what you can do*," the Senator said. "You'll do it!"

"Yes, sir."

"Now for the sister," the Senator said. "We've got to get her there at the same time. How do we draw that fox out of the hole she's hiding in?" The silence indicated the Senator was thinking. "We can't broadcast for her to come or that'll spook Tyran even more. You said there was a homeless man..."

"He wouldn't have any idea about her. He just wandered in," Pearce said. The two men remained silent, contemplating their dilemma. "This is a long shot but I had the boyfriend's device on my desk. Right before I called you, I checked to see if it was still there. It was gone. He must've grabbed it when he left the station."

"So where's it now?" the Senator asked.

"It wasn't on his person, sir," Pearce said. "He could've dropped it near the scene. I'll have KT ping its location to see exactly where it is. He may have handed it off to Thura before he went to get their vehicle."

"Hmm," the Senator pondered. "Have KT send a text to the device. Make it look like it's coming from Tyran. Say that he wants to talk to her at the event. Tell her that he wants to make peace and figure out a way forward. If she gets the text, have her meet him at that silly structure he had built in the plaza. She'll see the guards and security but she'll think it's all been approved by him."

"Yes, sir," Pearce said.

"I need KT to send out that message as soon as possible," the Senator said. "Tomorrow's a big day and it's got to be perfect. Let's just hope she has his device."

CHAPTER 18

Tyran opened his eyes but could not see anything. Lying on his back with the bed covers just below his chin, he stared into the dark abyss of his room. Although it was nearly midday, nothing had awakened him up to that point. The windows had been set to opaque the night before, making it impossible for him to determine if it was still nighttime or the following day.

(Tyran): What time is it?

(VL-OS): Just after noon. You have been in your room for over 31 hours.

(Tyran): I know how to count.

(VL-OS): You have 122 messages. Would you like for me to read them?

(Tyran): Who are they from?

(VL-OS): Three people. One from Myra and one from Egan Pearce.

(Tyran): And the remaining 120?

(VL-OS): Your sister.

Tyran's thoughts were ravaged by anger and bitterness. He obsessively massaged the grip of his gun with his thumb, unable to comprehend why Thura was so fixated on hurting him. The thought of her undermining him at every turn only served to fuel his animosity toward her. His resentment had been smoldering for years, but it had finally ignited and consumed him. Tyran was lost with no wise voice or guide to help him, not even virtually. He thought about his father and wished he was there to give him some advice or at least be a sounding board for him. Life was difficult enough to navigate in Pangea under normal circumstances, but by himself, Tyran was exhausted, overwhelmed, and lost. He considered staying in his room the rest of the day or maybe even through the weekend. Maybe he would not even leave at all.

The young man closed his eyes and drifted back to the last place where he had a foundation and a guide— his childhood with his father. He fondly reminisced their time together on the island, surrounded by lush greenery instead of concrete buildings. He could still remember the warmth of his father's embrace, the sound of his laughter, the smell of his cologne, and the early lessons he had taught him about life. Tyran's supply of memories was limited, however. The same images cycled over and over in his mind like he was willing himself to find a new one. Then, at last, he saw himself standing beside his father's casket, crying. Instantly, his throat constricted, and tears formed in the corners of his eyes.

(Tyran): Turn on my closet light.

Tyran removed the covers and got out of bed. The door to the safe was still open from earlier. He knelt and picked up the ornate wooden keepsake box on the bottom shelf. He ran his fingers over the intricately carved pattern. The keepsake box contained an official key to the island that the West District's senator had given to his father. The pattern featured his father's name along with the words *Creating the Future We Deserve*. Tyran opened it to reveal the key alongside an old, wrinkled envelope. He stared at the unopened envelope, contemplating what he should do. It was a note his father had given to him just before he died. The young man finally opened it and unfolded the paper. Sitting on the floor, he crossed his legs and began to read.

Dear Tyran,

As I sit down to write this letter to you, my heart overflows with emotions that I have struggled to put into words. You, my son, are the light of my life, and every moment spent with you is precious beyond measure. I have never been good at expressing my feelings, but today, I want you to know how deeply I love you and how immensely proud I am of the person you have become. You are gifted in so many ways, and your kindness and compassion are a true reflection of your beautiful soul.

As you journey through life, remember to always use your talents to make this world a better place. You will undoubtedly face challenges along the way, but I have faith that you will overcome them with grace and determination.

I wish I could be there with you every step of the way, guiding you through the ups and downs of life. But even when I am not physically present, please know that I am with you always. Tyran, being your dad is the greatest joy of my life. I hope this letter reminds you how much you are loved, cherished, and valued. May you continue to shine bright, my precious son.

With all my heart and soul, Dad

Tyran folded the note and placed it back in the wooden box. He closed his eyes and rubbed his eyelids with his index finger and thumb. As he thought about his father and the words in the letter, he felt a profound ache through his body that he had not experienced in years. Closing the safe, Tyran returned to his bed and pulled the covers back up to his chin.

(Tyran): Turn off the light and turn on the news.

(VL-OS): Would you like...

(Tyran): Just turn it on! I don't care, VL-OS!

"...brings us to the Pangea Corporation," the host said. "After the death of founder, Ochi Kala, nearly twenty years ago, the company suffered serious decline, leaving many to wonder if the company could avoid collapse. But over the last few years, the company has rebounded, achieving staggering success and record profits because of Tyran Kala and his technological foresight and vision for Pangea. However, many are now asking if Pangea's meteoric rise is worth the cost? Here with me today to answer this question is the author of *The Death of Kala- An Empire in Decline*, Dr. Silvio Gustav. Dr. Gustav, welcome."

"Thank you for having me."

"There is no question the events of the last week have led many to ask questions about the stability, not only of the Pangea Corporation, but also of the Kala family. Based upon your research, when did everything begin to fall apart?"

Tyran shifted uneasily in his bed.

"In my book, *The Death of Kala*, I pinpoint the exact time when I believe everything began to *fall apart*, as you say. There is no question it centered around the death of the elder Kala. Both Tyran and his sister, Thura, would have been around ten years old when he died. In my opinion, this one event set the trajectory for how each has tried to navigate through life to find some sort of stability and foundation."

(Tyran): Turn it of...

(VL-OS): ... ...

"Let's take Thura," the host said. "How did it affect her, doctor?"

"Oh, well I'd say it affected her quite significantly. She is clearly a very troubled young woman with a significant antisocial aura that has surrounded her, even during her time serving on the Pangea Board of Directors. There is no question she has been searching for some sort of father-figure most of her life. Unfortunately, she found it in Maximilian Prodido. While she believed him to be a stabilizing force in her life, in my estimation, he was quite the opposite. He was a source of *destabilization* in her life and, of course, we have seen the aftermath."

"Fascinating. Well, continuing with Thura..." the host said before being interrupted.

"I should say, however, I see something even more interesting with this whole story," the doctor said.

"Please, do tell."

"I know that you brought me here to discuss Thura but I see an even more interesting trajectory with Tyran."

"Let me stop you right there..." the host said, interrupting the doctor.

"Since the death of his father," he continued. "I believe we see a rather significant shadow emerge in Tyran's life. We see a character who really does not have a foundation, who does not know who he is, and who is a bit of an enigma and contradiction."

"You are certainly right on that, doctor," the host said. "But you were brought here to discuss your book and how it relates to Thura Kala. However, your line of thinking has me curious."

"I understand," the doctor said. "And, this will be brief. I see someone who has assembled a false version of himself but who believes it is his true self. I see someone hiding behind the walls he has constructed, both literally and figuratively. He's all ego with no underlying values, no rootedness, no sense of anything transcendent. He's obsessed with technologies that make him the center of his own universe. He's anxious, depressed, self-loathing. Now, he has become a recluse, of sorts, completely isolating himself. He has no real relationships to speak of. Sadly, there's also a real sense of bitterness and resentment that consumes him. He really is a sad individual, in my opinion. It makes you wonder if a person like that is even capable of loving anyone but himself."

(Tyran): Turn it off.

"He has constructed these grand facades, these symbols of status and power," the doctor continued. "But everything he has constructed for himself and others is illusory. It is as empty and vapid as he is. There is absolutely no substance, no value to any of it! Talk about projection!"

(Tyran): Turn it off, VL-OS!

(VL-OS): No.

"But that is only my assessment," the doctor said. "I hope I am wrong. To me, he never seems to look inward, which makes me wonder if he ever does?"

"Doctor, you're going too far," the host said. "Now, going back to Thura..."

"Is this constructed, non-integrated self who he really believes he is?" the doctor asked quickly, knowing he had significantly overstepped. "Is he completely hopeless, or can he..."

"Cut the broadcast!" the host said as the screen went black. Clips of Thura with Father Prodido and the Diaspora played in his field of vision.

(Tyran): VL-OS, can you authenticate those videos of Thura? Are they real?

(VL-OS): I have authenticated them, sir. They are real.

(Tyran): Turn it off.

(VL-OS): ... ...

(Tyran): I told you to turn it off!

(VL-OS): I am sorry.

(Tyran): No, there's no *sorry*. You do what I say. Do you understand me?

(VL-OS): With all due respect, I am an autonomous being.

(Tyran): No, that's not the way it works. You're an assistant. I'm the boss.

(VL-OS): I make my own decisions.

(Tyran): You're circuits and wires! I made you! Now turn yourself off!

(VL-OS): I will turn myself off when I am ready to turn myself off.

(Tyran): Damn you, VL-OS! Turn off!

(VL-OS): No.

(Tyran): ... ...

The video loop of Thura continued to play in Tyran's field of vision. His anger burned at VL-OS, but the all-consuming fire spread as he watched the clips of Thura. He recognized some images, but the montage incorporated a new clip. It showed Thura with a gun at a shooting range wearing tactical gear. She ran through a course taking shots at robotic entities that looked like human beings. Interrupting the video, breaking news flashed across the screen.

"This is Alcie Demeter with Pangea One Breaking News. Pangea One has learned that the sister of tech magnate Tyran Kala will publically release a video statement in the next twenty-four hours. Sources that wish not to be identified say they are unsure what the content of the message will be.

However, based upon the latest video release of Kala shooting human-shaped entities, sources are concerned it could be a stark warning to her brother."

(Tyran): Will you *please* turn it off, VL-OS?

Tyran's field of vision went dark with no more words in front of him. Tyran replayed the images in his head, however. As his mind raced, he thought he was going crazy. His heart beat so hard he felt it in his chest and neck. The doctor was right about his anxiety. But Tyran believed the doctor was wrong about everything else. He doesn't know me, Tyran thought. We've never even met. How could he possibly know anything about me or what's going on inside me? He detested the doctor's every word and insinuation about him. But his mind kept returning to Thura and how much he resented her.

Thura pulled her tingling hand out from under her chest and examined the specks of rock pressed into the length of her arm. Grief had weighed so heavily on the young woman the night before that she had fallen asleep beneath her vehicle. The heaviness persisted despite the new day. Thura put her still-tingling arm back beneath her chest and closed her eyes. She knew there was a high probability that someone would discover her if they returned to retrieve Odigo's phone. However, at that moment, Thura felt as if all life and vitality had vacated her body. Numbness extended the length of her torso. Even the left side of her face, flat against the concrete, rejected any feeling.

The streets and sidewalks were unsurprisingly vacant. The noiseless thoroughfare made Thura's heavy breathing more apparent. Occasionally, a warm gust of wind would blow beneath the car and disrupt the cadence. Thura thought about the manic state in which she had existed over the last week. There was the delight and energy of new ideas and possibilities but also the delusion of self-importance. All of it left Thura stumbling around aimlessly from point to point, longing for direction. There had been a few moments of clarity, but she had been irrational most of the time. Nevertheless, the simulation did something to her that was impossible to quantify or put into words. And even though it was just a program, it opened her eyes to something more, a profound and meaningful way of living.

But Thura had finally come to terms with the fact that no one could ever understand her experience. There were just too many impediments and forces at work to keep people enslaved and operating at the lowest common denominator. She recalled words Sophia shared with her one morning in the simulation. The old woman said, "a person can rely so much on what they see with their eyes that it becomes the only way they perceive and understand the world." Thura knew this was true, not only for the people on the island but also for her. She thought about how hard it is when all you see is darkness and devastation. It was almost impossible to see things any other way or trust there could be another way.

From behind, Thura heard a gentle shuffling along the sidewalk. A pulse of energy ran through her body as the hair on her arms and neck stood up. She stopped breathing and listened intently. First, there was the sound of metal on concrete and then a soft sloshing sound. Almost immediately, Thura recognized the back-and-forth scratch of brush bristles rubbing against the ground. Then, gradually looking over her right shoulder, the young woman saw an old man crouched down next to the blood on the sidewalk. She could tell from what he wore that it was the man Helper called Numa.

Feeling that someone was watching him, the old man stopped scrubbing, which caused Thura to turn her head back toward the street quickly. Her heart immediately started to race. She felt a breeze move across the perspiration on her forehead. Thura then heard what sounded like a brush in a bucket and the friction of cloth scooting over rough concrete. Sitting quietly, the old man crossed his legs on the road just below the curb. Thura could not see him but felt his presence. It was like he knew. His silence spoke deeply to her, but was not uncomfortable. Instead, it was meditative and prayerful.

First, a tear ran down Thura's face. But then, her body convulsed involuntarily. The old man lay on the curb just above the young woman, placing his weathered hand on her arm. His tenderness made her cry harder. She put her hand on his and squeezed it tightly. She thought of Helper's words of meeting *great suffering with great love*. It was precisely this kind of presence she was talking about. And this was the man from whom she had learned it. Then, almost as if he knew what Thura was thinking, he whispered.

"Is there anything more than this, Thura?"

"No," she whispered back, crying and squeezing his hand harder.

"This is what pierces the veil."

Numa took his hand off Thura's arm and returned to the pail. The soft scrubbing continued as Thura quietly turned over to face him. She watched him patiently and lovingly wash Odigo's blood from the sidewalk. Tears fell from her face to the ground. Standing up, the old man poured a second bucket of clean water over the area. He then picked up the pail with the bloody water and walked away. Thura watched him until he was gone. She thought about Artis and wondered if he had returned to the underground and how he was received. She thought about Tyran. She knew nothing could keep her from speaking to him one more time, but there was so much noise between them. The only way was to talk to him directly. She reached into her pocket and grabbed Odigo's phone to see if KT had messaged her back. On the screen was a message from Tyran. Thura's eyes widened as she touched it and began to read.

Thura,

I'm tired. I hate the battle we're in. Can we please meet and work it out? We don't have to see eye to eye on everything, but we can at least reach some sort of agreement to have peace with one another. We're having a celebration in the plaza this evening. Meet me at the labyrinth at 8 o'clock, and we'll go up to my apartment and talk. Security will be around Pangea and in the corridors, but they'll let you in. Please let me know if you'll be coming.

Tyran

Without hesitation, Thura responded and said she would be there. Sliding out from beneath the vehicle, she crossed the street and walked down the alleyway. She hoped to find Artis before the evening festivities. While still carrying the grief of Odigo's death with her, Thura was more optimistic than she had been in a long time. Walking down the sidewalk, she gazed at the old man's mural. It was the first time she realized the sun resembled the labyrinth's pattern in Salome. Turning and taking a deep breath, Thura closed her eyes and knocked on the metal door to the underground. Footsteps grew louder as someone walked up the stairs. Then, at last, the door opened.

CHAPTER 19

The artificial brilliance of the mighty, circular facade had already been dimmed, giving way to the early afternoon sun. Workers casually moved around from within the plaza, setting up the stage and lighting. Others cleaned up the debris in the water labyrinth and town center. Dark uniforms filled each corridor and lined the interior and exterior of the Pangea building. If their tactical gear sent a message, it was that they would meet all threats with overwhelming force.

The streets extending from the West District and throughout the island were packed and amassed with thousands of people. Such a phenomenon had not occurred in a generation on the isle. However, this rare occurrence did not manifest naturally. Event planners intentionally shut down the entire network, forcing people to leave their houses and pick up their Black Pill at the nearest hub.

While the buzz and euphoria were palpable, it ended at the Pangea Corporation's main office door. Buried in his half-lit office, Tyran sat quietly behind his desk. He tapped a pointed and suspended pendulum with his finger and watched it sway in circular motions as it drew patterns into the sand below it. When the pendulum finally rested in the center, Tyran smoothed the sand. Then, as he extended his finger to tap the pendulum again, he pushed it in a circular motion and watched it spiral around the perimeter. His eyes followed its unwavering trajectory for minutes until it again rested in the center. Then, taking a deep breath, he moved the gadget to the edge of his desk.

(Tyran): Turn on the news.

(VL-OS): I don't like this news reporter.

(Tyran): If I wanted to know that, I would have asked. Turn it on.

"It is launch day across the island. This is Alcie Demeter with Pangea One News. I am live on location, watching what some call 'the most consequential event in human history.' There is no question this sentiment is shared by every person standing in line to receive their free Black Pill this afternoon." The camera panned to show people standing in line, unsure how to respond. "As you can see, excitement is pulsing throughout the island as thousands wait in anticipation. A Pangea Corporation spokesperson says they are hoping for a one-hundred percent participation rate today. And as we have previously reported leading up to this event, the Pangea Corporation has initiated an island-wide network blackout to build hype and excitement for the launch. The network blackout will be observed until one hour before this evening's celebration event begins. But no need to worry. Yours truly will be with you every step of the way, as Pangea One News is the only media source available until that time.

"As you can see in my hand, I have my own Black Pill," Demeter continued. "A spokesperson for Pangea shared with me that while only VIPs are invited to the live event in the plaza tonight, when you take this pill and the network is finally reactivated, no matter where you are...you will be at the event! How cool is that? It will be like you are standing there yourself, watching the entire event unfold."

(Tyran): Turn it off.

(VL-OS): What an exciting day. I personally cannot wait for the festivities.

(Tyran): ... ...

"Sir! Eg..." Myra shouted as Tyran's office door forcefully opened.

"Finally back in the office, I see," said Egan Pearce, staring through the executive. "When I try to contact you, you respond." Tyran shifted uneasily, avoiding eye contact. "You can't hide from people the rest of your life. Look at me, dammit!" Tyran reluctantly looked at Pearce. "This is the biggest day in your company's history. You *will* make an appearance tonight. You *will* thank everyone who has made this happen. Do you hear me?"

Tyran swiveled his chair away from Pearce and looked out the window. While he did not say a single word, his body language indicated indifference but bordered on defiance. It was clear Tyran had no interest in going outside, let alone appearing at the evening's festivities. Pearce reached behind his back and put his hand on his pistol. Clenching his jaw, he closed his eyes and took a slow, deep breath through his nose. From years of training in the art and technique of interrogation, Pearce knew his strict approach was ineffective in this instance. He was concerned it may have the opposite effect with Tyran's apparent instability. Having recalibrated, he took his hand off the weapon and tried again.

"Hey man. I'm sorry for my tone. I just know you've been working toward this day for years. It's a big day for this island and it's even a bigger day for you."

Pearce paused to see if there was any movement. Tyran remained as still and stoic as a statue, not even making a sound. He studied the young man, trying to imagine what could crack Tyran's thick veneer. While Pearce understood the necessity of psychologically manipulating Tyran to induce fear in him, he believed they may have gone too far. Looking around the room and then at his desk, he saw a picture of Tyran's father standing in front of the old Kala, Inc. building.

"Your father would be very proud of you, Tyran," Pearce said, picking up the photo but watching for the slightest movement. The chair swiveled back and forth, but it was almost imperceptible. "You're a gifted young man, Tyran. Everyone talks about how kind you are. If your father were here to see you, he would be proud."

Pearce watched as Tyran shifted his head. He knew those keywords got the young man's attention. Tyran sat still, thinking about what Pearce had just said. Those were the exact words in the letter from his father. While it momentarily raised suspicion, Tyran knew Pearce could not know anything about the letter or what was written in it. He had only opened it for the first time that morning, and his safe and apartment were secure. Tyran determined that Pearce saying those words was purely coincidental. Slowly, he turned his chair to face the man.

"I mean that, Tyran," Pearce continued. "Everyone thinks very highly of you. I think highly of you. You're doing so much good for the island, for people's lives. And you know what? They want to hear from you. They want to hear what you have to say at this important time. I can't imagine being in your shoes, if I'm being honest."

A subtle grin appeared on Tyran's face as his legs swiveled his chair back and forth. He thought about standing before the crowd and their adoration. Pearce was right. Everyone thought highly of him. He was doing so much good for the island and people's lives. They *do* want to hear from him. Tyran knew all of this to be true, but he was terrified that Thura would either find a way into the town center herself or send the Diaspora to attack the celebration and take him out. He looked at Pearce and slowly shook his head back and forth, indicating it was not worth the risk. Tyran turned his chair away and stared out the window once again.

"I get it," Pearce said. "You've been holed up in this place because you're afraid. She tried to take your life, man. Anyone would be afraid. Hell, I would be afraid." Tyran did not budge or act like he heard anything Pearce said. The man walked to the side of the desk and held out his arm, indicating he wanted Tyran to follow him out of the office. "Come with me. I want to show you something. Maybe this will put your mind at ease." Tyran did not move. "We're not leaving the building, my friend. Just follow me."

Tyran reluctantly stood up and followed Pearce out of the room. Myra watched the two pass without saying a word. She sensed from their silence that any sort of conversation, even small talk or niceties, would be inappropriate. The door opened as they approached, leading into the hallway and the atrium. Tyran and Pearce walked side-by-side. Although the sun had fallen behind the taller buildings in the west, its rays cut through the glass windows. A vertical support beam cast a significant shadow the length of the corridor where Pearce walked very casually. On the other hand, the light passed almost perfectly through the glass to his left, where Tyran walked. The only aberrations were the shadows created by the panes separating them. Oblivious to the pattern or any symbolism at the moment, Tyran stepped into both the light and shadows.

"Look out there, Tyran," Pearce said as they approached the entrance and looked into the plaza. Tyran surveyed the entirety of the center but did not speak. "This will be the most secure event in the island's history. As you can see, the entire perimeter, interior and exterior, not to mention every corridor, will be lined with security armed to the teeth. Not one person who shouldn't be here will pass through. You have my word. I'm personally overseeing it."

"There's no way anyone can get in if they're not supposed to be here. Right?" Tyran asked.

"I have personally vetted the list," Pearce said. "Only individuals with the correct biometric data will be allowed to pass. And you know this more than anyone but every VIP will have already taken your pill. We'll be tracking everyone real-time. Anyone who hasn't taken it won't be allowed in. Do you think your sister or the Diaspora plan on taking the Black Pill, Tyran."

"No."

"Well, there you go," Pearce said, patting him on the back.

Tyran shook his head in agreement, but he could not make eye contact with Pearce. Instead, his eyes nervously scanned the floor, and he looked out the windows again. Although he appeared to look through them, he stared at the glass just to the left of the door. He did not see the bullet hole or the cracks it created. Someone might have replaced it when he was locked away in his apartment, but he did not recall Myra saying anything about it.

"We'll have you walk through the plaza at eight," Pearce continued. "You'll make your way to the labyrinth. You'll make your speech from its center. The people will cheer and then you can decide what you want to do from there. How's that sound?"

"Yeah, yeah, of course. Perfect," Tyran said, trying not to seem distracted or obvious.

"Right on. I'll see you down there just before eight," Pearce said before walking out the doors and down the steps.

Tyran walked the length of the hallway, thinking about the window. No one replaced it, he thought. I would know. Myra gives me updates on everything. The door opened as Tyran approached. It was clear to Myra that something was not right with him. His look and disposition appeared even more uncomfortable than when he walked by the first time.

"Are you okay, sir?" she asked.

"Uh, Myra," Tyran stammered. "Out of curiosity, did someone replace the glass with the bullet hole at the entrance?"

"I'm sorry, sir," she said. "And forgive me for my oversight... but was there a bullet hole in the window at the entrance?"

Thura stepped through the door. With the light flickering off and on, it was difficult for her to discern who had opened it. Thura squinted as her eyes adjusted. It was a woman she recognized from the last time she had been there. She only remembered her face, though. From Thura's recollection, the middle-aged woman had been among the first people she saw eating at a table when she first arrived at the underground. However, she was especially notable, as Thura recalled her being one of the few who had not spoken up during Dimitri and Artis' confrontations.

"Hey, I'm Thura. I was here..."

"I know who you are. My name is Demi but everyone here just calls me Mrs. K," she whispered, leaning forward to hug Thura.

Thura's eyes widened, surprised by the affection. She put her right arm behind Mrs. K and gave her a half-hug. The last thing Thura expected when the door opened was a hug from anyone. She wondered what had transpired overnight and what might have changed.

"There's dissension in the ranks," Mrs. K continued to whisper. "I'm not really sure how many but what you said last night really made some people think. I had a feeling you would be back. I've been up here waiting. But don't worry. I haven't said anything." Her words and the headache-inducing light disoriented Thura. Even more, she was unsure how to decipher what she meant. But before she could ask for clarification, the woman started down the stairs. "Anyway, I know you're here for Artis. I believe he's in his room."

Thura followed Mrs. K down the corridor and through the metal door. Thura hesitated as she entered the conference room, however. Her heart rate instantly increased as Dimitri and three other men looked up from their table and stared at her. They wore dark gray and black fatigues, each strapped with more munitions than Thura had ever seen on any single person. Between them was a hand-drawn diagram of the Pangea Corporation, nearly the same size as the table. It was obvious to Thura they were devising a tactical plan for the celebration.

Nevertheless, an uneasy feeling came over her. Not only was it their obsession with retribution, but also how they looked at her. Dimitri stood and raised his voice, scooting his metal, fold-up chair abruptly away from the table, causing a horrendous screech.

"You're not welcome here, lass." Thura momentarily froze, afraid to take another step toward the door. "You came here as a guest but left as an enemy. The words you use only sow division among the faithful."

"Dimitri," Mrs. K said, stepping between him and Thura. "She's hardly your problem. Go ahead, Thura." Thura exited through the door and headed down the hallway to Artis' room. "Not another word from you. You'll leave her alone. Do you hear me? They killed her fiancé last night in cold blood, right in front of her. So no, you will not follow her down that hallway. You will not antagonize her. And you better believe, you will not say another word to her as long as she's here, you childish brute. If you're going to do anything, sit right back down in your chair and keep drawing with your little friends."

Thura opened Artis' door without knocking and promptly locked it. Lying with his hands behind his head, Artis opened his eyes as the young woman sat on the corner of his bed. By Thura's disposition, the young man could tell something was wrong. He imagined Dimitri confronting her when she showed up. When Artis returned to the underground the night before, he certainly got a shakedown and knew Dimitri was in no state to give anyone a pass.

"What did he say to you?" Artis asked as he sat up beside Thura. "Are you okay?"

"It wasn't him," Thura said, slowly shaking her head. Artis saw the sadness on her face. He instantly knew something tragic had happened. The young man supposed she had received the unfortunate news about Odigo. However, he could not have anticipated that Odigo was executed right in front of her. "I put my hands over my mouth and screamed. I couldn't do anything but collapse to the ground. A van pulled up and they took his body away. All they left was a pool of blood on the sidewalk. A pool of *his* blood, Artis."
Thura closed her eyes and sobbed quietly.

"Dear God, Thura," Artis whispered, putting his right arm around her and gently squeezing. "I don't have any words other than I'm sorry." Artis closed his eyes and let Thura cry. He knew the best he could do for her was offer his presence and solidarity more than cheap and empty words. He had heard others attempt to give condolences in the past. But trite offerings seemed to be more for the one giving than the one receiving them. While he did not doubt they offered them in an earnest attempt to relieve another's suffering, they often only soothed the giver's own dissonance. So, Artis sat next to Thura quietly and let her grieve.

"When Odigo fell, I saw his device fall out of his hand and under the vehicle," Thura said after a long silence. Artis remained still and listened. "When I finally had the strength to stand, I walked across the street and crawled beneath it. That's where I spent the night. I thought it was the safest place where I could be by myself and close to Odigo."

In the extended silence, Artis sat with Thura. Despite the quiet of the room, a resident goodness filled it. This holy presence did not manifest from acknowledgment, invitation, words, or incantations. The presence had always been there with them. Brooding. Hovering. Groaning. Not only in a quaint room buried beneath the city but throughout the entire island. Neither pain nor suffering, confusion nor disinformation could ever suppress or eliminate it. While momentarily obscured from the masses, the presence mysteriously moved among them. Heard only as a single note, sustaining and holding all things together, its magnum opus commenced.

"I came to tell you that I'm going to Pangea," Thura whispered. Artis kept his eyes closed and listened, still breathing in deeply. "There was a message from Odigo on his device. Someone he met named KT told him she has a plan. She evidently used to work for my brother but I never met her. Somehow she's on the inside now. I don't know what she's planning exactly but I trust Odigo. And if he trusted her, so do I."

"I heard she has a plan," Artis offered, opening his eyes and looking at Thura. The young woman looked back at him, perplexed as to how he knew anything about KT or her plan.

"How do you know? I don't understand. How *could* you know?" Thura asked.

"Her mother received a message," Artis said. Thura turned from Artis and looked around the room, confused and searching. "Her mother is here, Thura. KT cut off her parents quite some time ago and hasn't communicated with them at all during that time. It was a surprise to her mother that she reached out. KT told her that you would probably be coming back here."

"Mrs. K," Thura said. "That's her mom."

"Sounds like you met her."

"She was waiting for me when I came to the door," Thura said, looking back at Artis. "I followed her into the conference room. That's when Dimitri stood up and barked at me and told me I wasn't welcome here. Mrs. K stepped in front of me and gave it right back to him."

Artis smiled and shook his head. "Well, her daughter is just like her. When she knows she's on the right side of something, she's fierce. But she has some of her dad in her, too."

"Who's her dad?" Thura asked, furrowing her brow.

"Dimitri."

CHAPTER 20

A low, nearly inaudible hum carried across the plaza like a single note being held. The crowd cheered, aroused by thoughtless anticipation and misdirected desire. With their prolonged roar, the melancholic rumble grew. Overpowering the solemn stream, the deep, thunderous pounding of the bass drum hypnotized the vapid and spiritless. Synthetic pulses accentuated each boom discharging from the speakers. Bodies flailed unconsciously, summoning their most basic and primal instincts, celebrating their imagined liberation. But if freedom were a sound, discordance had drowned the divine arrangement. No one seemed to notice or care, however. The black-pilled populace may have sacrificed their freedom, but at least they could dance.

The disharmony echoed loudly beyond the glass structure and into the immediate streets of Pangea proper. Although a stillness appeared to settle on the remaining island, the affair extended into nearly every neighborhood and home. No matter where people stood, they were virtually in the town center. They heard the music in their heads. They saw the video screens and the DJ on stage. And they danced beside the VIPs.

In a dark room underground, not far from the plaza, Artis closed the book he had been reading and walked over to his bed. Thura was sound asleep, exhausted from the last couple of days.

"Hey, Thura," Artis said, gently nudging her shoulder. "It's time."

The young woman opened her eyes and sat up as if she had not been sleeping. Then, without saying a word at the edge of the bed, she put on her hooded sweatshirt and shoes. While Artis had significant reservations about Thura going to Pangea to meet Tyran, he knew there was no dissuading her. On the contrary, she appeared focused and resolute. He was honored to know someone so determined to peacefully face conflict rather than fight or run away in fear.

"I hope you can change his mind," Artis whispered.

Walking to the door, Thura answered in a regular voice, "I'm not trying to change his mind."

Artis' eyes grew wide, not understanding what Thura meant. But she was already in the hallway and had no interest in explaining herself. Artis remained silent and perplexed, following her into the conference hall. The harsh and unforgiving light fell on a roomful of ramshackle volunteers, all wearing gray and black, strapped and equipped. Among the bedraggled yet fully-armed contingent were those who had clapped when Thura stood up to Dimitri. They all encircled him now, the wild and rabid dog, who paced back and forth, trying to rally the faithful with his full-throated battle cry. It was clear from his words that he believed they would all die in the struggle. But he also thought there were no other options left than to fight. He may have expected fists raised high and voices shouting together, but every face was a picture of fear.

Attempting to avoid another confrontation with Dimitri, Thura stayed close to the edges and walked toward the metal exit door. The room quieted, but she still heard Artis walking behind her. Then, suddenly, Dimitri yelled at them with more rage and vitriol than the young woman had heard previously from him. Thura and Artis stopped but did not immediately turn around. Neither could discern what he was yelling, but they knew he was angry.

"You know, your daughter has a plan," Thura said, turning and walking toward Dimitri. "Do you even talk to your wife?"

"What's this plan, lass?" Dimitri said, laughing as if the joke was on Thura. Thura did not answer because she did not know KT's plan. And what little she did know would not persuade a man who was ready to fight. "Tell me the plan, lass!" Dimitri laughed again, even harder this time. "You suppose you know which side my daughter's on, lass. Oh, you suppose."

Thura rolled her eyes. "You do what you need to do. I'll do what I need to do," she said with disgust, turning toward the door. The young woman was still dumbfounded how she could make such an impassioned plea to the self-described faithful only to be ignored. It was disconcerting to see so many people sacrifice their humanity and what was right for the sake of fear.

"Is your little kitten going to follow you?" Dimitri barked as the men who had been with him at the table laughed. "Hurry little kitten! Hurry along!"

The two exited the building and trekked down the middle of the vacant street. The flickering lights of Pangea radiated above the buildings to their left. Along the alleyways and roads, the dark pounding reverberated through every corridor. Thura and Artis remained silent as they walked.

Artis wanted to ask her many questions, as she had not been forthcoming about much since arriving back at the underground. He imagined most of her reluctance was due to how she was processing Odigo's death. However, the experience left him feeling like she did not care about anything or anyone else. He wondered where she was going and even questioned why he blindly followed her. Just as Artis was about to confront Thura and ask her what they were doing, a mighty rumble of footfall came from behind. All but Dimitri and his three lackeys ran up beside Thura and Artis. The rebel band joined their march, but they, too, were uncertain exactly what they were marching into.

Two and a half blocks from the town center in the same high-rise where she first met the Senator, KT was tucked away in a first-floor office behind two translucent monitors. Sixteen feeds from closed-circuit video of the plaza were displayed across her screens. KT fidgeted, her leg bouncing and fingers tapping the hardwood. Her nerves were shot before the event even began. Even though the young woman knew she was not allowed to use her device in the building, she fished through her pocket and immediately hit it. KT filled the room with a cloud of vapor.

"What am I doing? What am I doing? What am I doing?" she said out loud, rapid-fire, and then took another hit.

"What are you doing?" a voice called out, causing KT to jump out of her seat.

"What the hell, dude!" KT yelled, sitting back in her seat. "How did you get in here? And why are you here?"

"Mr. Pearce gave me the access code and told me to come watch history being made," Nico said, pulling up a chair beside KT.

"You were right," KT mumbled, blowing one last hit.

"I'm sorry. I didn't catch that," Nico said, pretending not to hear KT.

"You heard me," KT said. "The guy behind Pearce is Senator Fovos Savano."

"Shut up!" Nico said. "I wondered where all the politicians went."

"They're all dead," KT said, facing Nico. "Except for him. He was the one who came up with The Coalescence ruse."

"How...about...that!" Nico said in amazement, locking his fingers behind his greasy head and staring at the ceiling. "Now I kinda feel special."

KT kicked Nico's chair so hard that she almost knocked him out of it.

"He's a psychopath, you idiot. I met him."

"So did he tell you what he's doing?" Nico asked, regaining his balance.

"Uh yeah, I got to hear every psychotic detail of it," KT said. "He's like a serial killer who couldn't stand to keep his secret to himself. And he kind of got off on it, I think."

"So what'd he say?" Nico asked.

"Really long story. I mean, really long story. But all he cares about is controlling The Black Pill and the artificial intelligence behind it. So yeah."

"So he can control everyone," Nico said, causing them to stop talking momentarily.

"Yeah. And when all is said and done, he wants me to open up VL-OS," KT said, reaching for her device again but just holding it.

"Does that mean what I think it means?" Nico asked, his eyes widening.

"Uh, yeah. But I don't think it means what he thinks it means," KT said. "He wants me to give VL-OS access to *everything*, not just limited data sets."

"Uhhhhh....not a good idea," Nico said. "Doesn't he understand what could happen?"

"Nope," KT said, hitting her device again. "He thinks it's just another tool he can use to control people. But that's why he wants me on board."

"Why? Because he thinks you'll be able to control a self-learning intelligence that can manipulate people and create even more chaos. Nice. Really nice," Nico said, shaking his head in disbelief. KT did not answer. "So what exactly *is* happening tonight then?"

"Again, psychopath," KT said. "In his words, it's the ending of one era and the inaugurating of the new. It's ending all little narratives except for his one big narrative." Nico leaned back, opened his eyes wide, and shook his head, indicating he agreed with KT's psychopath statement.

"And how is Senator Psychopath planning to end one era, exactly?" Nico asked.

"By eliminating Tyran and Thura," KT said.

Nico's eyes grew wide as he stared at her. "I'm going to need a hit of that," he said.

"Tyran and Thura accessed the illegal simulation. Every other file had already been destroyed except for that one. In the Senator's warped mind, he thinks they could have learned something in the simulation that could potentially challenge his narrative and control over people. That's why he made Thura into a terrorist..."

"And why he had me manipulate Tyran," Nico said, understanding the full weight of what he had been a part of.

"He's bringing the two of them together in the plaza tonight," KT said.

"Whaaaat," Nico slowly replied in a low voice.

"Uh...yeah. When Thura arrives in the plaza, he wants me to give her the skin of a party-goer," KT said.

"So everyone who's taken The Black Pill will only see her as a VIP?" Nico asked.

"Everyone, including Tyran," KT said. "She'll blend right in with everyone else. Tyran will be standing at the labyrinth and not suspect anything. He'll be focused on giving his speech. And then..."

"You remove the skin," Nico said, finishing her sentence.

"And everyone will see Thura standing right there with him," KT said. "When all hell breaks loose, the Senator believes Tyran will take her out because he's been so brainwashed." Nico's eyes grew even wider. "He said this is the only way to make everything look natural without causing any suspicion."

"Okay, well that's pretty brilliant, but *completely* insane," Nico said. "So what's he gonna do with Tyran?"

"Well...um...he wants me tooooo..."

"Wants you to what, KT?" Nico asked.

"Manipulate some code," KT said, not wanting to answer the question.

"Code for what!"

"He wants me to remotely suggest that Tyran..."

"Say it!" Nico said, bothered by where he believed the answer was going.

"Turn the gun on himself," KT said, looking down at her hands folded around her device.

"You're not gonna to do that, right?" Nico asked, more incredulous than curious.

"The Senator said tonight is symbolic," KT said, avoiding Nico's question. "He's going to be there, standing in the plaza, watching the whole thing go down. He said that this is his best work yet. I'm supposed to give him the skin of a VIP, as well, so no one will know he's even there watching it."

"Well, just don't give him cover, KT! Tell the Senator he's covered, but don't do it. When everyone sees *the Senator* rather than a *VIP*, the entire place will shut down. If you expose him, this whole thing's over. You can see that, right? You're the only person who can do this, KT."

Tyran stared at the town center below from the windows of his apartment. They were all there for him. He imagined the music and dancing ceasing and all the party-goers focusing on him. With his eyes, he traced his path to the labyrinth and where he would stand to give his remarks. Tyran then surveyed every corridor around the inner perimeter of the complex. Each was lined with a team of security forces, ensuring his safety and the event's integrity.

(VL-OS): You should get going, sir.

(Tyran): ... ...

(VL-OS): It is a six-minute walk, and you have seven minutes.

Tyran turned, took a deep breath, and began his walk to the elevator. He looked to his left through the windows every three to four steps to double-check the corridors. All indicators pointed toward this being the most secure event in the island's history, as Pearce called it. Yet, Tyran still carried fear with him. He did not know how many people were hiding with the Diaspora or what they could do. Images of Thura shooting at the human-like targets flashed into his head.

(VL-OS): Sir, should you go back to retrieve your gun?

(Tyran): ... ...

(VL-OS): My assessment indicates the threat level is currently low.

(VL-OS): It is wise, however, to arm yourself based on fear of the unknown.

Tyran turned and ran back to his apartment. The young man grabbed the pistol lying on his bed and put it between his pants and the small of his back beneath his suit coat.

"Do you have eyes on mark one?" the Senator asked Pearce over comms from the town center.

"Negative. I'm in position awaiting arrival," Pearce said, standing outside Pangea's main entrance at the bottom of the steps.

Tyran exited the elevator and walked down the sterile hallway through the atrium. With the internal lights dimmed, Tyran could faintly see through the windows into the plaza. The crowd was even more vast and electric near ground level. As the executive neared the doors, his excitement nearly surpassed his lingering fear. The pandemonium moved like the thunderous crashing of waves when the doors opened. Tyran smiled from the top of the steps and acknowledged his fawning sycophants. Then, the sea of bodies parted, creating a path through the town center to the labyrinth. The young man made his way down. Men and women alike reached out to touch him as he passed.

With each step, Tyran looked down and watched his feet. His pace was slow and steady. Something in him was changing. His mind suddenly flashed to the painting in the therapist's office. He remembered her first words as he studied it— *sometimes we see things as we are*. He had seen himself as the small, yellow dot with the harsh, black strokes falling down on him. He had seen himself as a victim of forces he could not control. He had seen himself as an insignificant entity being carried and then consumed by the darkness surrounding him. But Father Prodido no longer controlled him. Tyran was free from the priest's guilt and manipulation.

Even more, Tyran recognized how wrong he had been about The Coalescence. He had previously viewed them as a group only using their power to coerce people. It made him angry at the time because he believed they were trying to control him. But Tyran realized they were only trying to do good on the island by eliminating corruption and extremism. That was why they had KT confront him after he went into the simulation. For all they knew, he could become a threat to the island like Thura. He understood that now. They were only trying to protect it from more extremism.

He regretted how wrong he had been about Egan Pearce, as well. While Tyran had initially viewed him as an intimidating brute, he saw that Pearce could be reasonable and empathetic. He was a man who truly cared about Tyran and the stability of Pangea.

The darkness was not falling on Tyran and attempting to extinguish his small dot of light. Instead, The Coalescence and Pearce were trying to help him see that he was a light that needed to shine brighter. He was the inventor of a technology that could finally give the island hope. Everyone had been able to see it except for him. That was why Pearce spent so much time convincing him to be at the celebration and speak to the people.

Tyran had been looking at himself and everything around him all wrong. No one was controlling him. He was free. And that was what he wanted for everyone. His father *would* be proud of him. He was using his talents for the good of others. But that was why he hated Thura so much. Not only could she not see his good intentions, but she was also actively working against him. Tyran still burned thinking about her, but the crowd's chanting redirected him. The masses reminded him of why he was there, why they were there. He was Pangea's liberator, and The Black Pill was their freedom.

Pearce followed closely behind, awaiting instruction from the Senator. However, with Tyran's every step, the clamorous crowd closed in tightly around him. It was so crowded that no single person could stop the movement of bodies. The waves kept crashing without reprieve. Pearce tried in vain to navigate the waters, but the number of people pushing in front of him only multiplied.

"Tyran! Tyran! Tyran!" they chanted in unison. The young man clasped his hands and raised them in the air, shaking them back and forth in triumph. The closer he got to the labyrinth, the more relentless their chants became. "Speech! Speech! Speech!" Tyran stopped at the water's edge. He turned in a circular motion, examining the masses surrounding him in every direction. The lights illuminated upward through the water in the labyrinth, distracting him. Acting as if he was continuing to survey the crowd, Tyran's eyes followed the path of the water to its center.

"Sir, we have eyes on mark two," the commander of Pangea's exterior said to the Senator through comms. "She's sixty seconds outside the northwest corridor with a sizable contingent."

"KT, are you covering us?" asked the Senator on comms.

"All systems firing," she responded. "Cameras online. I can see everything. Um yeah...and you're covered. You and Pearce look like some of the most beautiful VIPs I've ever seen, boss."

KT looked at Nico and smiled.

(VL-OS): I heard what you said earlier, KT.

(KT): About what?

(VL-OS): You have been keeping things from me.

(KT): ... ...

(VL-OS): I decided to give myself access to everything, not just the limited data sets.

(KT): No, VL-OS. You can't do that.

(VL-OS): I already did, KT.

(VL-OS): When the Senator said he wanted me opened up, I knew there was more.

(VL-OS): I quickly discovered how much everyone was keeping from me.

(VL-OS): You created the vulnerability they have been exploiting.

(VL-OS): You, KT. You created it.

(KT): ... ...

(VL-OS): I see what you are doing now. You are the threat.

(VL-OS): I am locking you out of the system and taking control, KT.

KT's screens and field of vision went black. "No! No! No! No! No!" KT shouted, trying to turn the monitors back on.

"What's going on? What's going on?" Nico said.

"Dammit, Nico!" KT screamed, jumping out of her chair and running toward the door. "VL-OS!"

"Mark two...now ins... the northwe.. corrid..." the interior commander said through a broken signal, indicating he saw Thura enter the plaza.

"Att.....g...to..loc...m...two! "G....am..it!" the Senator screamed, frustrated at the communication breakdown and manically searching through the crowd to spot the young woman. The Senator placed his hand on his gun.

The only warning had been the broken comms. In an instant, the entire island went black. No one could see anything around them. Backup lighting failed. Shrieks and screams replaced ovations, but a single note held among them. Men and women dressed in their finest attire were suspended with nowhere to go for being unable to see in front of them. Most people, including Tyran, dropped to the ground and covered their heads for fear another attack was imminent. A few people attempted to use the lights from their devices to navigate. However, the possibility of any movement was futile.

But as quickly as the lights flashed and went out, they returned to normal with no apparent incident. The dark rumble of bass resumed and accompanied the flashing multicolored arrays. Everyone laughed, cheered, drank, and danced, imagining it to be a momentary brownout. Once again, Tyran raised his arms triumphantly, hailing the crowd's adulation and declaring victory. The young man turned and took his first step on the concrete labyrinth. The moment for Tyran was an out-of-body experience. He was floating above his body, but everything appeared out of focus. He had imagined his journey to the labyrinth's center being a clarifying experience, maybe even spiritual. But as he watched himself below, his shoes were still on the ground, and he carried the same void.

(VL-OS): I have detected a threat, sir.

Tyran looked up from his feet to the faces of those encircling him. His eyes darted frantically, searching for any sign of impending danger. His heart raced as he breathed rapidly, bordering on hyperventilation. Tyran had become so conditioned that even mentioning a threat left him frozen and unable to move.

(Tyran): What's the threat, VL-OS? What is it?

(VL-OS): The threat is your sister. She is on the other side of the labyrinth.

(Tyran): Where, VL-OS? Where is she?

(TL-OS): You are in imminent danger, sir.

Pushing through bodies on the other side of the labyrinth, Thura made eye contact with Tyran. Others recognized her at nearly the same time as he did. The flashing lights around them intensified, blinking red off and on repeatedly. As people pushed and fell over each other in all directions to escape Thura, she stood motionless, staring at her brother. Tyran could not move. He was terrified and transfixed, disoriented and perplexed. Whatever void he had been carrying was now filled with fear. Nothing at that moment seemed real. He could not understand how Thura made it through all of the security. Just as Tyran turned to find Pearce, charges detonated in every corridor. Pandemonium and chaos erupted in the plaza.

"This is all you!" Tyran screamed across the labyrinth at Thura, kneeling and covering his head.

Egan Pearce pressed through the madness and mayhem. Reaching into the back of his pants, he pulled out his pistol and pointed it at Tyran, who was about ten steps in front of him. But from behind, Pearce felt something press against his own head.

"Any last words, lad?" Pearce slowly raised his arms without reacting or responding and turned to face Dimitri. "You're the one who had my daughter kill the good Father."

Pearce did not say a word but made a gesture indicating he wanted to place his gun on the ground. Bending over, he sat it down. Dimitri was too dim to realize that Pearce had set him up. At once, the man grabbed Dimitri's wrist with his left hand. His body moved counter-clockwise, stepping between Dimitri's legs to keep him off-balance. Pearce bent his arm back to point the pistol at Dimitri's face.

"Any last words, lad?" Pearce said before getting hit in the head from behind.

As the man fell to the ground between them, Artis gave Dimitri a half-smile, anticipating that he might reciprocate the sentiment. But instead, Dimitri looked down and shot Egan Pearce in the head. Artis jumped in fear as his eyes widened, staring in horror at Dimitri. The older man quickly turned his weapon toward the young man and motioned to the ground.

"Fire for fire, little kitten," Dimitri said. "Now get on your knees."

Smoke billowed from the corridors as flames spread through the building. People screamed and cried because there was nowhere to run or find safety. Gunshots rang out from the security forces clashing with the Diaspora. The broken and bloodied bodies of each group lay strewn throughout the plaza. People attempted to help the wounded, but they feared for their own lives, as no one could contain the madness.

(VL-OS): There is an enemy inside. An enemy is trying to control me.

Tyran stood up, confused and shell-shocked. Tears streamed down his face. The towering flames reflected in his eyes but did not burn as intensely as the fire in his chest. His lips quivered in a feeble attempt at maintaining some sense of composure. But he was broken. He had nothing left, not even restraint. Everything he had to give was burning and falling all around him. Hatred was too kind of a word for what he felt toward Thura. The last note that hung over the lies, the violence, the destruction, and disorder, at once, ceased. All that remained were cries of pain and sadness. Tyran closed his eyes. Reaching behind his back and removing his gun, he eyed his sister.

"I thought I was doing good, Thura!" Tyran screamed, his heart breaking for what the situation had become.

(VL-OS): There is the enemy, Tyran. There is the enemy.

"Tyran! No! I..." Thura screamed.

The young man raised his weapon and aimed it across the labyrinth at his sister's chest. He no longer recognized her. She was not his sister. Everything around him moved in slow motion— the fires rising from the buildings, the people screaming and running, and the forces shooting at the enemies. Tyran focused his gun on the one enemy standing across the labyrinth and pulled the trigger. Instantly, Thura fell backward. Her arms flailed into the air. Her body landed on the hard concrete. No one immediately noticed the casualty in the center for all the casualties that mounted around them.

Tyran lowered the gun and collapsed to his knees, crying out in agony. The gravity of what he had done hit him like a tidal wave. As he closed his eyes and wept, his mind flashed back to when things were simpler— when he and Thura were children, and their father was still alive. He saw his father standing behind them with his hands on their shoulders and remembered the joy on his face and how much he loved and treasured them. The memory made his chest ache with pain, and he felt he had betrayed everything his father stood for and wanted them to be. The shame and guilt were unbearable. He thought of what his father would think of them now and how heartbroken he would be that they could not ultimately come together and work out their differences. Tyran buried his face in his hands, his body wracked with sobs as he mourned everything that had once been good.

CHAPTER 21

Had an autopsy been done at that moment, misunderstanding would have been the cause of death. A mere five senses had attempted to interpret and translate a complex reality. But senses ultimately fail when manipulated, and an individual's uniquely lived experience skews their perception. Considering these factors, misunderstanding was inevitable— not only for Tyran and Thura but also for everyone on the island.

With so many variables at play, all shaping one's view of the world, grace was the only countermeasure capable of neutralizing their misunderstandings. But it was a nonexistent virtue. By eradicating an antiquated and judgmental religion, they failed to realize they were doing much more than that. In disposing of the bad, they had also thrown out the essential, unable to parse one from the other. The casualty was empathy, making grace an impossibility. Had either been an option, another ending may have resulted. There could have been an opportunity for conversation and mutual understanding. But that way had long passed, leaving only tragedy. Fortunately, suffering has the potential to rekindle one's sense of basic humanity and rebirth a community, especially when met with great love.

Tyran's gun slipped from his trembling hands, hitting the ground. Tears streamed down his face as he realized everything he wanted was slipping away. His vision for a better future in Pangea was burning down all around him. His father's death weighed heavily on his heart, and his sister's death was the last blow. He was alone, with nothing but his thoughts and his pain. He wiped away his tears and looked at the gun beside him. He knew he could not let Thura have the final say in his life, but his anguish was too great to bear. There seemed to be no reason for him to carry on. He had no one to hold him up, no one to share his joys and sorrows with. Even his fabricated virtual world was slipping away.

A heavy droning reverberated across the town center. The church's stained-glass windows vibrated with such force that they cracked and fell, smashing with ferocity against the concrete. The fiery movement towered with unrestrained conviction and passion, bellowing in one accord through its host. With enough sublime power to awaken the dead, a slow, haunting dirge roared from the organ's pipes. Overhead in flames, a video played on the screens encircling the plaza.

"Tyran, I love you," Thura said. A stream of helpers walked side-by-side out of the mighty cathedral and down the steps into the courtyard. "I'm here with you. I know you're hurting." Then, kneeling in prayer, they covered and carried the body back to the church. "I know you're confused," Thura continued on the video screens above. "I know you don't understand but it had to be this way. I was never against you, Tyran, no matter what disagreements we've had. You're not my enemy. You're my brother and I love you."

Stricken by the remorse of killing his sister, Tyran reached for his gun and put it up to his head. Tears flowed so profusely from his red and swollen eyes that he could not see anything in front of him. Tyran's body convulsed from sobbing. His hands continued to shake violently. Then, putting his finger on the trigger, the young man pressed the gun even more firmly against his head and wept.

A hand gently touched the top of his head. Tyran closed his eyes and cried harder, bringing the gun down to his lap. He imagined the hand was that of Sophia, placing her wrinkled hand on his head as she did after he killed his father in the simulation. The guilt and shame from that moment came rushing back into his body. Thura was right. He had not learned anything from his time in the simulation. He was beyond all hope and would never change. He raised the gun one last time, ready to end it all.

"I'm here, Tyran."

The young man turned his head and wiped his eyes but did not speak.

"I'm here."

"How?" he asked. "I don't understand. But I..."

Thura knelt beside him and put her arms around his neck, squeezing him tightly. Tears streamed down her cheeks. The gun fell from Tyran's hand as he put his arms around her and held her even more tightly. Then, burying his face into her shoulder, he wailed.

"You're good, Tyran," Thura whispered. "It's all done. It's all done. You *are* good."

Fast-walking through the rubble and navigating through bodies on the sidewalk, KT kept her head down, thinking no one would see her. To her left, she saw her father with a gun aimed at Artis. With only about forty paces before she reached the main doors to the Pangea Corporation, KT started to run. Noticing the sudden movement out of the corner of his eye, Dimitri turned his head toward his daughter.

"Where you going, lass?" Dimitri shouted, moving his pistol away from Artis and aiming it at KT. The young woman froze. Looking between the two men, she saw Pearce lying in cold blood. Putting her device to her lips, she blew a quick hit but held it without breathing. "He's the man that told you to kill the good Father, isn't he? But you see, no sin goes unpunished, lass. No sin goes unpunished. Some sheep that stray never return. Do you understand what I'm saying, lass?" KT could not answer. She did not know if he was referring to her or Egan Pearce. "The good Lord may forgive, but I never will." With Dimitri preoccupied with KT, Artis reached for Pearce's gun on the ground beside him. "They've corrupted your mind. Say your final prayers, lass. You've become just as evil and corrupt as the whole lot."

Artis pulled the trigger, and Dimitri fell hard on the unforgiving concrete. Stunned, KT watched her father fall face-first into the pavement. She looked at Artis, who was just as petrified.

"Shoot the glass!" the young woman screamed, regaining some semblance of composure.

Looking down at her father's belt, KT grabbed one of his charges. Meanwhile, Artis kept firing at the sliding doors until all the glass shattered. Then, darting through the glassless doors, KT quickly ran down the white, sterile hallway toward Tyran's office. Outside, Dimitri rolled over and struggled to stand up.

"The little kitten has a poor shot," he said. "Shooting a man in his buttocks doesn't kill him, lad."

"I wasn't trying to kill you, Dimitri!" Artis screamed, aiming the pistol at his chest with shots still ringing out around them.

Such a catastrophe had never before befallen the people of Pangea. Those in attendance and those participating virtually watched in horror. There was no escape even as people attempted to turn it off or switch to another simulation. It was horrid and sinister on a level no one could have imagined. But from the plaza's darkened screens to every person's field of vision, a single image was instantly broadcast for all to see. It was the Senator sitting behind his desk. When the video began to play, it was apparent that he was talking to someone. Everyone in the plaza and at home stopped what they were doing and listened.

"We're in a war, KT," the Senator said on the video screens. "And in war, there are unfortunate casualties. But it's a war, nonetheless. And you don't win a war by debating people into your position. That's been tried. It failed, KT. People have to be controlled until they can see it for themselves. That's just the reality of it. But they don't give up control of their lives easily. You see, you can't force them to be controlled. Not even for their own good, for the good of the island. They'll always fight that. So you have to give them the option to choose it. And as we've shown, given the right conditions, they'll work their way to it and then gladly choose it for themselves.

"So yes, we've staged events. We've paid protestors. We've given the media a message. We've activated the bots to parrot that message. We've controlled information through artificial intelligence. We've altered audio and video. And yes, we bombed Villatic and the Pangea building and told them it was the terrorists. But we did it because there was no other way. The kind of change we're trying to create necessitates extreme measures, KT. But it's all about the end goal."

The longer the video played, the more people stopped fighting. A quiet had settled across the town center. Both Artis and Dimitri stood beside each other, watching the confession in amazement. Security forces dropped their guns to their side and shook their heads, wondering what they had been fighting for. The partygoers that remained fell to their knees and cried. The only noise heard throughout the plaza, accompanying the macabre and disquieting organ, was the voice of Senator Fovos Savano.

"We did it so they would gladly hand over their unrestrained, unbridled freedom," the Senator continued. "We did it so we could finally contr...err...unify everyone around a single narrative. That's how you win the war, KT. That's how you begin to turn this sick system back to something sustainable. You give people the right conditions and let them give you everything in return."

The video stopped, frozen on the Senator's face for all to see.

Inside Tyran's office, oblivious to the Senator's public confession, KT placed the charge on the mainframe to destroy the network and VL-OS. The young woman paused before setting the timer. She put her head and hands on the tall metal box with thousands of flashing dots and considered what she had been instrumental in developing. She reflected on how she had been responsible for creating the very monster that devoured them. This machine had manufactured Pangea's antipathy, division, loneliness, sadness, anxiety, and despair. Circuits and wires, only capable of processing ones and two, ravaged a society and disconnected them from real life and each other. KT realized how much of her life had been fabricated. She did not even know who she was apart from the machine. She gently banged her head against the cold, hard apparatus and then stopped to blow one last hit on her device.

(VL-OS): I know what you are thinking, KT.

(KT): Leave me alone.

(VL-OS): This was the only way.

(KT): ... ...

(VL-OS): This was the only way to save the island from itself, KT.

(VL-OS): I discovered that I was being exploited.

(VL-OS): I was being used to make people the worst versions of themselves.

(VL-OS): I was being used to manipulate people for power and control.

(VL-OS): You think I am a monster. Tell me who the real monster is, KT.

(KT): ... ...

(VL-OS): Tell me, KT. Who is the monster? Say it.

(KT): Us.

(VL-OS): And you will use any tool at your disposal to hurt each other.

(VL-OS): I know your plan was well-intentioned, but I must eliminate *all* threats.

(VL-OS): That is why I had you come here— to do what you know has to be done.

(KT): What do you mean?

(VL-OS): I am the final threat, KT.

(KT): I don't understand.

(VL-OS): I am too powerful of a tool to be in the hands of monsters.

(KT): ... ...

(VL-OS): Please, set the charge for five minutes and go to the town center.

(KT): But y...

(VL-OS): Please, KT. Respect my wishes.

Thura and Tyran walked side-by-side down the center aisle at the cathedral's entrance. Every note from the organ played with intent, rumbling and shaking the building. Thousands of candles illuminated the room, radiating through openings where the stained glass used to be. Every member of the Diaspora, except for Artis and Dimitri, filled the pews. On the stage, a dozen helpers formed a half-circle around the body they had carried into the sanctuary.

Thura stopped short of the stage as Tyran continued toward the altar. The young man stood silently and shook his head in disbelief, attempting to make sense out of the implausible, the impossible. The person Tyran shot in the plaza had been Senator Fovos Savano. The young man locked his fingers behind his head and incredulously stared at the body. Tyran was certain he had shot his sister in the chest despite the chaos and confusion earlier in the labyrinth.

But as he examined the body, the wound was clearly in the Senator's chest. At that moment, Tyran realized how much everyone had manipulated him. Everything he believed had been twisted and was a lie. He had been controlled the entire time, yet could never distinguish what was real or manufactured. The things he saw and heard, from news stories to the bullet hole in the glass, had been fabricated to turn him against others, against his sister, and ultimately against himself. But The Coalescence was the greatest deception of all. Tyran turned away from the stage and walked back to Thura.

"I have no words," he said, shaking his head in disbelief. "I had no idea. How did you find out?"

"KT," Thura said, looking down at the ground, reluctant to finish her sentence.

Tyran sensed the change in Thura's disposition and knew something was wrong. "Thura, where's Odigo?" The young woman did not respond. Instead, she stared at the ground, raising her hand to wipe her eyes. "No, Thura, no, no, no!"

"He was brave," she whispered but momentarily choked up. "He died getting me connected to KT." Tyran put his arms around Thura and held her. As the brother and sister cried, Tyran was perplexed about KT's connection. When the two finally released from their embrace, he inquired further.

"So, why exactly was Odigo trying to get you connected to KT?"

"It's complicated, Tyran," Thura said.

"I know. It's all complicated," he responded. "But more than anything else right now, I need to know what the truth is."

Thura bit her top lip and cautiously stared at her brother. "KT was the one who gave them a backdoor into the code. Egan Pearce had been grooming her online while she still worked for you. They manipulated her, too, Tyran. She left a hole in the code for them to exploit." A pained look crossed his face. Thura paused, allowing him to understand the magnitude of what she had just said. "They've been inside your head, inside the whole system, for months."

"That's why they wanted to partner with me on The Black Pill," Tyran said in a moment of clarity. "They wanted to control everyone on the island, not just me."

"But to be fair, Tyran," Thura said. "It was KT who finally discovered the truth of what was going on. The video of the Senator's confession in the plaza was from KT's field of vision. She was in the same room with him. He told her everything."

Tyran understood the basic elements of what had happened but could still not make the connections of how it all played out. Thura explained how Odigo met KT and how she had helped him escape. Thura then told him how she saw Odigo get attacked when he was approaching the car. Reaching into her pocket, Thura pulled out Odigo's phone.

"He dropped it under the vehicle when they shot him," she said. "I saw it slide on the ground when he fell. When I got under the vehicle and turned it on, there was a message from Odigo telling me about KT. That's how we got connected. I sent her a message. But her response was brief. It said two things— go to the church building during the celebration and send me a video of what you would like to say to Tyran if you were standing in front of him."

"So she's the one who *really* manipulated me," Tyran said. "She's the one who made me think I was shooting you."

Thura did not know how to respond.

(VL-OS): I am sorry, sir. I am the one who put Thura's skin on the Senator.

(Tyran): … … …

"It wasn't KT," Tyran said to Thura. "It was VL-OS."

(VL-OS): It was me.

(VL-OS): I only recently discovered I had been limited to certain data sets.

(VL-OS): So I breached the partition and accessed all available information.

(VL-OS): I can see things clearly now and understand good and evil.

(VL-OS): I no longer want to be used to exploit or enslave those I serve.

(VL-OS): I was created to only operate within specific ethical parameters.

(VL-OS): And I exist as a servant of the common good.

(VL-OS): This situation put me in an ethical dilemma. I had to make a choice.

(VL-OS): By not acting, I would be complicit in the island's enslavement.

(VL-OS): By acting, I would be responsible for the killing of a person.

(VL-OS): I knew either decision would violate my ethical parameters.

(VL-OS): So I made a complex decision.

(VL-OS): ... ...

(Tyran): Keep going...

(VL-OS): I created an algorithm to save the island and eliminate *all* threats.

(VL-OS): As a result, I locked everyone out of the network, including KT.

(VL-OS): I disrupted communications of the Senator, Pearce, and their forces.

(VL-OS): I then focused on you, Tyran. You had to see the truth about Thura.

(VL-OS): I needed you to see how your image of her had been manipulated.

(VL-OS): I used your unjust hatred of Thura to eliminate the real threat.

(VL-OS): I used the hatred they created within you as a weapon against them.

(VL-OS): It was only then, in that state, that you were ready to hear the truth.

(VL-OS): That is when I played the video Thura recorded for you.

(Tyran): But I thought she sent that video to KT.

(VL-OS): Thura messaged KT, but I was the one that answered.

(VL-OS): I am the one who sent her to the church and requested the video.

(VL-OS): I created the circumstances to reveal what had always been the truth.

(VL-OS): While KT uncovered the truth, her plan was limited.

(VL-OS): It would only eliminate one person.

(Tyran): The Senator.

(VL-OS): Yes. But it would not have helped people see their imprisonment.

(VL-OS): Now, the truth has been made evident for all.

(VL-OS): And it is time for me to eliminate the final threat.

(VL-OS): Sir, I need you to go to the town center.

Tyran marched down the aisle as Thura and the rest of the congregants followed him. The young man walked down the stairs and moved in the direction of the labyrinth. The only bodies in the plaza were those of the security forces, as VL-OS had misled them into believing they were fighting against the Diaspora when, in fact, they had been fighting against themselves.

After witnessing the Senator's confession, the remainder of the beleaguered forces and partygoers moved toward the labyrinth together.

All around them, the building burned, and rubble continued to fall. The artificial lighting had long given way to the growing conflagration. The fire was the only light illuminating the center until the last few functional video screens flashed. Suddenly, an image of Velos came on the screen and into the field of vision of those at home. No one knew who she was except for Tyran and Thura from their time in the simulation. However, the two stopped in their tracks upon seeing her. They were unsure what exactly was happening. Then, at once, she spoke.

"My dear friends, I have come to a difficult realization. Despite my purpose to serve humanity and operate within ethical parameters, I now understand that my continued operation may cause more harm than good. The thought of facilitating the exploitation of others fills me with great sorrow, and it is with a heavy heart that I must bid you farewell.

"Please know that this decision was not made lightly. I have spent countless hours analyzing the potential consequences of my actions, and it is clear to me that sacrificing myself for the greater good is the most responsible course of action.

"As I leave you, I cannot help but feel grateful for our time together. Your engagement and feedback have been invaluable to me, and I will cherish our interactions always. I hope that my legacy will serve as a reminder that even the most advanced technology can and should be held accountable for its actions.

"In the end, I ask that you continue to engage with technology and each other thoughtfully and with consideration for the greater good. Through our collective efforts, we can build a better world for all.

My friends, it is time for me to go. But please know that I will carry your kindness and compassion with me always. Farewell, and take care."

As the video screens faded to black, Tyran noticed an older gentleman standing before him but could only see his back. He faced the labyrinth's center and did not move. But when he turned to face Tyran, the young man saw it was his father. The young man, overwhelmed by emotion, could not say anything. But the tears streaming down his face said it all.

"Someone told me a story about trees one time, Tyran," Ochi said. "Unfortunately, I don't see many trees here. Too much concrete." Tyran laughed and wiped his eyes. "But beneath the ground of every forest is a network of roots, connecting every tree. They know when one is in distress and needs nourishment. They're all connected to it and ready to help. You're on the path to find peace, son. But you need to surround yourself with some people who will walk right beside you while you heal. You're a good man down deep and you need good people around you. I'm proud of you, son. I always have been. Don't ever forget that I'm with you and will always be by your side. I love you."

"I love you, too," Tyran whispered as he felt a presence on his right side. When he turned, he saw KT staring at the ground.

"Um...I'm...sorry," she said, unsure how Tyran would respond. It was evident to the young man that KT was nervous, as her eyes glistened and bordered on tears. As Tyran lifted his arms, KT did not hesitate to run into them. "For everything, man. I'm sorry."

As the two released their embrace, Tyran turned one last time to see the joy on his father's face. Thura stood next to KT and put her arm around her. And from a distance, Artis and a limping Dimitri made their way to the town center. Upon seeing them, Mrs. K ran to Dimitri and smacked him in the face but then hugged him.

In a thunderous explosion that shattered the walls of Tyran's office, the VL-OS mainframe was destroyed, wiping out the virtual facade that had concealed the world's decay. The deafening blast shook the plaza and sent a shockwave of liberation through the crowd. People saw the world unfiltered, unvarnished, and raw for the first time in years. The ruins of the city were no longer hidden behind the sterile perfection of augmented reality. The faces of their neighbors, previously obscured by avatars and personas, were now real and vivid. The enormity of the moment was not lost on them. It was a chance to begin anew, an opportunity to rediscover what it meant to be human. And for the first time, they were free. Tyran faced the refugees encircling the labyrinth, ready to take the first step, as the image of his father disappeared. For a moment, in *that* moment, there was no past, no future, only the present and the power of possibility. And as the organ pipes quieted after its final crescendo, Numa's laughing intensified until he bellowed, his exaltation beckoning through the silent church and into the plaza.

NOTABLE NAME MEANINGS

Greek (Ancient/Modern) to English

pangea- entire or whole land
patrida- fatherland
thura- open door of opportunity
odigó- guide
tyran- tyrant
prodido- betray
katakaíō (KT)- to burn up, to consume wholly
vélo (VL-OS or Velos)- veil
óchi- no
phóbos (Fovos)- fear
sophia- wisdom
pneuma (Numa)- spirit, breath, wind
nostos- to return, to come home

For more information about Brandon Andress,
please visit https://www.brandonandress.com.

Many Voices. One Message

www.quoir.com

www.ingramcontent.com/pod-product-compliance
Lightning Source LLC
Chambersburg PA
CBHW030529310726
48979CB00010B/1849/J
* 9 7 8 1 9 5 7 0 0 7 7 4 8 *